D1613267

The
Memoirs
of
Josephine

The
Memoirs
of
Josephine

Anonymous

CARROLL & GRAF PUBLISHERS, INC.

New York

Copyright © 1985 by Carroll & Graf Publishers, Inc.

First Carroll & Graf Edition 1985

Original title: THE MEMOIRS OF
JOSEPHINE MUTZENBACHER

ISBN: 0-88184-161-7

Carroll & Graf Publishers, Inc.
260 Fifth Avenue
New York, N.Y. 10001

Manufactured in the United States of America

The
Memoirs
of
Josephine

PREFACE

BY JOSEPHINE MUTZENBACHER

When I remember the old popular saying that young whores turn into religious bigots when they become old, I must claim to be one of the few exceptions. Yes, I am old now, and have lost my good looks, and though I am wealthy, I often suffer from loneliness; but I don't regret my past one little bit and don't feel I have to do penance. I believe in God, but I dislike making a show of religion which is a private concern.

My sex education started very early in life, and theory and practice were never separated. I have experienced everything that a woman can in male company, be it in bed, on the floor, on tables or chairs, leaning against the walls of old houses, in the open field, in carriages and on trains, in military barracks, in prisons and bordellos.

Although I was born in the proletarian slum section of Vienna, I inherited from my parents a healthy body which stood me in good stead through the vicissitudes of my life and helps me now to enjoy a comfortable old age. Most of the girls who were my playmates in that shabby neighborhood of ours went to pot and died an early death in dreary orphanages, or became old-looking hags in their twenties, worn out by the daily drudgery which is the lot of proletarian wives. But my voluptuous body withstood all the miseries of poverty and seemed to thrive on the practice of every kind of sex activity from early childhood on.

My indestructible health was the firm foundation on which I was able to build a long and lucrative career as a prostitute. I was not only sexually precocious, but more observant than other slum children and I soon realized that as a matter of sheer survival I had to get away from the filthy proletarian suburb of my childhood. When I noticed that men wanted my body and were ready to pay for it, I tried to acquire customers among the socially prominent classes of society and when the men of social standing and erudition often showed some interest in "educating" me and teaching me good manners, I became an eager listener. Gradually I acquired a taste for culture and the finer things in life, especially when I noticed that low-born women like myself don't have to remain poor and ignorant nobodies all their lives, as we had always been told in our childhood. I also found out that most proletarian girls were driven to prostitution by social and economic conditions and not because they were just "naturally corrupt."

I must admit that—in my own case—it was my passionate disposition and my prematurely awakened body that pushed me in the direction that might have led to an early death in a hospital for the poor, but which led me to a life of wealth and enjoyment instead. I got around, as the saying goes, and I widened my cultural horizon by travel in foreign countries, all the while observing people everywhere and letting my judgment mature.

If, today, I want to write about the early part of my life, it is certainly not from any guilt feelings that may force me to unburden my soul, or any such nonsense. It is rather to mitigate my loneliness that makes me think back to the days of my childhood and young girlhood, and perhaps also the desire to find some entertainment in reliving my past and especially the memory of all those pleasures from which my aged body has excluded me for some years. I know that our dear old parish priest would like me to do penance in "confessing my sinful past," and base my writing on such an austere attitude. But, as I have said before, I don't feel any regrets, because that "sinful" life has saved me from suffocating in the slums and permitted me to live like any woman of good society.

Apart from all that, I have never found any truthful description of how prostitutes actually live, what they feel and think, and what they have to put up with. Thus, by writing this book and offering the reader a realistic picture of the "low-life," many of my former customers and all the noble, rich and carefree males of "good society" may learn a good lesson about what the average "girl for hire," that they greedily press into their arms, thinks of them and that what she often *has* to tell them are not her real thoughts and feelings, but a professional "line" to make them feel proud. It will do those gentlemen a lot of good to learn the truth.

CHAPTER 1

My father was a very poor journeyman saddler who worked from morning till evening in a shop in the Josefstadt, as the eighth district of Vienna is called. In order to be there at seven in the morning, he had to get up at five and leave half an hour later to catch the horse-drawn streetcar that delivered him after one and a half hour's ride at a stop near his working place.

"Suburbia" in the Vienna of the mid-19th century did not necessarily mean a residential section for the well-to-do middle-class, as in modern times. Rich people did live in the outer districts to the north and northwest, but the western and southern suburbs constituted what we called the "workers' ghetto." There, in gloomy tenement houses about five stories high, lived all the Viennese who were not white-collar workers.

Our tenement building, filled from top to bottom with poor folk, was in the seventeenth district, called Ottakring. Nobody who never visited those tenement houses can imagine the unsanitary, primitive living conditions under which we spent our childhood and adolescence, and—in most cases—the rest of our poor lives.

My parents, and my two brothers and I lived in a so-called apartment that consisted of one room and a kitchen. That was the size of all the apartments in our building and in most of the other buildings of the district. Most tenants had a lot of children who swarmed all over the buildings and crowded the small courtyards in the summer. Since I and my two older brothers made up only a "small" family, compared with the families around us having at least half a dozen brats, my parents could afford to make a little money by accepting roomers. Such roomers, who had to share our one room and a kitchen with the whole family, were called "sleepers," because the tiny rent one could charge them was for a small, iron

18

folding bed that was placed in the kitchen at night.

I remember several dozens of such sleepers who stayed with us for a while, one after another. Some left because they found work out of town, some, because they quarreled too much with my father, and others simply did not show up one evening, thus creating a vacancy for the next one. Among all those sleepers there were two who clearly stand out in my memory. One was a dark-haired young fellow with sad eyes who made a scant living as a locksmith's apprentice and hardly ever washed his sooty face. We children were a little afraid of him, perhaps because of his blackened face and also because he hardly said anything. One afternoon I was alone in our place playing with what was supposed to be a doll on the floor. My mother had taken my two brothers to a nearby empty lot that was covered with wild grass and shrubbery where the boys could play, and my father was not yet home from work. The young sleeper came home quite unexpectedly and, as usual, did not say a word. When he saw me playing on the floor, he picked me up, sat down and put me on his knees. When he noticed that I was about to cry, he whispered fiercely, "Shut up! I'm not going to do you any harm!"

He made me lie on my back across his knees and lifted my skirt so that he could look at my nude abdomen, especially at the spot between my legs. He kept looking and looking, and though I was still afraid, I did not move. Suddenly he heard my mother and the boys coming home and put me down on the floor and went into the kitchen. A few days after that he appeared again in the middle of the afternoon, but this time my mother was home. She seemed to be glad that the man had come so early and asked him to watch over me while she went buying some food. He promised to do that and as soon as mother had gone, he repeated the strange game of last time. Without saying anything he held me on his knees and contemplated my nude midsection with a fascinated stare. I, too, did not say a word, if only from fear. He repeated this strange ritual a few more times while he stayed with us. I had not the slightest idea what it was all about, and knowing that adults were strange anyway, I did not bother to think about it. Today, of course, I know the meaning of it and that's why I call that silent locksmith's apprentice my first lover.

The other sleeper whom I remember only too well was neither silent nor as easily satisfied as the locksmith. But I'll talk about him a little later.

CHAPTER 2

My two brothers were quite unlike each other, as if they came from different families. Lorenz, the older of the two, was nine, my senior by four years. He was an introvert and did very well at school and loved to go to church. Franz, the younger one, was almost seven. In contrast to Lorenz, he was always gay and outgoing and preferred my company to that of his brother.

When I was seven years old I had a very remarkable experience. (That was two years after the bewildering episode with the taciturn locksmith's apprentice.) One afternoon Franz and I decided to visit the children of our neighbor, a widower who was at work all day and had to leave his son and daughter to themselves. Anna was a thin, blonde girl of nine whose pale complexion was not improved by the addition of a harelip. Her brother, Ferdinand, called "Ferdl" for short, was a robust and well-built thirteen-year-old, blonde like his sister, but much healthier looking, with red cheeks and broad shoulders.

We had played a few harmless games as we usually did, when Anna suddenly suggested we should play "Father and Mother." Her brother laughed and said: "Yeah, she always wants to play father and mother and nothing else!" But Anna kept insisting and, without much further ado, took my brother, Franz, by the hand and declared:

"You are my husband and I am your wife."

At the same moment Ferdl took my arm and said: "Well then I am your husband and you are my wife!"

Anna got hold of two pillow-slips and twisted them into the likeness of babies in swaddling clothes. Handing me one, she said:

"This is your child!"

I obediently took the imitation baby in my arms and began to rock it as I had seen mothers do with their sucklings. Anna and Ferdl burst out laughing.

"Hold it! You can't start out like that! First you have to *make* a child, then you have to be pregnant, then you have to give birth to it, and then, when it has been born, you can rock it!"

I remembered that I had already heard of

women being "pregnant," and that it meant they would give birth to a child. I also knew why women often had big bellies, but all this was pretty vague in my mind and, although Franz and I did not believe in the stork any longer, we still didn't know how children were "made." Both of us looked kind of silly, because we didn't understand what the "game" was that we were supposed to play.

Anna seemed to know what to do next. She tried to unbutton the fly of Franz' pants.

"Come on, Franz, pull that tassel out of your pants!"

She didn't wait for him to make up his mind, but with a deft movement of her hand freed his "tassel" from its hiding place behind the fly. Ferdl laughed as if it were a big joke, but I didn't know what to do. My feelings were all mixed up. I looked at Franz' tassel with as much astonishment as fascination, also with curiosity and a little uneasiness. But I also felt a strange excitement that was new to me.

Franz himself stood quite still and didn't know what exactly was happening to him, but the touch of Anna's hand on his bare tassel made it stand up stiff like a small pencil.

"Quick, Franz," Anna was whispering, "come on, now!" With that she flopped down on the floor, lifted her little skirt and spread her legs apart. At the same time I felt Ferdl's hand between my legs while he urged me in a hoarse voice to lie down. I did so obediently and as soon as I pulled my skirt over my belly, Ferdl knelt between my legs and rubbed his stiff tassel against my belly. I had to giggle because in his excitement Ferdl moved his tassel all over my abdomen and tickled me quite a bit. His weight on my chest felt a little heavy, and I began to find this "game" very silly, but Ferdl's heavy breathing roused a peculiar sensation in me that I had never felt before. It was almost pleasurable, and that's why I didn't insist on getting up, and even became quite serious after a while.

Suddenly Ferdl stopped moving and lay still on me, then we both got up and he showed me his tassel which I took between my fingers and curiously eyed the small drop of liquid that appeared on its tip. Ferdl pulled the foreskin back so that the rosy glans became fully visible. I amused myself by moving the foreskin back and forth and watching the glans appear and disappear like the head of a turtle.

Franz and Anna were still lying on the floor and at it, full steam. I noticed that Franz' face had become quite red and his breath was quick and heavy as that of Ferdl had been a while ago. Anna's face, too, had changed and reddened, her eyes were closed and she looked as if she felt a little sick. But I was mistaken, because when Franz stopped moving and they both lay still for a few seconds, Anna opened her eyes and seemed quite contented. Both got up from the floor and joined Ferdl and myself on the sofa. While we sat there together, Ferdl kept his hand under my skirt and stroked my cunt and I saw that Franz did the same to Anna. We girls, in our turn, played with the tassels of the boys, who enjoyed it very much. The tickling that Ferdl's fingers aroused in my cunt did not make me giggle any more. On the contrary, I felt a vague pleasure of a kind I had never experienced before. A voluptuous warmth spread all over my body as if Ferdl's fingers were touching me everywhere.

That's why it came as a disappointment when Anna interrupted our preoccupation with one another and insisted that we continue to play the game in its logical sequence. She took the two imitation babies, alias bunched up pillow-slips, shoved one under my dress and the other under her own.

"You see," she said, "now we are pregnant!"

We promenaded around the room showing our big bellies and got a great kick out of it. So did the boys. After a while we "gave birth" to the babies and rocked them gently in our arms and then handed them to our "husbands" so that they could admire them and rock them, too. To all outward appearances, we were playing like any innocent children and having great fun.

Suddenly Anna got the idea that she should suckle her baby. She unbuttoned her blouse and went through the motions of a mother suckling her child. Her nipples were already quite noticeable and her brother began to play with them, encouraging Franz to follow his example.

"It's too bad," said Ferdl, "that Pepi (that's my nickname) has no teats yet."

I began to envy Anna and wished to grow and become older much quicker. Now Ferdl and Anna gave a lecture on "how to make babies." They told us that what we had been doing was called "fucking," and that our parents did the same thing when they were in bed with each other, and that's what made women pregnant so that they could have children.

Ferdl was already an expert in these matters and seemed to know everything about fucking and making babies. I was astonished to hear that our cunts were still too undeveloped to let a boy's prick enter there and that only when we became older a lot of hair would grow around it and the hole would at last be able to open properly so that a prick could get into it completely.

When I refused to believe this, Anna assured me that Ferdl was telling the truth, especially since he had fucked Mrs. Reinthaler, when he caught her alone in the attic one afternoon, where she was hanging up some freshly washed linen to dry.

"That's why Ferdl knows it so well," said Anna, "his prick went right into her hole, all the way."

Mrs. Reinthaler and her husband, a streetcar conductor, lived on the uppermost floor of our tenement building. She was a smallish, thick-set woman with black hair and a pretty face, and very friendly with us children. Ferdl told us the whole story.

"Mrs. Reinthaler had been doing her washing in the laundry room in the basement and came upstairs carrying a basket full of wet linen. When she saw me sitting on the last step in front of the entrance to the attic, she said to me, 'Hello, Ferdl, you are a strong boy! Why don't you help me carry this heavy basket right into the loft?' Well, I did, and when we had put the basket down, Mrs. Reinthaler gave me a strange look and asked me what I wanted for helping her. I told her she didn't have to give me anything for this little help, but she suddenly took hold of my hand and pressed it against her full breast.

"'Doesn't that feel good?' she asked and her eyes were glittering. I knew at once what she was getting at because my sister and I had been doing it with each other for some time. Correct, Anna?"

"Correct," said Anna, as if such a thing were a matter of course.

"And so I wasn't as dumb as Mrs. Reinthaler seemed to believe," continued Ferdl. "But I wasn't too sure how far she wanted me to go, and so I just squeezed her teats for a while. She liked it all right and she opened her blouse and put her naked breast in my hand and let me play with it. She laughed and suddenly grabbed my already stiff prick and said, 'If you won't tell anybody I'll let you do something else!' I assured her that I wouldn't say a thing. 'Promise?' she said. 'Sure!' I said. She went to the door of the loft to make sure nobody was coming upstairs and then she ran back to me and laid herself across the full laundry basket and pulled her skirt up to her waist and pulled me down on her belly. I didn't have to do a thing. She grabbed my prick and stuck it into her cunt where it disappeared. I could feel that my balls were hitting against her skin. I also felt the hair of her cunt rubbing against my belly. So you see? I really know all about it."

Anna didn't want Ferdl to stop talking about this exciting adventure. "Was it good?" she asked him.

"Yes, quite good," he said in a matter-of-fact tone. "Mrs. Reinthaler liked it very much. She kept pushing back at me and pressed me against her and made me play with her teats all the while. When it was all over, she jumped up, pushed her skirt down and hissed at me, 'Now get the hell out of here, you louse, and if you say one word to a soul I'll bash your head in. Now scram!' "

Ferdl was frowning. "I don't understand why she was mad, all of a sudden?"

"Never mind!" said Anna impatiently. "Look. Ferdl, why don't we see whether you can stick it into me the way you could do it with Mrs. Reinthaler. We haven't tried it for some time."

Ferdl groped under her skirt and played around for a few seconds, but when he tried to stick a finger into her hole, she said:

"No, let's try the real thing. Come on, we'll play father and mother again!"

Franz went over to Anna and grabbed her, but she pushed him away.

"No, this time Ferdl is going to be my husband. You try it with Pepi!"

While Anna pulled her brother down on her, I took Franz' little tassel out of his fly and I still remember how excited I was when I felt it become stiff and hard. I massaged it a little and Franz rubbed his hand against my cunt, but since we knew now how the thing was done, we flopped down on the floor and I directed Franz' little prick between my thighs so that it rubbed against my cunt. I wanted to feel it there and not sliding up on my belly. Franz did a good job and I began to enjoy it so much that I rubbed against him, too. That went on for some time until Franz collapsed on me and seemed quite exhausted. We lay there without moving for a few moments until we heard a whispered dispute going on next to us.

When we got up we saw that Ferdl was still lying on Anna and that she had put her legs around the small of his back.

"Hold still," we heard Ferdl say. "I'm sure

it will go in all the way!"

"Yes," said Anna, "but it hurts!"

"It will stop soon. It always hurts in the beginning. Just let me try. You'll like it!"

Franz and I lay down on the floor on either side of the two so that we could see whether Ferdl's prick was really going in all the way. We noticed to our amazement that Anna's cunt was really open and that Ferdl's prick was almost half in. But he moved it back and forth so clumsily that it slid out again. I grabbed it and pushed it back into its place and tried to help by pushing it in further. But when Ferdl pressed forward with all his strength, Anna yelled so loudly that we were frightened. She got up and flatly refused to continue our "game." Ferdl, by that time, was so excited that I had to let him lie on me and rub his prick against my slit until he was satisfied.

By now I felt a little sore between my legs and was glad that the time had come to go back home. Like the Reinthalers, we lived on the top floor and when Franz and I went up there we saw Mrs. Reinthaler and another woman standing in front of her door, gossiping. We couldn't help bursting into loud laughter and quickly disappeared into our apartment and banged the door shut behind us before the two women had time to turn around.

CHAPTER 3

It was from that day on that I began to regard children and adults, men and women, with a new awareness. Although I was only seven years of age, I was completely awakened sexually, a strange situation for so young a girl, and all the more so as this new awareness became manifest in the way I walked, and looked at people. My whole existence became a silent challenge to every male to grab hold of me and possess me. The word "sex-appeal" had not been invented yet, but that was exactly what seemed to ooze out of my very being, and that is the only explanation I can find for the astonishing fact that even mature and usually reasonable men could not keep their eyes and hands off me when they saw me for the first time and lost all caution and every inhibition in taking their pleasure with me.

I am not bragging, or giving in to undue vanity, when I say that even now certain men seem to get quite excited in my presence, no matter that my youth is gone, and that my face and body have lost much of their former attractiveness. Yes, even today when I take men. like that to bed with me, they seem to become sexually drunk in my embrace. This natural sexual appeal in my nature must have been noticeable when I was still quite young and innocent. Otherwise, why should that taciturn locksmith's apprentice have always taken me on his lap to contemplate my nude abdomen?

It was a few days after our informative visit with Anna and Ferdl when all three of us children happened to be alone at home. Franz and I decided to tease our older brother, Lorenz, who never paid much attention to us and antagonized us by his sanctimonious, "goody-goody" behavior. Franz asked Lorenz whether he knew where babies came from and also how they are "made." Lorenz looked quite perplexed and said: "Why? Do YOU know the answer?"

Franz and I laughed, and I quickly took Franz' tassel from his pants and began to stroke it, while Franz put his hand on my slit. Lorenz didn't say a word but kept watching us with a serious face. Franz and I lay down on the bed and demonstrated our new knowledge exactly as we had learned it from Anna and Ferdl. Lorenz watched us quite calmly and never said a word, even when Franz and I had finished. I went over to Lorenz and wanted to open his fly and said: "Come on, you must try it with me, now!" He pushed my hand away and said to our amazement:

"I've known about fucking for quite some time. You don't really believe that I'd have to wait for you two to teach me something new, eh? You know, of course, that fucking is a mortal sin, don't you! Fornicators go to hell!"

His words scared us at first, but after a while we asked him whether he really believed that our parents would have to roast in hell for doing it.

"Certainly," said Lorenz, making a stubborn face, "fornication is a mortal sin and all who do it must go to hell!"

This time we laughed because we sensed his stupid piousness which made him talk that way. But Lorenz repeated his contention and when we teased him about it, he threatened to tell on us. "Wait till I tell father and mother about it! I'll also tell our teacher and the priest!"

We were a little subdued by his talk and decided never to do anything in his presence. Nevertheless, Lorenz somehow knew that Franz and I continued to do it with each other, also that we played around with other children, but he kept silent and avoided being with us.

Yes, we played the new "game" as often as possible. Whenever we were with Anna and Ferdl, Franz did it first with Anna and then with me, while Ferdl fucked me first and then his sister. If we didn't find Anna and Ferdl at home, Franz and I played our game alone. We did it day after day and couldn't talk and think of anything else. Our greatest wish was to be able to do it like real grown-up people. Anna and I wanted to have an adult man lying on top of us, and Ferdl and Franz dreamed of doing it with Mrs. Reinthaler.

One day, when we had come to visit Anna and Ferdl, we met two other visitors, Mizzi and her brother Poldi. Mizzi, a thirteen-year-old, well-developed girl, was Anna's cousin. I envied her for the already pointed breasts under her thin blouse. We all talked about our interesting new game and Poldi, quite big for his twelve years, bragged about his pubescent sister. He lifted the front of her skirt and said:

"Look! She already has hair on her cunt! Just like a grown woman!"

We regarded the triangular tuft of hair below Mizzi's belly almost with respect. There was a grown woman, we thought. And we felt sad about the bare places between our own legs. Next, Poldi helped Mizzi to shed her blouse and let us admire her firm young breasts. Each of us stroked and fondled them so that Mizzi became quite excited. She lay back on the bed, closed her eyes and reached for her brother and for Franz who stood next to her. Obligingly the boys took their stiff pricks from their flies and pressed them each into Mizzi's groping hands. Ferdl placed himself between her legs and tickled her slit with his stick. She stretched

31

her body and exclaimed:

"Ah, I can't stand it any longer. Quick, Poldi, do it to me!"

The next moment her brother was lying on her and guided his prick into her hole. The rest of us were standing close to the bed and watched very attentively how some "real fucking" was being done. Mizzi and Poldi said that grown-ups did it exactly as they were about to perform for us right now. Each one of us was excited in his, or her, own way. Mizzi still held Ferdl's prick with one hand, while Franz had put his into Anna's hand.

To my amazement Poldi kissed his sister full on the mouth. I hadn't known that kissing was part of fucking. I also noticed that Poldi kept caressing Mizzi's breasts until the nipples stood up quite stiffly. When Poldi's prick disappeared completely in Mizzi's cunt, I checked with my fingers to find out whether my eyes were not deceiving me. When I felt the root of that hard prick right on top of Mizzi's tuft of hair and then coming out again and sliding back the next moment, in and out, in and out, I became strangely excited. Poldi's prick was much bigger than my brother's and even Ferdl's, and I got a vague idea of what an adult's prick must look like.

But, most of all, I was surprised at Mizzi's reaction. She wildly moved her hips, countering Poldi's thrusts with some of her own, and wriggled her legs and feet, and kept sighing and moaning as if she were in great pain. But I soon noticed it was anything but pain that caused her groans and contortions. Especially when she gasped:

"Push harder, Poldi! Deeper! Deeper! Ah,

that's good!"

As soon as Poldi had finished and pulled out his limp prick, Ferdl and Franz struggled to get between Mizzi's legs first. Each tried to push the other back, and Mizzi watched them with a delighted smile, but when it began to look like a real fight, she quickly decided:

"Stop! I'll have the little one first!"

She meant my brother. Franz pounced on her like a madman and began to rub his little prick against her slit as he always did it with me. Mizzi grabbed his little pencil and stuck it into her hole. Franz stopped moving and seemed quite bewildered at this new experience. But Mizzi began to move her hips wildly so that Franz' prick slid promptly out of her hole. I grabbed it with my right hand and put it back where it belonged, and Franz seemed to understand what was expected of him in this, for him, new situation. But now a new difficulty arose when Mizzi insisted he should caress her teats as Poldi had done a while ago. When Franz tried to knead her breasts, he stopped fucking her and when she, quite impatiently, reminded him of moving within her hole, he forgot about her breasts. It was too much to expect of Franz to act like an experienced fucker on this first real try of his, and Mizzi sighed:

"What a pity! The little one can't do much!"

Now it was Ferdl who intervened by saving Franz all the work with Mizzi's teats. He caressed them and kissed and sucked the nipples so that Mizzi sighed with pleasure, while Franz began to move in her quickly and rhythmically so that she threw up her legs and moaned lustfully:

"Ah, now it's good! Ah, that little prick feels really good, now! What a good little prick!"

When they had finished, Ferdl quickly climbed on Mizzi without letting go of her breasts. She greedily grabbed his stiff tool and when he didn't find the opening immediately I helped him and kept my hand there so that I could feel him enter completely. I held his balls so that I could feel his prick move in and out, faster and faster. He did it quite skillfully and declared: "Ah, that's fine! Just as it was with Mrs. Reinthaler!"

Ferdl's thrusts became almost violent so that the bed began to shake and squeak. Mizzi was groaning and Ferdl's breathing became so loud that I thought it could be heard on the staircase. A strange sensual atmosphere pervaded the room and was distinctly felt by Anna, Franz and Poldi who were looking on with a fascinated stare, their faces flushed scarlet.

When Mizzi and Ferdl had finished at last, Anna and I demanded to have our turn, but Anna was quicker than I and threw herself on the bed and called for Poldi, who seemed to interest her very much, to mount her. Mizzi, who had got up from the bed with the bounce of a ballet dancer after a good performance, seemed as fresh as a daisy, and yet she had been fucked by three different pricks during the past hour. She smoothed her skirt down over her legs, but left her breasts uncovered and declared, laughingly, that now she wanted to enjoy herself by watching us perform.

Anna was still lying on the bed, her skirt pulled up to her belly and her legs spread apart, but Poldi did not pay any attention to her

34

invitation and began to play with the nude breasts of his sister. He lifted them with his palms, pressed them together and worked on the nipples with his tongue. Soon Mizzi began to emit lustful groans and leaned against a large chest of clothes. With one hand she worked on Poldi's stiff tool and with the other she caressed his pubic hair. If Anna was still hoping to get Poldi to mount her she must have been disappointed to see him so busy with Mizzi's teats. After a few minutes, Poldi lifted his sister's skirt and let her guiding hand deposit his prick in her insatiable hole. The two started to fuck so violently that the hangers inside the clothes-chest were bumping against each other. This was the first stand-up job we had ever seen. As a matter of fact, we hadn't even known that such a thing existed. When Poldi was through, it seemed quite natural that Franz should be the next to try this new position and this time Mizzi kept her hand near her hole to see that Franz wasn't going to slip out again. At last, Ferdl tried this new variation of the exciting game and proved that he was a fast learner.

I realized to my amazement that Mizzi had stood these six lays without getting tired. Now I wished more than ever to grow up quickly and be able to do it like Mizzi. Anna felt grossly neglected and got up from the bed. She got hold of Poldi's prick and assured him that her hole was already big enough to do a good job and that he should try it. Poldi did not seem convinced. He lifted her skirt and groped her with his fingers and at last said she was not quite ready for the task. But Anna didn't want to give up so easily. She kept massaging Poldi's limp prick; it didn't have the desired effect.

I had turned to Ferdl and tried to infuse some life into his tired tool and he let me play with it for a while, but it stayed down. My self-esteem was greatly hurt, especially when Ferdl let his hands slide over my flat breasts and exclaimed:

"You just don't have any teats!"

"To hell with you!" I thought and looked around for Franz whom I discovered lying again on Mizzi in one corner of the room. He kneaded her breasts as if he wanted to practice this special caress for further occasions. I opened his fly and pulled his stiff little pencil out, but he asked me to help him put it into Mizzi's hole. This was too much! Being twice rejected, I stuck my tongue out at him and said he should put his little worm into her without my help. He did it, too, and now we had to watch Mizzi enjoying her seventh fuck with great glee. It was the wildest of all and lasted a full half hour. Anna and I were glad when it was time for us to go home. We felt miserable and cursed that damned Mizzi with her large teats and her thick tuft of hair on her cunt. It became clear to us that we could not afford to risk having older girls around if we wanted to be included in that wonderful game.

Thank God, Mizzi and her brother lived too far away to visit us often, and so Anna and I *had* to be good enough for our partners. We didn't pretend to play father and mother any more, but practiced screwing for the pleasure of it, without having to give any excuses to anybody. We had learned enough to be kept busy every day and tried to fuck lying down and standing up, too. Sometimes it became a little painful for Anna and myself, because the boys had tasted the real thing and always tried to drill their pricks into our holes, but without much success.

This pastime of ours lasted all summer. Later Anna and Ferdl moved to another part of town and I didn't see Anna again until many years had passed. But before our two friends left we had the opportunity to enrich our sexual knowledge on a special occasion when Mizzi and Poldi had come on another visit. This time they brought a fifteen-year-old boy with them, Robert, who immediately took charge of our games. When he showed us his big prick we noticed that he already had a lot of hair around its root. We three girls were delighted with this almost mature emblem of virility and kept stroking it gently and also caressing the large balls we had taken out of his fly. Mizzi, always the greedy one, asked Robert to start with her, but he said, "No, I want to fuck Pepi first!"

I still remember how proud and happy I was to be chosen, instead of that full-bosomed Mizzi. I climbed quickly on the bed, pushed my skirt back and opened my thighs as wide as I could. Robert came to the bed and groped my still hairless cunt and exclaimed:

"It's still too small for the real thing! I'd have to rub against her slit on the outside."

"Sure, she's only a rub-job!" Mizzi said very quickly, and pulled him by the arm. "She hasn't even two hairs on that little box. What do you want with her? Look at my box. I'm a real woman, you can stick it in as far as you want to!"

"Shut up! I said I want to fuck Pepi first, and I'm going to do it!" Robert declared with firmness.

I was lying quite still and kept looking at his face that had become flushed. He hadn't stopped rubbing his fingers against my slit, and for the first time I felt what it meant to be fucked by a real man, or rather what it *could* mean, if I were a few years older and had a riper body.

Robert suddenly said:

"Now all of you, do what I tell you. I'm going to show you something new."

He seemed to think it over for a few seconds and then asked me to lie exactly in the middle of the bed, while Anna had to lie on my left, next to the wall, and Mizzi on my right, near the edge. Robert knelt in front of me and commanded: "Okay, Pepi, now turn around! Yes, on your belly! You, Anna, lie a little higher! Yes, your belly should be next to Pepi's shoulder! That's good, and you, Mizzi, take your blouse off!"

Mizzi almost tore her blouse to shreds. She couldn't get it off fast enough. I saw that her nipples were dark and quite stiff. Now, Robert pushed Anna's skirt over her waist, and then he uncovered my fanny beyond the small of my back. With his right hand he gripped my belly very gently so that my fanny was raised a little and stuck his big tool between my thighs which, at his request, I squeezed tightly together. It was wonderful to feel his hot prick between my thighs and touching my slit, too.

Robert removed his hand from my belly and began to move his prick slowly backward and forward. Soon I felt a thrill running through my whole body and wished this would go on forever. To my own surprise I began to sigh and moan as I had heard Mizzi do it, the last time, and I responded by pushing my fanny against Robert whose rhythmic thrusts had become slightly faster. When I heard Mizzi and Anna beginning to moan like myself, I wondered what was happening. I had my head buried in the pillow and could not see a thing. I didn't *want* to see anything. All I wanted was to feel that vigorous prick moving between my thighs, and down to my slit.

I lifted my head a little and saw how Robert's right hand was fingering Anna's slit. He must have been doing a good job, because she wriggled from right to left and moaned louder and louder. With the other hand, Robert played with Mizzi's nipple which had become so stiff that it looked like a little prick. He himself was beginning to breathe hard and kept fucking me in the same, slightly increasing tempo. Ferdl and Franz were standing beside the bed, their faces quite red, and looked on.

Mizzi, who was producing the loudest moans, suddenly screamed:

"Ah, I can't stand it any longer! I want to get something into my cunt! Hey, you, Ferdl, Franz, stick your pricks into me, ah, I want to be fucked! Quick! Come on, Franz, you little squirt, give it to me!"

When Franz saw her blindly groping hand, he quickly put his stiff thing into it. She pulled him close, and he quickly knelt on the bed next to Robert, and soon was fucking her like an expert. But he was not expert enough to play with her breasts at the same time. He needn't have worried, because Robert kept tickling Mizzi's nipple as before, which was driving her mad with pleasure. She grabbed her brother's bare prick and put it between her lips so that Poldi experienced the first blow-job of his young life. Ferdl, who seemed to be the only one left out of the group-fucking, crawled next to Anna and put his tool into her mouth and began to move it quickly in and out. His sister not only did not resent it, but began to suck Ferdl's fast moving cock as if it were a lollipop.

I realized that all seven of us were getting great pleasure out of what we were doing and decided to remember this clever device for the future and perhaps add a few innovations of my own. Sex, as I saw more and more clearly, invited one to invent endless varieties.

That wonderful stiff, hot prick of Robert's moved faster and faster, his breathing became almost a rattle, and suddenly, I felt a hot liquid squirt between my thighs and I yelled:

"Hey, you are pissing! Stop it!"

Robert, without stopping, grunted:

"Nonsense! I'm coming! That's the best of it!"

Now he stopped moving, and we all disentangled ourselves from each other. Each wanted to know all about this business of "having to come" and squirting a lot of liquid from the prick. Robert explained that that was what every adult man had to do when he was about to finish fucking, and that it was the highlight of the whole thing. Ferdl, Franz and Poldi were assured by him that as soon as some hair would grow around their genitals, they, too, would be able to ejaculate a lot of liquid. Now, as long as they were younger, only a drop appeared on the tip of their cocks.

Mizzi was not a bit interested in Robert's

educational lecture to the boys and interrupted with an impatient demand: "Come on, Robert, now you've got to fuck me, but good!"

"Relax, kid!" said Robert, who took great pride in having become our teacher. Besides, the other boys and Anna and I wanted to watch how Robert managed "to come."

He was only too willing to give us an immediate demonstration.

"If you want to see me come, you'll have to do a hand-job on me!"

We didn't know what he meant. We knew now what regular fucking was and also what a blow-job was, but a hand-job was still new to us. Robert didn't hesitate to show it to us. He sat down on a chair, spread his knees apart and began to masturbate himself. (Of course, I learned the proper term for it much later.)

We caught on pretty fast, and we three girls tried our skill at this new hand-job. Mizzi improved on the technique by sticking Robert's tool into her mouth and worked on it so greedily that Robert was afraid he might come too soon for us to see anything. He pushed Mizzi aside, and when Anna thought she could take over now, he grabbed me by the hair and pressed his prick against my face. I did not hesitate and received that big thing between my lips. It was quite different from feeling it between my thighs and soon I realized that the voluptuous sensation caused by the in-and-out movement of this thick, silky stick must be similar to what a grown woman feels inside her cunt during a regular lay. As a matter of fact, I did feel some sensation in my cunt as if there were some secret connection between mouth and genitals. Today I know that a woman's sex apparatus is not limited to her cunt, but extends all over her body.

Robert disliked letting go of me, but he wanted to be fair and let Anna have a go at it, too. But Anna had hardly touched that twitching prick with her lips, when Robert began to ejaculate. The first squirt had gone into Anna's mouth and she quickly spit it out. Robert replaced Anna's lips with his fingers and kept masturbating until the last squirt of white liquid had left the opening in his penis. We all crowded around him to watch this astonishing spectacle and marveled at the distance his sperm was ejected. One big splotch landed smack in my face, and I was so excited that I didn't feel any disgust. Each one of us showed great excitement, especially Mizzi who kept pestering Robert:

"But now, now you're going to fuck me, eh?"

Robert's tool had become quite limp and seemed to need a good rest, and Robert himself said as much, but Mizzi acted hysterical and didn't want to give up. She squatted on the floor between Robert's knees, and began to suck and lick his tool as if her life depended on getting it hard again. It was no use, and almost with tears in her eyes she kept exclaiming: "But you WILL fuck me when it gets hard again, won't you? You will fuck me, won't you?" Robert didn't pay much attention to her wailing.

We others didn't have much time to pay attention to Mizzi's problem, we were too busy practicing blow-jobs. This newly-learned variety of the great fucking game impressed us quite a bit and Anna and I had to serve the boys as willing guinea pigs. Anna took on Franz, while I put Ferdl's stick in my mouth. It was far easier to take care of than the thick and long tool of Robert's, but it was also far less exciting. A boy's penis can never be a good substitute for that of an adult. Besides, Ferdl was so uncontrolled that he pushed his thing right down my throat and moved in and out with such wild motions that I might have been a piece of wood with a hole in it. I had to grab his prick and direct the procedure with a firm hand. When he came, he didn't really come the way Robert had. The little drop that appeared on the tip of his penis was hardly noticed by my tongue. On the other hand, I again felt that certain sensation in my cunt as if Ferdl's prick had been down there instead of in my mouth.

Anna was still busy sucking Franz' tool, and so I had to take on the waiting Poldi who had already "invented" this variety with his sister without any instructions and demonstrations from outsiders. He was more disciplined and skilled than Ferdl and moved in my mouth in an even tempo as if he were fucking a cunt. I became so strongly aroused that I would have yelled with lust as Mizzi had done a while ago; only the moving prick in my mouth prevented me from giving sound to my intense pleasure. Without being aware of it, I had begun to lick Poldi's tool with my tongue which, unfortunately, had the result that he came immediately. He, too, had become very excited and, at the final moment, pressed my head against his body. I could hear the blood beat in his veins, which, together with the twitching of his tool in my mouth, gave me a sort of ecstasy that I'd never felt before. I didn't let go of Poldi's prick until it had become quite soft in my mouth.

Mizzi was still lying between Robert's knees, desperately sucking away at his limp tool and still without result. Robert's face didn't register any concern with Mizzi's efforts; he seemed so detached, as if he were reading a newpaper. Anna and Franz were still going strong at their blow-job, but suddenly Anna released my brother's stick from her mouth and said:

"Let's try it now the regular way. Perhaps it will go into my cunt."

Franz didn't have to be asked twice. He pushed Anna on her back and mounted her with great enthusiasm, and we all went over to where they lay to watch them. Franz was more impatient than considerate in his attempts, and yet Anna did not utter a sound of protest. She and her brother had been trying to accomplish this feat during the recent weeks, and this seemed to have loosened up the opening of her hole to some extent, because when Franz' little prick, still covered with saliva from Anna's mouth, drilled away between her legs, something gave, and Anna shouted:

"Ha, he's in me!"

"Yes, I'm really in her cunt," echoed Franz.

I asked Anna whether she was feeling any pain, but no answer came. Those two were far too busy screwing like a couple of lunatics to pay any attention to what was going on around them. Only after they had, at last, finished, was I able to have Anna tell me that "this was the best thing she had ever felt in all her life."

Meanwhile Mizzi's continuous efforts had the desired effect. After sucking and licking Robert's tool for about half an hour, nature took its course, and it was standing up, hard and rigid, and Robert condescended to mount Mizzi who behaved like one obsessed. She played with her own breasts, and grabbed Robert's fingers to put them into her mouth, sucking at them, one after the other, then she groped down to where Robert's prick was trying to do a good job and got hold of it for a second, as if to make sure that it was really fucking her. She also arched her body, from time to time, and threw her fanny around on the mattress so that Robert was almost thrown off her. Suddenly he bent down and began to lick and suck at her right nipple, just as we had done earlier with his prick. Mizzi was beside herself and began to scream and to sob:

"Ah, you are wonderful . . . oh, fuck me, fuck me, every day I want to be fucked by you . . . ah, THAT is what I call a prick, a real, wonderful prick . . . push it in deeper, deeper . . . ah, suck my other nipple, too, yes, the other nipple . . . yes . . . that's good . . . push faster, faster . . . you must fuck me tomorrow again . . . every day you must fuck me . . . ah . . . ah . . . Jesus, Mary and Joseph . . . ah, aaah . . ."

Robert worked in her like a piston in a cylinder, and at last he came, grunting with pleasure. Mizzi was lying below him as one dead.

Without doubt, Robert had become the most important person in our little group. Each of us had profited from his visit, especially Anna who was proud to have been fucked "like a grown-up." But we were too excited to pay any attention to the success of any special individual in our group. It was Robert that our attention centered around. He told us that he had been fucking regularly for the past two years. It was his stepmother who had "trained" him. His father was paralyzed and needed a lot of attention. That's why Robert was made to sleep alone in the kitchen, on a small collapsible iron bedstead. One evening he was alone in the kitchen. He heard his stepmother talking with his father in the adjoining bedroom telling him to try to sleep. Suddenly she came into the kitchen and sat down next to Robert on the bench in the dining-nook and began to stroke his face and hair, then her hand slid over his shoulders and arms to his thighs which she groped and squeezed and, at last, she opened his fly and got hold of his prick that had become quite stiff.

Feeling the hand of the still young woman playing with his tool, Robert was strongly aroused and grabbed for her breasts. She quickly opened her blouse and pressed his palms around her bare teats, guiding his fingers to the stiff nipples and showing him how to tickle them. Her breathing became so loud that the father called from the bedroom:

"Hey, what's going on out there?"

"Calm down," the stepmother called back. "Robert is helping me to push the flour barrel into place. It's heavy, you know."

After caressing Robert's prick for a few more minutes, she thought it wiser to join her husband in the bedroom, but an hour later, when she knew he had fallen asleep, she came into the kitchen again and crawled into Robert's small bed. She knelt over him, with her knees on either side of him, pushed her nightshirt back and inserted his tool into her hole. The boy remained motionless, but when he felt the large teats of the woman touch his face, he grasped them and began to play with the nipples as she had taught him a while ago. She also encouraged him to take the nipples between his lips and suck at them like a baby. He felt her moving on him and instinctively he pushed against her until he was screwing her as she had intended him to. He felt her come and then she dropped down on him with her whole weight, exhausted.

Next evening the game repeated itself, and all the following nights the stepmother joined him as soon as the father had fallen asleep. One night, she didn't leave the bedroom and Robert became more and more horny. There was a clear full moon shining through the window and Robert got up and spied through the glass panes in the door leading to the bedroom. He saw the stepmother squatting over the supine figure of his father. She was completely nude and put her nipples, alternately, into the mouth of the paralyzed man. Robert could not see whether his father could move his body, but after some time he heard the groans of both of them and realized they had come.

Now he was greatly excited and called for his stepmother to come and feel his head. "I think I'm sick!" he added. She came out at once and realized that he must have seen everything through the panes in the door.

"Did you see us do something?" she asked.

"Yes, everything!" said Robert.

She lay down next to him and pressed her teats into his waiting hands.

"This time you will lie on top of me," she promised him. Robert did not wait any longer and helped her to strip off the nightshirt until she was as naked as he had seen her in the bedroom, a while ago. He hardly needed the coaching she wanted to give him. He was frantic with desire and mounted her without delay. Once he had his prick in her, he began to poke her like an old-timer, but suddenly he heard his father call out from the bedroom:

"What the hell is the matter with the boy?"

"He's quite hot all over his body," the stepmother called back. "Maybe he has a little fever. I'm cooling him down."

"You giving him a cold compress?"

"Sure," she answered, while Robert didn't stop fucking her for a second, "he'll be all right in the morning!"

Soon the father had fallen asleep, and the two kept at it with such abandon that the bed began to squeak loudly; it was quite a noise. They had to pause to make sure that the invalid in the bedroom had not heard anything, then went right back to enjoying the lay. When Robert had finished, the stepmother wanted him to mount her again, but his little tool was still limp. She quickly took it in her mouth and began to suck it. It was a new caress for the delighted boy who soon was ready for another treat. But the full moon seemed to have affected the stepmother as it had Robert, and she made him get up and sit on the kitchen chair, then she straddled him, burying his prick in her cunt. He nearly suffocated under her weight, but this time, she did all the moving and Robert thought he would faint when both of them finished. It was a little too much enjoyment for a beginner like him.

It was already dawn when the stepmother

put on her nightshirt and went back to the bedroom. Although Robert had sunk into a profound sleep, he was too weak to get up the next morning. His father was convinced that he must have felt "feverish" last night and advised him to stay in bed all day.

All that had happened two years back, and Robert had been fucking his stepmother regularly ever since. When he finished his story, all of us looked at him with respect and admiration. After all, he was just as good as a real adult.

But the story had also stirred us up a great deal and we were ready to start experimenting again, all the more so as we had heard something new: the reversal of positions. We girls wanted to know what it felt like to lie on top of a male. Robert said we shouldn't think that this was all there was to it, but that there were many more ways of doing it.

"For instance," he said, "I sometimes fuck my stepmother from behind!"

I said that he had done it to me, too, and that's why I knew how pleasant it is.

"Yeah, but I fucked you only between the thighs; when I screw *her* from behind, I stick it right into her hole."

I realized that there were a lot of unknown pleasures in store for me and could not wait to be a few years older.

Anna and Mizzi were eager to try lying on top of the boys. Franz had to oblige Anna, because his little tool was the only one she could tolerate getting into her newly opened hole. Mizzi had to try it with her brother Poldi, but I had no luck with either Ferdl or Robert; neither could make their pricks stand up. I was determined not to be a mere onlooker again and started sucking Ferdl's prick until, at last, it became stiff. I mounted him and he cooperated very nicely, rubbing his tool against my slit. Robert didn't even try to get another hard-on, because, as he said:

"I have to save something for my stepmother. She still comes to me every night and I'm not going to disappoint her. What's more, I'm still learning a lot from her!"

We understood that quite well and looked at Robert with the same awe as third-graders look at a college boy.

Shortly after the memorable session with Robert, our two friends, Anna and Ferdl, moved with their father to another part of town.

CHAPTER 4

Franz and I had no playmates left and we would have had to play our sex games only with each other, but that was quite impossible because we were never alone. Lorenz, or my mother, were always at home, and even when they went out for a while, we couldn't take any risks.

As I slept in the same room with my parents, I decided to do a little observing now that my knowledge of what marriage meant had so greatly increased. Of course, I often heard their bed squeak at night and my father grunting and my mother sighing, but I couldn't distinguish anything in the darkness. Knowing what all those sounds meant, I became excited every time I heard them, and rubbed my fingers against my slit. One night I discovered that I could make myself come that way if I carried on long enough.

Sometimes I heard my parents whisper to each other, and immediately afterwards the bed began to squeak and I knew that it had taken some persuading of one or the other to start the game. My mother was often quite tired when she went to bed and had to be awakened by my father when he was late, and sometimes also drunk, and then wanted to have his maritally guaranteed pleasure. Sometimes it was my mother who had to prod my father into mounting her, but he never needed much persuasion except when he was in a drunken stupor and slept, snoring heavily, until the next morning. Sunday being the only day when father didn't have to go to work, it was usually on Saturday nights that he could afford to linger in some tavern and come home quite late and quite drunk.

One Saturday night, when mother and we children were already sleeping, some noise woke me up. The light was on and I saw father was so drunk that mother had to help him get out of his clothes. When she had got everything off him except his shirt, he groped for her breasts, but she pushed his hand away. My father was a strong man and could assert his strength even when he was soused. He grabbed my mother around the waist and whispered hoarsely:

"Come on, woman, open up!"

"No, you are full of beer. Sleep it off!"

He tore her nightshirt off and pushed her across the bed.

"Quick, open your legs!"

Mother gave in and spread her legs apart

and hissed at him:

"Turn the light off. The children might wake up!"

"Nonsense! They are all asleep! Come on, stick it in for me! Damn it!"

"First turn the light off," mother insisted.

Father had already put his stick into her and began to move. The light was left on, and after a while I heard mother say:

"Ah, that's good, really, tonight you've a real good hard-on . . . not so fast . . . take your time . . . and get it deeper into me, deeper . . . ah, that's the idea, yes, yes, now quicker . . . quicker . . . come on, speed up . . . ah, now make it come, make it come . . . now . . . now . . . ah . . . !"

Father grunted and gasped, and then both were quite still. After a few minutes the light was turned off, and soon I heard them both snoring away as they always did when they slept soundly.

I cautiously got up and sneaked over to the sofa where Franz was sleeping. He was wide awake and told me he, too, had watched the whole scene and felt like doing it himself. With that he slipped on top of me, but I quickly turned around on my belly and told him I wanted him to fuck me from behind, the way Robert had shown us. We were careful not to make the slightest noise and when we both had come we admitted to each other that fucking at night, and in the nude, was much better than otherwise. From then on we often did it at night when we were sure that the others were fast asleep.

It was several months after Anna and her brother had moved away when mother rented the bed in the kitchen to another sleeper. He is the one of whom I said I wanted to talk about, earlier. He must have been about fifty, but tall and with a good physique. I didn't know what he did for a living, because he stayed at home for the greater part of the day and often had long chats with mother in the kitchen, and when everybody had gone out, I used to be alone with him.

He had a long beard of curly hair, and I often speculated on how much hair he might have between his legs. On Sunday I could watch when he washed himself in the kitchen. I discovered that his chest was all covered with black hair and that made me somewhat afraid of him, although I still wanted to know what he looked like below his belly.

I shouldn't have been afraid of him at all, because he was always very friendly with me, chucked me under the chin, or stroked my hair, and I soon started to cuddle against him when he did that. One afternoon, when I was again alone with him, I began to feel more horny than ever and wished that big Robert was there and could do it to me. I went into the kitchen where Mr. Eckhardt—that was his name—sat on a chair reading the newspaper. He pulled me close and began to stroke my hair as usual, but this time I combed his beard with my fingers and, feeling all that hair, I became more and more excited. The way I looked at him seemed to act as a signal. He lowered his hand and touched my dress exactly where it covered that heated spot between my legs. He could have done it quite unintentionally and that's what I'd have thought still two years ago when I was really innocent. Now I was anything but innocent and knew exactly what was going on, and that's why I smiled at him provocatively so that his next touch on the same spot was more firm and demanding. I stepped right between his legs and gave him the same smile and, suddenly, his face became quite red. He pulled me into his arms, hugged me, and kissed me full on the mouth, while his hand slipped under my skirt and began to ·work on my slit with an artistry that I can still remember. It was as if all his five fingers were competing with each other to tickle every part of that critical spot so that it felt as if he were already in me, though he wasn't.

When I began to rub my belly against his hand, he took one of mine and pressed his tool into it. I was startled to find that my hand was too small to close around it, and when I looked at it I was startled again, because it was so big and thick that I could not imagine it would fit even into the hole of a grown woman. Nevertheless, I began to play with it and massage it, up and down the way Robert had shown us when he masturbated. Mr. Eckhardt kept kissing me passionately and suddenly he came; it was like a volcano erupting. His semen splashed in big splotches on the floor, and some of it into my hand. I, too, came, since he had redoubled the speed of his fingers on my cunt so that I nearly swooned.

When we both had calmed down, Mr. Eckhardt seemed startled at what had happened. He pressed me into his arms and said:

"You going to keep your mouth shut about this?"

I only smiled and nodded assuringly. He gave me another kiss and then got up and left the apartment. During the next few days I didn't see him very often, but when he saw me he seemed to avoid my eyes as if he were ashamed of the secret we both shared. This reaction of his gave me a peculiar feeling and I tried not to be alone with him again. On the other hand, I also felt that I did not dislike him at all and that my momentary running away from him was not what I really wanted.

One afternoon I was playing with my brothers in the courtyard when I saw Mr. Eckhardt go upstairs. I knew that my mother was not at home and I sneaked upstairs after him. My heart beat a little faster when I cautiously opened the kitchen door and saw him sitting there at the kitchen table. He reached out for me as soon as he saw me and I noticed his hands were trembling with desire. I actually threw myself into his arms and soon his skilled fingers were tickling my slit again, giving me a real treat. When he let me hold his prick, I took a good look at it. It was twice as long and thick as the one of Robert's and I noticed that it was slightly curved.

Today, after having seen thousands of these joy sticks of all sizes, having handled them and tasted them within my receptacle, I must say, in retrospect, that Mr. Eckhardt's specimen was quite extraordinary, what one may call a woman's dream, and had I been only a few years older, I'd have been able to get some real enjoyment out of it. In those days I had to limit myself to a good hand-job, and it wasn't even very good, because my hand began to be tired after a while and slowed down. But Mr. Eckhardt kept covering me with kisses and urged me on:

"Ah, don't stop, my darling, my little dove, go on, my angel, go on, don't stop now, for God's sake, keep rubbing it, quick, quick . . ."

Hearing him using all those endearments made me quite proud and I redoubled my efforts to bring this hand-job to a good finish. My diligence was soon rewarded. He ejaculated with such force that his semen hit me almost in the face which was leaning over his tool and had become quite heated what with all that effort. Seeing that large prick spurting such a great quantity of semen gave me a good idea what a real adult male should be like and it made me itch between my legs more than ever.

A few days later Mr. Eckhardt and I were again using our hands on each other and he repeated the string of endearments, like "darling," "sweetheart," "my little mistress," "my angel," "my little dove" and many more. I was giving his tool an exceptionally good work-out, while he did the same on my slit. When he noticed how I responded by swinging my hips back and forth—I was about ready to come—he whispered hotly:

"O God, if I could only fuck you . . ."

I almost startled him by letting go of him at once. Quickly I lay down on the floor, spread my legs and gave him the most inviting look I was capable of. He bent down and looked me over and then gasped:

"No, that won't work . . . you are still too young."

"But that doesn't matter," I insisted. "Come on and try, anyway!"

Trembling with desire, he shoved one hand under my fanny, raising my abdomen a little, and rubbed his prick against my little box, while I kept the moving tool in place. His thrusts became faster and he asked:

"Have you ever done this before?"

I should have told him of my games with Franz and Ferdl and Robert, but something made me say instead: "No!"

Without stopping, Mr. Eckhardt whispered:

"Oh, come on, darling, why don't you admit that you have done this before? I can see you are not new at the old game! Come on, tell me the truth! Who was it who did it with you? Tell me! Did you do it often? Did you like it?"

I was swinging my hips like mad and breathing hard, not only with pleasure, but because some of his weight was on my chest. I also felt the twitching of his prick signaling he was about to come. But I kept up my denial and said:

"No, no, I've never done it before! This is the first time . . ."

"D'you like it . . .?"

At that moment his semen splashed all over my belly and ran down my thighs.

"Sure, I like it . . ." I assured him.

"Stay where you are," he ordered and got up. He pulled his handkerchief from his pocket and cleaned up the liquid mess on my body. He continued his questioning:

"Listen, kid, I know what I'm talking about! Of course, you have known something about this. Don't lie to me!"

But when I — God only knows why — remained firm in my denial, he said:

"Well, you must have seen somebody else do it!"

That gave me a way out and I nodded.

He pressed on: "Who was it?"

I pointed toward the bedroom and said:
"My mother and father."

That seemed to interest him very much and he said:

"Ah, your folks! Tell me, how did they do it?"

He kept on questioning me until I had told him everything in great detail. While I was talking he put his fingers back to work on my slit so that I came another time.

This adventure made me very proud. Now I had done it with an adult, a real man. But I was careful not to tell Franz anything about it, although we often speculated how good all this must be with grown-up persons as partners. I always made mention of Mrs. Reinthaler so that Franz became obsessed with the idea of being another lucky one who could help her carry her laundry basket up to the drying loft.

CHAPTER 5

Since I had done it with Mr. Eckhardt, I developed a definite interest in grown men and always turned around when I noticed some especially virile looking fellow in the street and began to imagine how it would feel if such a man would take me on his knees and do it to me.

The way I looked at men didn't go unnoticed. Many turned around and looked at me as if they didn't believe what they couldn't help noticing. Some stopped and kept looking, and one day a handsome young fellow beckoned me to follow him. This unexpected event made me horny as hell, but I didn't dare accept the invitation.

Greatly encouraged by the memory of that fellow, I spent my afternoons on a large field behind our tenement house, called the Prince's Meadow. Mother used to take the boys there, sometimes, because they had lots of space to roam around and play behind a row of shrubs. Ordinarily one met only a few people there during the day and it was a good place for a quick lay, provided I could find another man like Mr. Eckhardt crossing my path.

One afternoon I had strayed a little farther afield than usual and the sun was already below the horizon when I turned around to go home. At that moment I saw a soldier coming from the opposite direction and I immediately slowed down. When we were face to face I gave him my special smile. He looked surprised, but I continued to walk slowly. I had noticed that nobody else could be seen within a radius of half a mile. I turned around and saw the soldier still looking after me. I gave him another smile and walked on. When I turned around again the soldier beckoned me and I felt a burning tickle between my legs, and my heart beat a wild tattoo. But I was too afraid to go to him, and merely stood still. Now the soldier ran toward me and whispered in a serious manner:

"You alone here?" And when I nodded silently, he added hoarsely: "Okay, let's go!"

Although I was trembling with fear, I followed him at once. I couldn't help myself. My curiosity and my horniness drowned out any idea of caution.

He led me behind some shrubbery and, without saying a word, he pushed me on my back and the next moment he was lying on top of me. I felt his hard stick pushing against my slit and quickly put my hand in front of it. But he pushed it away and kept trying to put his prick into me, groping with his hand for the right aim. His vain attempts began to hurt me, but I didn't say anything. I thought it had to happen at some time or another and the sooner the better. Once when his prick slid over my cunt it felt quite agreeable, but when he tried again to force his entrance the pain returned. Now he became angry with impatience and plain lust, and tried to force his way in.

With one hand he spread my slit apart and with the other he guided his missile and drilled so vehemently that I feared he'd tear my cunt apart. Just when I was about to scream, he flooded me with his semen. The next moment he got up, adjusted his pants and, without giving me a second look, walked away and left me lying there.

When I, at last, came out from behind the shrubbery, I saw him standing at a great distance, making water. For him the little incident was over, and he didn't think of it anymore. It was getting dark and I hurried in the direction of our building.

I had hardly walked a hundred steps when I felt somebody tapping me on the shoulder. Quite startled at the sudden touch, I turned around. It was a dirty little boy, smaller than I and probably younger. He stood there clad in torn pants and shirt and gave me a triumphant, malicious look.

"Hey, you," he said, "what were you doing with that soldier, eh?"

"Nothing!" I said furiously.

"Nothing, eh?" He laughed an ugly laugh.

And then, with a sneer: "I've seen everything!"

"You haven't seen a damned thing, you bastard," I yelled, but my poise began to give and I added lamely: "Really, there wasn't anything!"

He quickly put his hand between my legs and said:

"You bitch you, don't lie to me. You were fucking there in the grass, I seen it."

He was quite angry and kept knocking his hand against my box.

"What do you want?" I asked in a softer tone of voice. I saw it was futile to deny what he must have actually seen.

"What do I want?" He had stepped quite close to me. "I want to fuck you, too! That's what I want!"

I pushed him away from me and yelled:

"Get the hell away from me! Scram!"

Suddenly he slapped my cheek. "I'll show you, you whore! Don't ever push me again! You bitch! You like to fuck with soldiers, but you think a guy like me can be pushed around. I'm going to tell your mother about it. I know damned well who you are."

I quickly turned and began to run away from him, but little as he was, he caught up with me in no time. He grabbed me by the shoulder and was about to slap me again, when I said:

"All right, let's do it!"

We stepped behind the shrubbery by the wayside and he quickly pushed my dress back and mounted me.

"I've been waiting the whole damned afternoon to meet a girl I can fuck," this apparent seven-year-old said.

"How could you have seen me?" I inquired.

"There was nobody around."

"I was hidden in the grass when the soldier took you on. That's how."

He had a small, thin prick, but he used it quite cleverly, and I began to wonder why I had refused him in the first place. And because his prick was so very small, I got the idea that he could succeed where the soldier had failed. I grabbed the little stick and guided it right to the opening of my hole which was still wet from the soldier's ejaculation. And because of this natural lubrication, and perhaps also because the soldier's large tool had done a little advance-drilling, the boy's miniature prick suddenly slipped halfway in. I pushed against him and moved my hips and, lo and behold, for the first time in my very young life I had a male's member actually in me, no matter that the male was still a child.

I still felt some pain, but I was too proud and vain to say anything. The boy liked the whole thing very much and fucked me in little thrusts with the regularity of clockwork. It took quite some time until he had finished, and he took off without any further regard for me. I tried to get back home as fast as possible.

It was a Saturday, and my parents had gone to the tavern for a glass of beer. My brothers were already asleep and I tried to sneak by Mr. Eckhardt's iron bed in the kitchen. He was still awake and called me over to him. He pulled my hand underneath his blanket and I soon felt his prick getting hard when I touched it. Since he always slept in the nude I could feel his large balls, his thick pubic hair and his thighs and became aroused myself.

"Well, don't you want to fuck?" he whispered. I didn't want him to touch me as I was still wet between my legs. The soldier and that shrimp of a boy had left their tokens.

"No," I said, "not tonight."

I kept jacking him off and hoped that once he'd come he'd leave me alone. But he tried to get his hand under my dress and when I tried to evade him, he asked:

"What's the matter with you tonight?"

"Oh, my brothers could wake up. Let's be careful!"

And yet the feel of his big tool in my hand had made me quite horny again and I didn't resist when he lifted me up on the bed and let me mount his stiff prick. I rubbed myself against this pulsating, silky pillar of flesh and quite forgot about being still wet about my box. Mr. Eckhardt didn't notice anything. He was quite worked up and again called me his angel and his sweetheart, and when I came so violently that I felt my whole body twitch, he came too and wetted my shirt so thoroughly that I felt the moisture all night. This had been quite an eventful day for me, just as remarkable as when Robert had taught us what real fucking and masturbating and blow-jobs meant.

CHAPTER 6

My brother Franz was still watching Mrs. Reinthaler every day and I did some spying on my own, so that I could supply him with all the information that could further his secret plans.

I often saw that pretty, fat woman standing in front of the building entrance, talking and kidding around with all sorts of men and I couldn't help thinking that she was also laid by them.

The man with whom I saw her most was Mr. Horak, and as far as he was concerned it turned out that my suspicions were justified. Mr. Horak was a driver who transported loads of beer barrels to and from our building to various taverns and restaurants. I forgot to mention that the large cellar under our building was rented to a brewery and used as a subsidiary warehouse.

Mr. Horak was about thirty, tall and athletic, with a round, red face. He had a little blond moustache and his hair was cut so short that it looked as if he had shaved it off. He also wore a tiny gold earring in one ear, which impressed me very much. It was said that the piercing of the ear improved the eyesight. I never found out whether it was true, or mere popular superstition. In those days Mr. Horak appeared to me as the acme of virile beauty and proud maleness. He always wore a nicely pressed white blazer, or a regular summer suit with a vest, ornamented with a heavy silver watch chain with a pendant: a little horse also made of silver. I admired it very much and would have liked to wear it as a charm on a silver bracelet. As a matter of fact, when, many years later, I had some money, that was the kind of bracelet I bought for myself.

One day, when I came home from school, I saw two people standing inside the house entrance talking to each other. Sneaking a little closer, I heard laughter and banter, and when I peeked cautiously around the front door, there were Mr. Horak and Mrs. Reinthaler carrying on like a couple of kids who had just reached the age of puberty. Mr. Horak wore his white blazer and he tried in a playful way to grab Mrs. Reinthaler's breasts that were quite visible through her thin red blouse, which she hadn't tucked in, but let hang loose over her skirt. Mrs. Reinthaler always waited until Mr. Horak had got hold of one of her large breasts and squeezed it a little bit and then slapped the back of his hand to make him let go. When he grabbed both breasts at the same time and pressed them together, she pushed him away, but not very violently.

He stooped and pretended to lift her skirt and she reacted with a little scream and then they both laughed very heartily for a while as if enjoying a good joke. I couldn't hear them after that and when I peeked around the corner I saw them talking quite seriously, but could not make out what they were saying. Suddenly Mr. Horak disappeared in the direction of the staircase and after a few seconds Mrs. Reinthaler was following him. I sensed I was going to make a useful discovery and sneaked after them. Both had gone down to the huge cellar where the beer barrels were stored.

There was not one spot in that tenement building that we children had not explored at some time or other. We knew every nook and cranny in all the hallways, in the drying loft and in the cellar. That's why I could choose a spot behind a ledge in the wall that proved an ideal observation post. In front of me was a short corridor that ended in the storeroom which was receiving plenty of daylight through a few large grilled windows close to the ceiling.

Smack in the middle of that storeroom I

could see Mr. Horak and Mrs. Reinthaler pressed against each other in a passionate embrace. His hand was under her blouse playing with her large teats which I could see shortly when she took her blouse off. She pressed herself still closer against him and opened the buttons of his fly releasing his rigid prick which was very long and thin and of a strange paleness. Mrs. Reinthaler's hand wasn't exactly small, but it could hardly be seen when she began to massage that very long specimen that resembled a giant asparagus in its thinness and paleness.

I could hear the heavy breathing of Mr. Horak and saw how he pushed Mrs. Reinthaler against a barrel and lifted her so that she could sit on top of it. He stood between her legs and was still busy with her breasts, kneading them and tickling the nipples.

"I can't stand it any longer," gasped Mrs. Reinthaler, "give it to me right now!"

I was wondering how they were going to handle that, because it was a new position in my own short experience. It was quite fascinating to watch Mr. Horak lift the legs of the fat little woman up on his shoulders and insert his long thin tool into her. She was leaning against the wall and gasped and moaned before he started to move in and out with clock-like precision.

"Jesus, Mary and Joseph!" Mrs. Reinthaler exclaimed with delight, "ah, you are pushing it right up to my stomach . . . this is wonderful . . . !"

Mr. Horak, standing between Mrs. Reinthaler's legs, kept his head slightly forward so that he could feast his eyes on those mighty hemispheres with their large and stiff nipples which he licked a little, now and then.

Mrs. Reinthaler was in sheer ecstasy, sighing and moaning and intermittently kissing the crew-cut top of her lover's head. He really must have known what he was doing, because she almost screamed with delight:

"Ah . . . ah . . . I'm going out of my mind . . . you are the only guy who knows how to fuck . . . the only one . . . ah, my husband doesn't know anything about fucking like this . . . ah . . . I'm coming again . . . I'm coming all the time . . . ah, ah . . . now . . . now . . . I'm coming again . . . ah . . . don't come yet . . . please, don't come yet . . . go on like this . . . ah . . . now . . . now . . . again I'm coming . . . nobody has ever fucked me like this . . . nobody . . . I can feel you in me up to my throat . . . I've never had such a prick in me . . . what a wonderful prick . . . a woman would be a damned fool not to let you fuck her . . . ah . . . I'm coming again . . . this is paradise . . . ah, keep pushing, faster, faster, ah . . . Mr. Horak you must always fuck me . . . we must do it in the nude . . . d'you hear . . . both in the nude . . . in some hotel . . . d'you hear . . . ?"

He was far too busy to answer her. His tempo was speeding up and when she lifted her behind at the acme of delight, he grabbed it with both hands and tripled the speed of his motions. Mrs. Reinthaler seemed feverish and could only sob with pleasure. I was so fascinated by the spectacle that I almost stepped out of my hiding place and had to pull myself together to get back behind the ledge in the wall. The savage wildness of that intercourse reminded me of two big dogs I had once watched in the street. I began to understand why adults considered a good lay the most desirable thing in their dreary lives, and also why men began to lose their heads when I gave them my "come on" smile.

"Now!" gasped Mr. Horak, giving Mrs. Reinthaler a last deep thrust, and then he came, grunting like a boar. He leaned his head on Mrs. Reinthaler's large bosom and tried to get his breath back. After a while he slowly pulled his prick out of her inundated hole and stepped back.

Mrs. Reinthaler seemed more dead than alive and it took her several minutes to sit up straight. Slowly she slid off the barrel and as soon as her feet touched the ground she fell around Mr. Horak's neck and kissed him repeatedly.

"Ah, Mr. Horak, nothing like this has ever happened to me before. It's really incredible. I still can't believe it. Nobody in the whole world can fuck like you do! You're the greatest!"

He nonchalantly put a cigarette in his mouth and struck a match.

"How often did you come?" he asked.

"I hardly know. Five or six times, at least!"

He smiled contentedly and played with her nipples so that they became stiff again.

"Well, and how often do you come when your husband lays you?"

She sniffed contemptuously:

"That one? What does he know about a good lay? I never come when he fucks me. All he wants is to come quickly. He climbs on me and sticks it in and in a few seconds he shoots his gun off. Then he turns around, farts and falls asleep. And while he's snoring I have to do a hand-job on myself. All he does is stimulate me without making me come. If I didn't do it to myself afterwards, I couldn't even sleep."

Mr. Horak, still playing with her two globes, laughed loudly and said:

"That's just too bad if a man can't give satisfaction to his pretty wife. Perhaps he doesn't know how! Why don't you tell him what you need?"

"That doesn't do any good! We've often discussed this, but he says I just don't know what I'm talking about and that all men do their fucking the way he does it. A woman, he says, is not supposed to have the same pleasure as a man. He's as ignorant as hell! So, well, he has no reason to complain if I try to get what I need with other guys."

Horak let out a guffaw and kept playing with the stiff nipples in front of him.

"Believe me," Mrs. Reinthaler continued, "I've honestly tried to do something about that stupid man of mine. I thought, okay, he comes too fast when we do it the first time. So he might do it longer when we do it the second time. But there never is a second time. He can't work up a hard-on again. I've even tried to do a blow-job. But—nothing doing!"

"A blow-job?" Horak asked with interest.

Mrs. Reinthaler got a little red. "Well, I took his thing in my mouth to make it hard. Boy! I had to suck it for ten minutes until it became stiff again, and then, when he stuck it into me—bang! He comes at once! And the whole works was for the birds!"

Mr. Horak's face had a preoccupied expression. He didn't seem to listen to Mrs. Reinthaler's confessions and let go of her breasts.

"That blow-job," he said suddenly, "you mean you're taking his prick into your mouth?"

"Sure thing!" She became red again.

"You mean I could fuck you in the mouth? I've never heard of such a thing!"

He grabbed her big white breasts again. I remember that I found those huge globes quite attractive myself and wished I'd have some like it when I was older.

"Ah, come on now!" Mrs. Reinthaler pretended to be coy. "I bet lots of women did a blow-job on you. You can have all the women you want, can't you?"

I couldn't help agreeing with Mrs. Reinthaler. I wished Mr. Horak would want to do it with me, and, God knows, I'd have done anything he wanted me to.

"No," he said, "I've never fucked a woman in the mouth. I wouldn't know how to do it. Why don't you show me?"

Without letting go of her breasts, he pushed her again toward the barrel. She sat down and he was standing in front of her, playing with her nipples so that her breath became quite audible again.

"But you don't need that," she said pantingly. "Your prick gets stiff without any help."

"That's where you're wrong!" he said, pulling his limp tool out of his pants. "See how much I need it?"

She grabbed it greedily and began to massage it with her fingers, while he worked artfully on her teats.

"You're getting me all excited again," she panted. "I've got to go home soon."

He didn't seem to listen but was kneading and fondling her breasts as if he were following a system, and the result came soon. With a sudden movement she put his tool in her mouth and began to work on it.

Now it was Mr. Horak's turn to emit all sorts of lustful sounds.

"Ah, Mary and Joseph! That's good!" he groaned.

At this moment I heard steps coming down the staircase, and quite forgetting that I was not supposed to be seen or heard, I quickly shouted to them:

"Watch out! Somebody's coming down here!"

Those two stopped moving and stood as if paralyzed, staring at me as if I were an apparition from another world. I couldn't help seeing the comic part of the situation. Mr. Horak standing there with his stiff prick sticking in the air, and Mrs. Reinthaler putting her hands over her nude teats.

Mr. Horak was the first to get hold of himself and quickly stowed his tool inside his pants, and then helped Mrs. Reinthaler to slip into her blouse.

I had approached them out of an instinctive fear of the "somebody" who was coming down the cellar steps. The couple kept looking at me like children caught stealing apples from the neighbor's yard. Both were embarrassed and startled. The steps came closer and, at last, we saw the manager of the building walk past us and, giving the three of us a friendly "hello," he went to some corner and picked up a pushbroom and went upstairs again.

As soon as we were alone, Mrs. Reinthaler hid her face in her hands as if she were actually ashamed of me, and Mr. Horak kept staring at the wall without saying anything. I thought it would be best to leave them now, but when Mrs. Reinthaler noticed that I was moving away from them, she quickly grabbed me by the shoulders and whispered fiercely:

"What did you see?"

I hardly raised my voice. "Oh, well . . . THAT!"

"Whaddya mean by THAT?"

"Well . . . y'know . . . just THAT!" I said.

Mrs. Reinthaler's grip on my shoulders became quite firm. "You didn't see nothing! D'you hear? Nothing!!"

I was a little afraid, but a strange excitement had gripped me and made me contradict her boldly.

"I DID see it!"

She shook me by my shoulders. "I said it was nothing! D'you hear? NOTHING!"

"Well," I said, squirming a little under her firm grip, "if you call all that fucking with Mr. Horak 'nothing,' then I've seen nothing!"

In spite of my boldness I thought I'd better leave now, but Mrs. Reinthaler held on to my wrists. Both were a bit white in the face and stared at each other more or less helplessly.

Mr. Horak suddenly pulled a silver coin out of his pants pocket and, without looking at me, offered it:

"Here! Take it! But don't tell a soul what you've seen! D'you hear me?"

I was flabbergasted. Instead of being slapped in the face, as I had expected, I got paid for my secret spying. Suddenly all my anxiety disappeared. I knew now that these two were afraid of me. I took the coin and laughed:

"Gee, thanks!" And I wanted to run.

But Mrs. Reinthaler called me back. "Hey,

wait a moment. I want to tell you something!"

I stopped and saw her walk up to Mr. Horak and whisper something to him. Both were quite red in the face and seemed to get more excited the longer they talked to each other. Mr. Horak didn't seem quite convinced of what she must have told him, but she suddenly stopped whispering to him and turned to me:

"Come here, Pepi!"

When I stood before her, she put her arm around my shoulder and said in her most friendly manner:

"Be a good girl, Pepi! Tell us what you've seen here!"

I didn't say anything, and she kept asking:

"Now, Pepi, you must be able to say what you've seen. IF you've really seen something!"

Again I was silent.

"See? You can't say what you've seen, because you really didn't see anything! True?"

"I've told you what I've seen!" I said hesitantly.

"Then be a good girl and describe it, if you want us to believe you. Don't mind Mr. Horak! He said that he'll give you another silver coin if you tell us the truth. And, maybe, he'll also show you something you might like, eh?"

I became interested in that offer, but somehow I was too embarrassed to speak up before Mr. Horak. I put my mouth close to Mrs. Reinthaler's ear and whispered:

"Well . . . you were sitting on this barrel here . . ." I stopped. Mrs. Reinthaler urged me on.

"Yes . . . and what next?"

"And, well . . . Mr. Horak was standing between your legs . . ."

"Yes . . . and then?"

I grasped one of her breasts and went through the motions of kneading it just as Mr. Horak had done. She gave a little sigh and said:

"Okay, and what else did you see?"

I again brought my mouth close to her ear: "And then . . . and then you took that thing of Mr. Horak's in your mouth . . ."

She began to cuddle me in her arms and rock me like a baby.

"Well . . ." Her voice became low and sweet as if she were really talking to a small child. "And do you know what 'that thing' is called?"

I wanted to show off my knowledge and said: "Sure, I know!"

Mrs. Reinthaler kept rocking me and went on in the same crooning voice:

"Well, why don't you tell me, kiddo? Come on, say it!"

I pressed a little closer against her, but still stalled: "No, I'm afraid . . ."

"Aw, come on, kiddo!" she crooned. "You know we love you, don't you? I'm your friend! You can tell a friend, can't you?"

With that she unbuttoned Mr. Horak's fly and pulled out his prick that was as long and erect as I'd seen it a while ago. She sat down on the barrel and put me on her knees.

"Well? What is this?" she kept asking and fondling that big long prick in front of me.

When I didn't talk, she took my hand and put my fingers around Mr. Horak's prick. I willingly let her guide my hand and closed my fingers around the warm stiff piece of flesh and began to massage it very slowly. When I looked smilingly in Mr. Horak's face he blushed and I heard his breath become faster. Mrs.

Reinthaler put my head close to that stiff beauty and I, tentatively, put my lips around the tip and slowly took some of it into my mouth. I began to suck it just as I had learned from Robert and when that hot, pulsating prick touched my palate, I wished I could feel it deep inside my body and be fucked by Mr. Horak like Mrs. Reinthaler.

I felt Mr. Horak's hot hands caress my face and then slide down to feel my breasts that were, unfortunately, quite undeveloped. He comforted himself by grabbing the teats of Mrs. Reinthaler, reaching over my head, while she put her hand under my skirt and began to tickle my slit with experienced fingers so that I got more and more excited and sucked away at that throbbing prick with increasing speed. It was a pity that I could lodge only one fourth of its total length in my mouth, but I was doing quite well to judge from Mr. Horak's moans. Mrs. Reinthaler, who seemed to be a past-master at doing hand-jobs on a cunt, had also begun to emit all sorts of excited sounds. Now she said to Mr. Horak:

"Don't come yet! I'd like to get something out of it, too!"

He pulled his tool out of my mouth and after Mrs. Reinthaler had let me slide off her lap, she quickly stuck that long thing right into her cunt and, with a deep sigh, she turned to me and asked:

"D'you know . . . ah . . . that's good . . . d'you know what we're doing now?"

"Sure!" I said. "I've said it before. You two are fucking, aren't you?"

Her reply got lost in a long and deep sigh of pleasure. Mr. Horak put his hand under my skirt now and I quickly moved quite close to him so that he could do anything he wanted to. And while he kept working in Mrs. Reinthaler, his fingers probed on my slit and his index finger actually slid into the hole a tiny bit. That dirty little boy on the Prince's meadow had done a good job of opening it up to some extent. Mrs. Reinthaler moaned louder and louder and I soon followed suit. That large red hand on my slit did an excellent job and I began to tremble all over and became far more excited than I was before, when I could be nothing but an onlooker. I think the three of us came at one and the same time, because we stopped moaning simultaneously and were still for a minute.

Mr. Horak put his industrious prick back in his pants and remarked:

"Y'know, this kid here acts like an old-timer!"

Mrs. Reinthaler turned to me with a friendly smile and said:

"Of course! I guessed as much. Tell me, Pepi, how many times have you done some fucking, eh?"

I didn't feel like admitting anything and said:

"Never! This was the first time!"

Mrs. Reinthaler was not convinced.

"Come on, kid, don't lie to me. I've got eyes in my head, and Mr. Horak here wouldn't call you an old-timer for nothing. You don't have to be afraid to tell the truth. How often did you do it, eh?"

I told her the story I'd used when Mr. Eckhardt became too curious about me.

"I've watched my parents often, at night. That's all!"

Mr. Horak said he had to load a few barrels of beer on his wagon and remained in the cellar, while Mrs. Reinthaler and I began the long climb upstairs. I took her hand in mine. Somehow I felt a new kinship with that pretty, fat little woman whose sexual ecstasy I had watched a short time before. She had revealed to me what a woman can feel with a man. That was quite different from the likes of Mizzi and Anna who were groping beginners like myself. I suddenly realized that there was a lot to learn from an experienced woman like Mrs. Reinthaler. Hadn't she told Mr. Horak how she often spent sleepless nights because her husband couldn't satisfy her? How she had to masturbate in order to fall asleep?

Yes, I was going to be Mrs. Reinthaler's friend and confidante. I shared an important secret with her and I knew that she wouldn't betray me as long as I kept my mouth shut about her and Mr. Horak. She had been doing it with other men, too, she had said. It became clear to me that a woman needed regular sex to feel good and that it wasn't sinful at all to give the body what it needed to be healthy. I suppose it was in those days that I laid the foundation of a solid psychological attitude about the role of sex in human life and that's why today, at my advanced age, I don't feel the slightest regret about my past. After all, I never stole anything and never broke the law in any way. I merely fitted into the social conditions of my time and I find that nothing has changed much since those days of my childhood and youth.

Walking up those many stairs with Mrs. Reinthaler I began to feel closer to her with every step. By sharing a man with her, so to speak, I had become her "colleague." I pressed myself against her and whispered:

"You know, that wasn't really true what I said."

"What d'you mean?"

"Well, I mean . . . that I've never done it myself."

She was all ears: "So you *have* done it, eh?"

"Yes!" I said in a small voice.

She laughed. "I knew it!"

I didn't say anything, and she went on:

"You've done it . . . often?"

"Yes."

"How often?"

"Oh, perhaps ten or twelve times . . . or more."

"Hm, and with whom?"

Now I played my trump card. "With Ferdl!"

She acted unconcerned. "Which Ferdl d'you mean?"

I knew immediately that she wasn't as calm and indifferent as she pretended. And right then and there I decided to put in a good word for my brother who was still dreaming of that sensual woman and wanted to be "chosen" like Ferdl.

"Oh, you know that older boy who used to live here. That brother of Anna. You did know him!"

"I don't know what you're talking about. I never knew a Ferdl who lived here!"

She was acting as best she could. But I decided not to give up so easily.

"Just try to remember. Sure, you knew him!"

She looked at me sideways. "I can't remember."

I knew I had to "help" her remember.

"You know, it was Ferdl who used to give you a hand carrying your laundry basket upstairs."

She gave a slight start.

"O yes . . . I believe I know now what you're talking about. Yes . . . so that was Ferdl."

I didn't want to stop there and said:

"Y'know, Mrs. Reinthaler. Ferdl used to tell me things about you . . ."

She pulled her hand away from mine.

"Now, shut up! D'you hear?"

And that was all I could get out of her. I decided it was wiser to obey her and shut up. I could press home my advantage some other time.

CHAPTER 7

A few days after this memorable occasion, I met Mr. Horak on the staircase leading to the cellar. When he didn't seem to take any notice of me, I greeted him very politely.

"How d'you do, Mr. Horak?"

He turned around and when he saw me, he quickly looked to the right and left to see whether anybody else was near. When he had convinced himself that we were alone, he said:

"Hi, Pepi! Want to come with me? I've got to get some barrels out of the cellar."

He didn't have to ask me a second time. I followed him down to the cellar, but he stopped in the dark hallway that led to the storeroom and caressed my cheeks and stroked my hair. Then he pressed my head against the fly of his pants. I knew an invitation when I saw one and briskly took his already rigid tool from its prison, and, following a natural inclination, I began to massage it quite deftly. He sighed:

"Gee, kid, you know how to do that! How come?"

I accepted his praise without reply and groped carefully for his testicles inside his pants. It was a gigantic bag, almost as big as a baby's head, and the feel of it excited me very much. With my right hand I kept stroking his prick and with my left I carefully fondled his bulky nuts. His prick was hard as a rock and pulsated in my palm.

"Put it in your mouth," he begged.

I didn't want to. Not because I didn't like doing it, but because I'd have preferred to have it in a more suitable place than my mouth.

He began to plead.

"I'll give you a silver coin, if you do it!"

I pushed his hand with the coin away and said:

"I don't want any money!"

"But you took it the other day."

"That was different. Now I know better."

He seemed at a loss for what to say.

"But . . . isn't there anything I could give you?"

I hesitated for a second.

"Yes, there's something! Do with me what you did with Mrs. Reinthaler."

He gasped audibly.

"What??? You mean . . . I should fuck you?"

"Sure! That's exactly what I want!"

"But . . . listen, kiddo . . . you're still a child! Wait until you get older!"

I kept masturbating him as I'd learned from Robert, and I began to rub my cunt against his knee.

"I don't have to get any older," I informed him. "I *know* you could fuck me right now!"

"But . . ." he said, growing less certain, "you don't even have any hair on your hole. You don't know what you're saying, kid!"

"I do, too!" My mind was made up. "Hair or no hair, I *know* you can do it with me!"

He must have caught a note of desperation in my voice, because he stroked my hair again very gently and inquired:

"Tell me, Pepi, have you done it before?"

"Ha! And how! Many times!"

I noticed how the rate of his breathing increased. He pulled me up and made me straddle his right hip, the way one sometimes holds children. Our chests were pressed against one another and I put my arms around his red neck. He got my skirt out of the way and soon I felt his prick probe the opening of my slit. I began to move my fanny so that it would be easier for him to get in. His face was pressed against my cheek and I felt how he pushed and pushed down below, but without much success.

"No," he said at last, "it's no good. But . . . wait! I know what we could do!"

He put me down on the floor and sat down on a small barrel. He pulled another, smaller, barrel in front of him and told me to lie with my belly on it and he would take care of the rest. I turned my head and saw how he put some spittle on the tip of his prick, and I thought he'd do the same thing that Robert had done when he saw he couldn't fuck me regularly. I was already glad to be able to feel the same sensation again.

Mr. Horak got up and stood right over me,

but, instead of sticking his prick between my thighs, as Robert had done, he tried to get it into my rectum. I was about to let out a yell, but he put his hand on my mouth and whispered:

"Keep quiet! I'll be very careful. Just speak up if it hurts!"

At the same time he put his right hand in front of me, down below, and let his fingers work on my cunt with great agility.

"Well? Does it hurt?" he asked.

It did hurt a bit, but since his fingers gave me a very welcome pleasure I said: "No!"

His prick went into my fanny very gradually and I thought I would not be able to stand the pain, but, at the same time his clever fingers were working in my cunt and counteracted the painful sensation somewhat.

As Mr. Horak told me afterwards, he could get his prick in only halfway, which, considering my youth, was not bad at all. Suddenly another sensation mingled with the feeling of pain and almost neutralized it. It was a vague kind of pleasure, perhaps caused by the psychological aspect of the situation; an adult man was fucking me, and it didn't matter that he penetrated my rectum instead of my vagina, as long as he penetrated me somewhere.

This new kind of awareness of having a real man taking his pleasure with me, filled me with unspeakable delight and I, instinctively, pinched my buttocks around Mr. Horak's prick. He misunderstood this physical manifestation of my pleasure.

"Oh! Do I hurt you?"

My heightened excitement prevented me from answering him immediately. He pulled out of me and asked again with great concern whether it hurt me.

"No, no . . ." I had found my speech again. "Put it back in! Go on fucking me! Quick!"

I didn't have to say it twice. This time he could slide in more easily than before. His motions were slow and deliberate and I could feel he had added some more spittle. His hand went around my middle again and my cunt became quite moist under the ministration of his fingers.

The human mind is a strange thing. The situation made me think of the brutal soldier who had practically deflowered me, and that little boy who came right after him, on that evening on the Prince's Meadow. I also thought of Robert who had opened my hole a tiny little bit during that first trial, and then of Mr. Eckhardt who had given me quite a bit of pleasure. All these mental images increased my general excitement as if all those males were fucking me now at one and the same time. Again the great pleasure forced me to pinch my buttocks around Mr. Horak's prick, but this time it had quite a different effect on him. His motions became faster and he bent down to my ear and whispered:

"That's good . . . my darling . . . yes . . . pinch your little buttocks together . . . you're doing it very well . . . ah, that's really good . . . you're a sweet kid . . . if you want to we can do it every day . . . d'you hear? . . . every day . . . you can come down here in the cellar with me . . . ah, you're a sweet little whore . . .!"

I decided to take him at his word.

"Every day?" I asked, gasping under his thrusts. My sphincter kept pinching his prick and he showed his pleasure by increased moans.

"Ah . . . yes, you darling little whore . . . every day . . . I mean it . . . every day I want to screw you . . ."

I liked this conversation more and more and wanted to egg him on. All this talk while being fucked increased my pleasure tremendously.

"You really want to fuck me every day, Mr. Horak? You can't do that!"

"What! I can't do that! Why not?" His motions had become stronger and faster.

"You know, if Mrs. Reinthaler comes down here . . ." I said shrewdly.

"To hell with her! You with your little asshole and that naked little cunt are much better!"

"You just say that to make me feel good!"

"No, I mean it . . . ah . . . that's good now . . . !"

He was already so deep in me that I could feel his big balls touching the back of my thighs with each thrust. I felt a perverse joy to hear him depreciate Mrs. Reinthaler. Therefore I reminded him of her various attractions:

"She has such beautiful big teats . . ."

He breathed hard and his hands were both busy on my slit.

"To hell with her teats! I don't need them! Pretty soon you'll have some yourself!"

I noticed the more I contradicted him the hornier he became.

"Oh, that will take a few years!"

"Not that long, no! You must have sex as often as possible. That will make your teats grow much faster."

To hear all these encouraging remarks made me pinch my buttocks together several times in succession, and the effect on Mr. Horak was instantaneous. He stopped talking and merely gasped:

"Ah . . . ah . . . now . . . now . . ."

The next moment I felt something hot squirting into my bottom and I knew that he was coming. His prick kept twitching in me and deposited wave after wave of his warm seminal fluid. It felt like the licking of a warm tongue in my intestines. His fingers hadn't stopped for a moment to work on my cunt and I came with a vengeance, mingling my moans with his, and pressing my buttocks together.

At last Mr. Horak pulled his tool out of my rectum and I could change from my bent-over position to standing up straight. I felt how lots of the seminal fluid ran out of my behind and down my thighs and legs so that I was wet and uncomfortable. Mr. Horak, who stood there like one slightly drunk, pulled a handkerchief from his pocket and dried my legs and then began to wipe his glistening prick, but I took the cloth from his hand and attended to his prick myself, using great care as if I were touching something very precious—which it was, as far as I was concerned.

He looked at me very tenderly.

"You know," he said, "you are really like an experienced whore. I've never seen anything like this!"

"But Mrs. Reinthaler has beautiful teats, so big and white . . ."

I wanted to see whether he'd still react in the same way as when he was in the heat of fucking. To my joyful surprise he did:

"Never mind her teats! I like you much better!"

I felt quite proud, but wanted to make sure that he meant what he said.

"That's fine! But . . . suppose she does come down here again . . ." My voice trailed off.

"What d'you mean . . . ?" he inquired.

"I mean, who are you going to fuck, her or me?"

He laughed. "Of course, I'll fuck you! You can be sure of that!"

"Yes, but what's Mrs. Reinthaler going to say?"

"Whatever she wants to! I don't care!"

He sounded reassuring and I turned toward the stairs:

"Okay, I've got to go now."

"But why so soon? Stay a little while and let's talk, shall we?"

He sat down on that barrel again and made me stand between his knees.

"Now tell me," he said, "who was it you've fucked with?"

I was a little tired from all the excitement and was afraid I might give him the wrong answers. No matter how much I liked to be called his "little whore," I instinctively knew that a man gets more pleasure out of seducing an innocent girl. On the other hand, I wanted to encourage Mr. Horak to continue this new relationship which I found so fascinating, especially as he treated me like a grown woman.

"It doesn't matter who it was, because nobody can fuck so wonderfully as you do!"

"That's nice, but how have you done it with others?"

"I hardly ever did it with others."

"Now, now, tell the truth! You already admitted that you did it with others."

"Well, yes . . . but compared with you . . . it's really nothing!"

'Okay, now tell me who was it?"

I hesitated. "Well . . . a stranger . . ."

"A stranger . . . ?"

"Yes, a soldier."

"But where?"

"On the Prince's Meadow . . ."

"But . . . but . . . how did that happen . . . ?"

"He just pushed me in the grass and lay on top of me."

"Jeez! Why didn't you yell?"

"I was afraid!"

Mr. Horak put his arms around me and whispered into my ear:

"Or—perhaps you liked it a little bit, eh?"

"Oh, no, I didn't!" I protested.

"But you like it with me, don't you?"

In reply I hugged him and kissed his red cheeks. He laughed happily and released me. When I had reached the staircase, he called after me:

"See you soon, little darling!"

CHAPTER 8

After my experience with Mr. Horak I never thought of Mr. Eckhardt any more. All my thoughts and hopes centered around the tall, handsome driver who'd treated me like a real woman, and I hardly went out with my brothers any more, but stayed around the entrance to the cellar to watch for my "lover." But for several days there was no sign of Mr. Horak.

I didn't want to get out of practice and let Franz do it to me whenever we could be unobserved. At night I tried to watch my parents to find out whether they, too, knew the various positions I had learned so far. I discovered that they did their stuff in several different ways. Once I saw how mother made father fuck her from the rear, another time I saw my father being straddled by mother. One night, when the squeaking of the parental bed had woken me up, I heard a whispered conversation going on between them.

"It's much nicer to do it in the nude like now," mother said.

I could make out in the semi-darkness that father had put her legs on his shoulders and pushed into her like a bull in heat. It seemed to be one of his better nights.

"Ah, I'm going to come now," I heard him say.

"Not yet, wait . . . wait just a minute . . ." mother implored him.

But it didn't seem to do any good. I heard him grunt and slump down on the bed with his full weight.

"Damn it," mother complained, "I told you to wait! You didn't give me any time to come myself!"

After a while mother inquired:

"How about trying it again?"

"Not right now," my father's sleepy voice answered. "Later, perhaps."

Mother became angry.

"You and your 'later'! That's what you always say, but then you start snoring and that's all! You phony!"

"What d'you want me to do? I just can't right now . . ."

"It wouldn't be necessary if you'd held it

back another minute, you idiot!"

"Aw, let's just rest a while. I'll try again pretty soon."

It was obvious that father felt guilty about not being quite the man that he ought to be. Mother was still breathing heavily. It was also obvious that she was fully stimulated and unrelieved. After a few minutes' silence she said:

"Can't you get it hard again?"

"Not now! Later!" he grunted almost inaudibly.

I heard mother sit up in the bed.

"Come on, I know how to make it stand!"

I saw her shadowy figure bend over father's body and get busy with her hands and mouth, perhaps with both. He grabbed her breasts tentatively a few times, but otherwise lay still. About fifteen minutes must have passed when I heard my father say in an angry voice:

"Cut it out! You see it's no use! I'm dead tired. Let's sleep now!"

Mother was almost crying.

"That's the limit! What kind of man are you, anyway? Something should be done about this . . ."

"You can't do a damned thing about it. Just leave it alone and go to sleep, d'you hear?"

Mother was sobbing and kept working on that limp tool.

"My hand's beginning to hurt," she whined. "I'm going to try something else . . ."

This time she actually worked on it with her lips, because I heard the sucking and smacking sounds for a while, but it didn't seem to have any effect at all. Suddenly she almost yelled:

"Damn you and that weak prick of yours! You call yourself a man? When you're horny you slam it into me and move a few times and, bang!—you come at once and don't think for a minute that I want to get something out of it, too! What the devil do you think you've got a wife for? So that you can come when you feel like it, and to hell with her?"

Father was silent. But mother went on in the same excited tone of voice:

"What am I going to do about this? First, that miserable fucking of yours gets me all worked up, and now trying to get your prick stiff again has made me only more horny . . . and what am I going to do now? Why did you marry if you don't know what a woman needs? Every time it's the same story. You want to fuck, you move in and out three times, and then you come and want to sleep. You oughta be a rabbit, not a man! What would *you* say if I pushed you out of me just before you could come, eh? I know what you'd do . . . you'd go to some whore and help yourself. Men have it so much easier. But what can I do? What would you say if I let some other man fuck me . . .? Speak up, you!"

"I don't care! Let me sleep!" father grunted.

"All right!" Mother raised her voice. "If that's the way you feel about it, I'm going to help myself from now on, and if you think I can't find a good man to give it to me . . ."

Father sat up abruptly and pushed mother down on the pillow and touched her between the thighs. She became silent at once. Soon she moved her body up and down and sideways and moaned under the apparently expert treatment of my father's fingers. With his other hand

90

he played with her breasts and soon my mother whispered:

"That's good . . . stick your *whole* finger in . . . deeper . . . yes . . . now . . . now . . . ah . . . I'm coming . . . !"

When it was over, my father turned to the wall and growled, already half asleep:

"Thank God! That's that!"

A few minutes later both were snoring contentedly. But I couldn't fall asleep and lay there wide awake. My imagination was working full time and I wished somebody would come to me and give me a good passionate screwing.

CHAPTER 9

Sex had become a daily, if not an hourly necessity with me. The little prick of Franz was nothing more than a stopgap for my strong desire to feel an adult prick in me. It was not easy to get men to pay attention to me. But the neighborhood boys were a different matter. When I looked at any of them in that certain way, they seemed to get the message. Most of them responded by knocking their hand against my cunt and smiling at me. If I didn't like the boy, I pushed his hand away, but if he looked like a good lay, I put my hand on his fly and felt his prick getting stiff. Mostly I went with them down to our cellar, but often they took me to the cellar of their buildings, too. I was not afraid to be seen accidentally by Mrs. Reinthaler, or Mr. Horak, because those two knew very well that if they didn't keep their mouths shut, I'd not keep silent about them either.

I wasn't much interested in the girls at school. When I tried to discuss sex with them, they either bragged that they had already been fucking, or—they didn't know what I was talking about. The latter came mostly from better homes where the parents and children didn't have to share the same bedroom. Girls and boys like myself were conditioned by the poverty of our families. Lack of any sort of privacy made us precocious and knowing, before our bodies were only halfway ripe.

Looking back at those days, I realize that today's children of working class families are not so much exposed prematurely to the facts of life as they were in my youth, although they are still initiated in sex much earlier than kids of well-to-do families. In my childhood, boys and girls like my brother and I were all sexually aware and eager to practice that premature knowledge. Boys did it with their sisters and girl friends as a matter of course. They had never heard the word incest, or taboo, like the rich kids who had the opportunity to listen to the conversations of educated adults. Brothers and sisters of the poor proletarian class saw each other as males and females and would have been quite surprised if they had been told that blood relationships should make them see one another differently. When I could do any reading in my later years I discovered that the children in primitive societies felt and acted exactly as we did.

Among the eight or ten boys with whom I did it in our cellar, in those days, there were two that I still remember quite distinctly. One of them, as I'll show later, was somehow connected with my dealings with Mr. Eckhardt.

His name was Alois.

He was a very handsome, blond boy and, being the son of our landlord, he always wore costly clothes, mostly dark brown or blue suits made of velvet, or corduroy. He always wore shorts, though he was already twelve and rather tall and strong for his age. His well-shaped calves and the strong thighs I could see where his corduroy shorts ended, did something to me. I believe I was really in love with him, not merely sexually attracted. I trembled every time he walked past me and longed to be taken into his arms. There was something proud and aristocratic in his bearing, which made me feel ashamed of my poor shabby dress, but ashamed or not, I couldn't help always staring at him when we accidentally passed each other. He usually gave me a brief and sharp look and then turned away indifferently. Even if I'd had the courage to talk to him it would have led to nothing, because he was always accompanied by his governess, a small and very fat creature whose right shoulder was higher than the other.

One afternoon the unexpected happened. I had been lying in wait for some boy, any boy, who might walk by the entrance to the cellar, when Alois appeared without his chaperon. I was trembling with longing and horniness. He looked most attractive in his blue velvet suit, his bare knees and the lower part of his thighs, white and pink, and already slightly muscled. His handsome face and blond hair stood out against an open-neck sports collar, and, to my utter surprise, his blue eyes were looking at me without wavering. He stepped up to me without saying anything. My heart was beating so loud that I thought he must hear it too. I managed to smile without being able to say even one word. He remained serious and kept looking at me. At last I managed to ask in a subdued voice:

"Have you seen our cellar . . .? You've never been down there, have you . . . ?"

"No, I haven't. Let's go down there together!"

He'd said that without changing the serious expression on his face, but when we were half-way down the stairs, he suddenly whispered:

"Are you sure nobody can see us down there?"

I felt a freight train drop off my chest. Now I knew that we fully understood each other. But I still didn't dare to touch him.

"There's nobody there. I know it!" I assured him. My voice wasn't quite steady. It was hard to believe that my dream was, at last, coming true.

Alois was silent again, and when we had reached the semi-dark corridor that led to the storeroom, we stopped and faced each other without saying anything. I suppose both of us were a little afraid of taking the first step, but I didn't mind waiting. I was so infinitely happy that I merely stood there with bated breath looking at Alois' handsome face.

Suddenly he lifted his hand and gently stroked my cheek. It was a new approach: affection. I'd never experienced it before and, shyly, I returned his caress, marveling at the velvety softness of his complexion. Now his hand moved to my breast in the same caressing manner, and after a while it strayed lower and, at last, rested on my cunt, but still on the outside of my dress. I felt his hand pressing more and more strongly, and I opened my legs a little bit.

"Would you like to?" Alois whispered.

His tender and affectionate manner, so different from the uninhibited greed of other boys, woke some virginal shyness in me. Instead of eagerly agreeing, I said hesitantly:

"Well . . . but if somebody should see us . . . ?"

Alois must have known that I wanted him desperately and merely pretended to be concerned about somebody catching us in the act. After all, it was I who'd assured him that it was quite safe to do it in the cellar.

With a firm hand, he lifted my dress and placed himself between my legs, while I leaned back against the wall. I felt his hard prick grope for the entrance to my hole. His face still had the same serious expression and I'd have given much to see him smile. When his glans touched my slit, I came at once; so great was my excitement. But my horniness was not in the least diminished. I thought it was quite convenient that my cunt had become lubricated in a natural way and would make everything easier.

Alois was calmness itself. With a sure and deliberate movement he grabbed my buttocks and pressed me against himself so that only my shoulders were still supported by the wall. The next moment I groaned in pure ecstasy and closed my eyes, overcome by the voluptuous sensation in my body. Alois had entered me completely with only one quick and adroit thrust and I felt his stone-hard, rather short and thick tool rest in me for several seconds without moving. Then he began some quick, short thrusts, pulling his prick back only an inch. He left it within me and I became more and more excited, because this was the first time anybody had let me feel his prick within me so constantly and distinctly that we seemed to have become one entity. It was perhaps the first time that I began to understand, instinctively, the difference between mere fucking and sexual union. Alois and I were certainly united, and the newness of it drove me crazy with joy.

I didn't think that my ecstatic feeling could be heightened, but that's exactly what Alois accomplished. Without pulling his prick back more than an inch, he started a circular motion that made me come twice, quickly, within a few minutes. I moaned quite loudly and unashamed. I'd never felt such pleasure before.

Suddenly Alois said:

"And now: Finish with relish!"

Before I had time to ponder this peculiar phrase, he had changed his movements. Slowly he pulled his prick back and then pushed it in, equally slowly. He repeated this four or five times and then I felt him come. His warm, thick prick was twitching within me and I came again, for the fifth and last time.

As soon as Alois had finished, he pulled his prick out of me and dried it neatly with a snow-white handkerchief and put it back inside his fly. Then he gave me a friendly tap on my cheek and remarked:

"You certainly screw much better than old Clementine!"

Not knowing who that Clementine might be, I kept silent, but it did not surprise me that such a fine and elegant boy could screw whomever he wanted to. Before he left me he said casually:

"Come to our apartment, tomorrow afternoon. My folks go on a little trip, and we'll be by ourselves!"

I was so overcome by that magnanimous invitation that I could only nod and give him a big smile. After he'd gone upstairs, I lingered for some time in that dark cellar hallway, telling myself that I hadn't dreamed the whole thing and, what's more, that I was going to see Alois again. How lucky can you get, I thought.

The apartment of our landlord was on the first floor where the more affluent people resided. Affluent in those days meant to have more than one bedroom and a kitchen for a family with children. I had heard Mrs. Reinthaler tell another woman once that our landlord had two bedrooms, one for himself and his wife, and one for Alois. She also mentioned a living room, but never having seen one, I didn't know what it meant. I was soon going to find out about it in person.

The next afternoon, I knocked very shyly at the door of the landlord's apartment and a smiling woman, the cook as I later found out, let me in when I said that Alois was expecting me. I'm still not quite sure whether her smile was mere friendliness, or whether it meant to say: "I know why you've come to see our young master."

I was shown into what she described as the bedroom of the young gentleman. It was a large room with elegant white furniture and, above all, a very large and wide bed such as I'd never seen before.

Alois received me very graciously and with

the same serious facial expression that seemed to be second nature to him. When I had admired his huge bed, covered with a silken blue spread, he called my attention to the large sofa that looked quite impressive with its blue-white cover.

"I sleep in the bed," Alois explained, "and my governess sleeps on the sofa."

Then he proceeded to show me his various toys and illustrated children's books. He had lots of beautifully painted tin soldiers and his parents had also given him a uniform of his own, a saber and some toy rifles. I was so overwhelmed by the elegant room and the many things that belonged to Alois that I wondered whether one could have sex in such gorgeous surroundings. It was all so different from our own drab lodgings, or, for that matter, all the living quarters I had seen so far.

After we had been alone for a while, the door opened and that elderly little governess came in. I knew that she always accompanied the boy on his way to school and back. In those days it was customary not to let even boys go unchaperoned, provided they were the sons of middle-class people. No boy under fifteen or sixteen was ever seen alone in the street. A parent, or a relative, or a tutor, male or female, had to accompany them wherever they went. The idea was to prevent any "corrupting influence" coming, naturally, from poor people like us, to spoil their innocent little minds. Rich people's children had therefore hardly any privacy, and as far as corrupting influences went, most parents never suspected that some of those whom they trusted to protect their children from "corruption" were wolves in sheep's clothing.

When Alois' governess had entered, my hopes for a repetition of yesterday's pleasures vanished. She didn't seem to take any notice of us and sat down on the large sofa and began to knit at some half-finished shawl. Alois and I had remained sitting at the table, all covered with tin soldiers, which he had cleverly arranged in battle formation. Suddenly he got up and went over to the sofa. Without much ado, he grabbed one of the big teats of the governess and began to knead it. I hardly believed my eyes and thought she might slap his face, but she merely pushed his hand away and grunted mildly:

"Don't, Alois . . ."

She squinted over to where I sat and eyed me carefully. Alois was not impressed by her protest and grabbed her breast again.

"Don't worry," he said. "Pepi understands!"

The governess let Alois knead her breast now without any resistance and went on knitting.

"Yes, I believe she understands what you're doing, but—how d'you know she won't talk?"

Some instinct told me the time for action had arrived. I got up from my chair and went over to the sofa. With a smile at the governess, I took her other breast and went to work on it. It was a flabby teat and not one that would excite a man, I thought. Under the administrations of Alois' and my hands, the fat ugly little person became quite red in the face and stopped knitting.

Alois took his prick out of his pants and made the governess squeeze it with her thick fingers. She began to play with it, but not the way I

99

had learned to. She held it with her thumb and middle-finger and with her index she gently touched the glans so that the prepuce receded gradually.

"Are you familiar with this?" she asked with what was supposed to be a smile, but which looked more like a grimace.

"Sure!" I nodded.

"And what is the name for it?"

"A prick," I replied obediently.

"And what does one do with a prick?"

"Fucking," I said promptly. For a moment I thought I was in class and being questioned by a teacher.

Her breath came a little faster and her index finger kept tickling the glans which was quite red and swollen now.

"Very good, my child! And what does the prick fuck?"

"The cunt!" answered Alois for me. He began to find that question-and-answer game a little dull and wanted some action. He opened the woman's blouse and began to play with her two flabby breasts that were so different from the majestic hemispheres of Mrs. Reinthaler.

"Come on, Clementine!" he demanded.

Now I knew who Clementine was, the name he had mentioned yesterday when speaking about his sex life. But the fat little woman wanted to play the game as she and Alois seemed to play it all the time. She was the teacher and Alois the pupil to be examined.

"Now, Alois, what does the prick do in a cunt?"

"Fuck," said Alois as calmly as he always spoke.

Clementine's voice became more and more

excited:

"Good! And what else is it called?"

Alois enumerated obediently: "Screwing, poking, banging, balling, jazzing, jelly-rolling, honey-fuggling, laying, digging, dipping!" His face was dead serious.

Clementine became more and more excited.

"And what else can the prick do?"

"Ass-fucking, being blowed and sucked, fucking between the teats, also in the armpit, between the thighs, from the front and the rear . . ."

"And what is Alois going to do now . . . ?"

With that, Clementine reclined and shut her eyes. Alois tickled her nipples that were as long as my little finger. He put them alternately in his mouth and sucked them so that Clementine twitched with her whole upper body and especially with the very shoulder that was on the side of the breast that Alois worked on at the moment.

Alois proceeded quite deliberately, almost scientifically, as if he were following a specific formula, without deviating from the sequence. After a while he lifted her skirt up to her waist where he folded it neatly to make it stay in place. Clementine had put her head against the back of the sofa and kept twitching like an epileptic during a fit.

Alois stepped between her fat little thighs and with one quick motion had thrust his firm prick into her hairy cunt, after folding back the thick labia with one hand. Then he mounted on her, while she put her palms around his behind and pressed his abdomen close against hers, so that his prick stuck firmly in her cunt, no matter how hard he might be pushing into her. His fingers kept busy with her nipples.

I saw he was following the same procedure he had used with me in the cellar. Clementine breathed heavily through her nostrils like a bulldog, and after ten minutes she announced:

"Finish with relish!"

Her hands released Alois' buttocks, and he immediately made his prick move slowly in and out of her cunt. She raised her ass up, then fell back, and reared up again, in wild delight. Alois, with the most serious and serene face in the world, kept moving his prick very slowly in and out, so that the ugly, fat Clementine began to twitch and thrash around as if she were actually having a fit. After eight or ten in-an-out motions, Alois saw how Clementine's face suddenly relaxed, while her body went into a slump. His face became quite red and after another two thrusts he fell forward on Clementine's naked breasts. He had come, too.

For about one minute both were lying there without moving, and I was already tempted to lift my dress and give myself a good hand-job. But the next moment Alois got off Clementine and wiped his prick on the lining of her skirt. Then they invited me to sit down on the sofa with them.

Clementine gave me a searching look with her squinting eyes and asked:

"Well? How did you like it?"

I merely smiled without saying anything. Alois, sitting on her other side, looked over to me and watched me closely.

"Have you ever seen it before?" she went on questioning me.

My answer was again a smile.

Clementine didn't give up so easily:

"Have you ever done it yourself?"

I had no inhibitions to deny it before Clementine. On the other hand, I didn't feel like simply saying yes. That's why I managed to produce what I hoped was an embarrassed laugh, which could be taken for an admission.

"Well," said Clementine, "we can make quite sure what the situation is!"

With that she lifted my skirt and examined my little cunt.

"Jeez," she exclaimed. "That little box must have been opened quite a few times."

And before I could prevent it, she stuck her little finger into me and said:

"Ah, one can really get in!"

And turning to Alois, she repeated:

"Yes, one can get in!"

When she saw that I trembled a little, she asked me point-blank:

"Would you like to be fucked by Alois now?"

"O yes!" I said quickly. I had already been afraid I would be left out in the cold.

"Now, Alois," she turned to the boy, "how would you like to fuck this pretty little girl? What do you think?"

Alois got up and was about to come over to my side when she stopped him:

"Not yet! First I've got to fix your little prick so that you can do it!"

She was right, because his tassel hung quite limply between his legs and needed some new stimulation. A boy of his age should have been ready again by now, but it seemed that his Clementine overdid her "training" of him and tired him out to soon. I watched closely her method of "reactivating" his tool and decided to remember every detail. It might come in handy with other males.

First, she took it between her lips and licked it so that it became nicely lubricated. Then she bedded it in the furrow between her breasts and pressed them together with her hands. It looked as if Alois was sticking his prick into a pair of buttocks. I didn't like to see how Clementine herself became stimulated again by this procedure. She was quite capable of using this new state of readiness for her own pleasure. I was ready to intervene at the critical moment, but apparently the woman took just as much pleasure in talking as in fucking. She had to accompany her attempts at rejuvenating Alois' tool with all sorts of childish prattle.

"What is Alois' little prick doing now? He is fucking some teats? Some nice big teats? That feels good, doesn't it? Ah, now it begins to get stiff . . . good boy, Alois . . . good, little prick . . . Clementine takes care of his prick, doesn't she? . . . Who was just fucking very nicely? Alois? Loisl? Yes, Loisl is lucky to have Clementine! Some other governess wouldn't do all that for him, would she? . . . Let herself be fucked by a little boy like Loisl . . . But Clementine takes care of her Loisl . . . he can fuck her as often as he wants to . . ."

("Yes," I thought, "or rather, as often as Clementine wants to . . . that shrewd bitch : . .")

Now she turned to me:

"You know, Pepi, at night, when everything is quiet, Loisl leaves his bed and comes over here to me on the sofa, and we do it together . . . yes, Loisl can do it very well . . . Clementine has taught him how to do it well . . . and Loisl is an excellent pupil . . . aren't you, Loisl . . . ?"

104

"Loisl" had his eyes closed and didn't seem to pay any attention. I was already despairing of getting a good lay today, when he suddenly pulled his stiff tool from Clementine's teats and asked:

"Well . . . what about fucking Pepi now . . . ?"

When I saw how his thick little prick was pulsating with readiness, I had to control myself not to put my hand around it. I wasn't quite sure what that peculiar, ugly Clementine might do. The way she looked, she actually seemed to reflect whether she should permit Loisl's revived prick to satisfy somebody else instead of herself. Looking back, I believe that she decided it was better to ensure my silence about the goings on between governess and the landlord's son, and that my silence was worth her sacrificing another lay. On the other hand, she might also have derived some pleasure from merely looking on. At last, she made room for me next to her on that sofa and asked me to lie on her lap, and when this seemed an awkward position for what was to be done, she said I should merely put my head on her knees and stretch out along the sofa. Alois, with his usual serious mien, folded my skirt back very neatly and then mounted me with deliberate care. He spread the labia of my cunt with his fingers and the next moment his warm tool was completely within me.

It was like yesterday, only much better and more pleasurable, because during a standing-up job a prick can't get in up to its root as when we do it lying down.

Again I felt more than mere horniness when Loisl (as Clementine nicknamed him) began his short thrusts without pulling back more than half an inch each time. He awoke all the tenderness I was capable of and I wanted to stroke his cheek, or merely touch him to let him know how I felt about him, but the presence of that weird woman stifled all such manifestations in me. She closely watched all my facial expressions, which she could easily do since my head was on her lap. I felt her greedy, close observation of me as an intrusion of my privacy, the privacy of my feelings. I wouldn't have minded it in the case of any other boy. She must have sensed that I was in love with her Loisl.

Her mania for constant talking took over again. As soon as Loisl was in me she inquired:

"Is he completely in you?"

"Yes, completely!" I whispered almost defiantly, wanting to imply that he filled out my little hole much better than her bigger, reamed-out old cunt.

Now, she squeezed her hand between Loisl's and my belly and played, alternately, with my clitoris and his balls. I could hardly breathe on account of her pendulous teats that were lying on my face.

Soon she sat up again and asked:

"Well, does it feel good, Pepi?"

I tried to ignore her and kept my eyes shut. She went on, indefatigably:

"Loisl knows how to fuck, doesn't he?"

"Yes, yes . . . !" I replied and began to let my fanny dance up and down.

"Have you ever been fucked like that?" she continued her interview of me.

"No . . ." And I meant it, because this was a very intense pleasure and one quite new to me. After all, I was being laid by a boy I really loved.

"With whom d'you do it, usually?" the interview went on.

"With Ferdl," I said, because he and Anna were not here any more, but Clementine seemed to be well informed about tenants who've moved away, and insisted:

"There must be others. Who else?"

Her tone had become quite matter-of-fact, like a schoolmarm's examining in the classroom.

"With Robert . . ."

"Who else?"

"With my brother . . ." I confessed hesitantly.

The thrills which Loisl's ministrations sent through my body affected me like a truth-drug and I was afraid that I would betray all the other names of the boys and men I'd done it with.

But, luckily, Clementine's attention was now gripped by another idea. She opened my blouse so that my tiny undeveloped breasts lay bare before her. Moistening her middle finger with saliva, she began to tickle my nipples quite gently. It felt like a tongue licking me and soon my nipples stood straight up and helped me imagine what my breasts would look like in a few years.

That tickling of my nipples and Loisl's circular motions in my cunt—as if he were reaming it—drove me wild with lust and, losing all inhibitions, I began to shout:

"Ah . . . ah . . . I'm coming now . . . ah . . ."

From that moment on, I didn't care whether Clementine was talking or not, because I couldn't think any more, or pay any attention to anything but what I felt coursing through my whole body like heavenly balsam. The sensations did not come merely from my cunt, but from all over, from every part of my nervous system.

Today, in retrospect, I am able to judge what that particular experience with Alois meant to me. Up to then, fucking had been merely a very pleasurable pastime, the best of all of them, but being fucked by that fine, blond, elegant boy, who was so different from the crude kids I knew, made me realize that fucking and what people call love can go together. At the same time I also realized, though only vaguely on account of my great youth, that a woman could become sexually dependent on a man if she seriously loved him. I felt, also only vaguely, that a woman could make a man dependent on her, if she is a good lay and doesn't love the man. A prostitute who wants to go places and have a successful career must keep this truth in mind. A good lay is one thing, and love something else. Too many men—and women—have suffered emotional disasters by confusing the two things.

Alois, when he saw my huge excitement, decided to wind up the situation according to the ritual he had learned from Clementine:

"Finish with relish!" he quoted.

And, also according to ritual, he pulled his prick slowly out and moved it slowly back in, repeating the maneuver five or six times. This calculated stimulation and Clementine's working on my nipples had a tremendous impact on me. I stretched my body and threw it around and came three times in quick succession. Then I felt the warm spray of Loisl's sperm spurt into me, and I came a fourth time. It was wise of Clementine to press the palm of her hand firmly on my mouth to prevent me from yelling like mad. I'd never felt such intense and concentrated lust before and kept licking and biting Clementine's palm, but she didn't seem to mind, understanding quite well what I felt.

I was so exhausted that I had to keep lying on the sofa for another hour. It occurred to me then and there that fucking could also become bad for one's health if one overdid it. And that's exactly what happened to Alois, being constantly used by his governess.

From my lying position I saw how she had made him stand on the sofa seat, while she, standing before him, had again taken his limp and tired tool between her long teats, trying to revive it. When it did not affect him, this time, she took the prick in her mouth and sucked it like a piece of sugarcane, with loud smacking noises. Not noticing any immediate result, she stuck her head between his legs and licked his testicles and the sensitive skin between the fanny and the genitals, which visibly affected Loisl, whose whole body began to tremble, though his face remained as serious as ever.

When she put his prick in her mouth again, he began to move very slightly and put his hand on her head. After another five minutes he actually had another hard-on, but if Clementine had thought she could make him screw her again, she miscalculated. He put his prick into her mouth again and ordered abruptly:

"Leave it in!"

To my astonishment, she obeyed and let the boy fuck her in the mouth with his short thrusts. Clementine let him perform patiently and soon began to twitch all over her body, but without letting Loisl's prick slip out of her mouth. Only once did she release it and begged:

"Come, Loisl, let's fuck . . . come now . . . !"

Again I was surprised to see Loisl's reaction.

"I said, leave it in your mouth, damn it!"

His voice showed his anger. It was the first time he had betrayed any emotion since I met him.

Soon he pronounced his ritualistic formula: "Finish with relish!"

But when he started his teasingly slow in-and-out motions, Clementine let it slide out of her mouth a second time and begged:

"No, don't let it come yet . . ."

He wanted to force his prick back into her mouth, but she resisted this time and gasped and panted.

"No, Loisl must fuck me . . . little Loisl must be a good boy and fuck his Clementine . . . not in the mouth . . . but down there where it's much, much better . . ."

Alois didn't want to, and both started to wrestle with each other, but the smaller boy had no chance of winning out over that fat governess. With great force she grabbed him by the hips like a child and forced him on his back on the sofa. Then lifting her skirts, she straddled him and buried his prick in her heated hole and began to swing her hips wildly up and down. Her flabby breasts covered Loisl's face and he actually disappeared below that sex-crazed woman. I was witnessing a regular rape. Now and then I noticed that the boy had taken one of her nipples between his lips, which

110

showed that he had been well trained by her. Her fanny flew up and down sixty times a minute and, at last, she sank panting and groaning on top of the boy so that I couldn't see him at all.

I had lain on the other end of the sofa, still tired and quite unaffected by the spectacle before my eyes. I dimly wished I could take Loisl away from that ugly, old woman and let him rest up for a few days. I was at least as horny as that obscene Clementine, but I would renounce my desires for a while to let the boy recuperate. While I was thinking this way, I realized that I really loved him. Although I became—as people say—"only" a prostitute, I came to know quite early that love means to think of the other one first, something that most of my later customers, even the noble and cultured ones, didn't know. Most of the "fine" ladies, the so-called respectable ones, I had occasion to meet—incognito, of course—during my long life, loved their husbands only to the extent of the jewels and costly furs they received from them. Women who are ready to sacrifice some of their comfort for the man they "love" have always been rare. More often than not a woman sacrifices her life for the man who deserves it least.

When Clementine and Loisl had rested a while and then restored order to their clothes, the cook brought a tray full of all sorts of goodies that I'd never seen before, like hot chocolate with whipped cream and delicious little cakes. I began to get a slight idea of how the other half lived. The only pleasures we people of the poor working class could afford were sex and drinking. The latter was reserved for men, mostly. When my fortunes, in my late twenties, had made me, to all appearances, a member of the rich middle-class, sex was not so compelling any more as the only pleasure. By then I had learned to enjoy elegant dresses and comfortable living, also cultural pleasures like good music and stageplays and, above all, informative reading. Sex, when used as a profession, must be treated with intelligent discrimination. That's why frigid women often become the best and most successful prostitutes. I don't mean street girls, but those that are "kept in furniture" by a respectable man of good society who usually leads a double life.

When Clementine, Alois and I had finished our mid-afternoon snack, I announced that I had to leave now. Clementine put a few of the remaining goodies in a brown bag for me to take home and insisted on coming with me as far as the door of the apartment. In the semi-dark anteroom she quickly touched her hand to my cunt and said:

"You're going to be a sensible girl and keep your mouth shut, aren't you? If you keep everything to yourself, you may come back soon and . . . you know what!"

With that she pressed a silver coin into my hand and gently shoved me out of the door.

CHAPTER 10

The other boy who still sticks out in my memory of those early days was a classmate of my older brother, Lorenz. He was thirteen, tall for his age, slender and very proportionately built. I was attracted to his shock of black hair that was matched by a pair of jet black eyes which made him look like a handsome Italian. He was always pale, perhaps because he studied a lot and was very serious about doing his homework, as I could notice when he often came to us, or rather to Lorenz, to help him study and vice versa. Both were checking on the other's homework and correcting any mistakes.

The boy's name was Schani, which was a nickname for Sandor, a Hungarian first name. He lived in the same street, only a few buildings removed from ours. Being a friend of my pious older brother, I thought Schani was also chaste and very religious, and that's why I never dared to say anything more than a conventional "hello" to him. He was always friendly, nodding his head when I greeted him and when he left again.

One day Schani came to see Lorenz who had gone out. So were mother and Franz, my younger brother. Schani wanted to leave when he heard that Lorenz wasn't there, but I took heart to invite him in. He hesitated first, but when I said that Lorenz might be back any minute, he stepped over the threshold and walked slowly into the kitchen. I saw that he was just as embarrassed as I was and when I led him into the bedroom, he followed me in the same slow manner he had come in the front door.

I was crazy about his black eyes and told him so. He smiled good-naturedly and didn't mind when I cuddled up to him. Getting bold, I put my arms around his neck and pressed my abdomen against the front of his pants. I expected him to press me against him and to grope under my skirt, but he only smiled vaguely and remained passive.

I thought he needed more encouragement, and therefore I quickly lay down on the large bed and invited him to join me. He stepped close to the bed and just stood there. I gradually lifted my skirt to reveal my nakedness underneath and kept watching his face. When my slit was completely uncovered, he looked at it, still smiling and standing there without moving a finger. I became excited and wanted to take his tool from his pants, but he stepped back and said, almost sadly:

"Leave it alone, it's useless . . . !"

"But why . . . ?" I almost yelled the question and jumped from the bed.

"Just because . . . ! I couldn't do anything!"

I thought: "Aha! He's got the same mania for religious purity as my brother Lorenz." But somehow it was not the same attitude of moral indignation that Lorenz always carried with him like a phony halo. I decided to take the bull by the "horns."

"Show me!" I commanded and grabbed his fly. He tried to shake me off, but I held him firmly and soon his long, thin, but very stiff prick was in my hand. With my other hand I lifted my skirt and wanted to stick that rigid stick into my slit, but he pushed me away and said in an almost frightened tone:

"Don't . . . I just can't . . . !"

I was utterly surprised and felt helpless before that mysterious behavior of his. My feeling of frustration made me angry:

"You are lying! I know you can do it, but you don't want to!"

"I'm not lying," he said in a sad voice,

"you've got to believe me, I really can't do it!"

"This is ridiculous!" I said, getting angrier by the minute. "If you don't want to, just say so. That would be better than lying to me!"

He put his tool back in his pants and buttoned his fly. "I assure you," he said in his sad, soft manner, "I'd really like to do it, but . . . I just can't afford it!"

Now my anger gave way to curiosity.

"What d'you mean, you can't afford it?"

"I can't talk about it!"

"That's nonsense!" I became angry again. "You just don't want to fuck and are using a cheap excuse! I've said before you needn't lie, if you don't want to!"

"I'm really not lying to you," he said, giving me a pleading look. Suddenly he touched my cunt throught the material of my skirt, but then drew back and repeated:

"No, I just can't do it's . . . it's those damned women . . . !"

I was flabbergasted. *"What women?"*

Schani began walking around the room and spoke as if he were talking to himself:

"Those damned bitches! They don't leave me alone! I had to fuck them twice, today! Twice . . ."

"Who the hell are you talking about?" I was really curious now.

"Twice already . . . ! And if I fuck you now . . . then I can't get a hard-on tonight again, and if I don't get a hard-on she'll beat hell out of me!"

"She? Who's she?"

"Mother!"

"Your mother?"

"Yes!"

"You mean . . . your mother beats you up if you can't get a hard-on?"

He nodded sadly.

"That doesn't make sense to me. Why would your mother beat you up if you can't get a hard-on . . . You don't have to fuck your mother," I added facetiously, "or do you?"

Schani suddenly became furious and yelled:

"You said it! Those Godforsaken women . . . they're no good . . . they're bitches, each one of them . . ."

"And you've fucked her twice already, today?"

"No, not her! She doesn't come home before tonight!"

"So . . . who the hell did you fuck twice?"

"My sisters . . ."

"What? Your sisters? Both of them?"

"Yeah . . . both of them! And if I fuck you now then I won't get a hard-on in bed tonight and mother will know at once that I've done it with Wetti and Rosa. And then she beats me up!"

By now, Schani felt like telling me the whole story, a story which, of course, will shock all those "respectable" people who have not even a notion of an idea of the living conditions in the poorer districts of Vienna, or any other European city, for that matter. Incest was as natural with us as with animals, or some primitive tribes in South America. I've read quite a bit about it and can understand, today, to what extent inhuman and unhuman social conditions can kill all sensitivity in people. I know that even among some native tribes there is such a thing as an incest-taboo, but not in all

116

of them. And if some of my readers assume that a "religious education" should have prevented poor working-class people from becoming as sexually primitive as savages, I want to remind them that, first, organized religion could not prevent deep human urges like sex from asserting themselves, and, second, that any of my readers should do some honest soul-searching and ask himself whether he could guarantee his reactions if he had to live and grow up with parents, brothers and sisters who have to sleep, eat, wash, and so on, in one kitchen and one bedroom. That was the average "apartment" of the Austrian workingman's family.

Schani's story reflects the conditions of those days quite faithfully.

"I never knew my father," he began. "He died when I was just a baby. So . . . my two sisters and mother were my family as long as I can remember."

I knew his sisters, Wetti and Rosa. I also knew his mother, a small, lean woman in her late thirties who must have been very good-looking in her youth, but who, like all workers' wives, began to fade once she was over thirty. Schani inherited her beautiful dark eyes.

Rosa, the older sister, was eighteen, a blonde, slender girl with a lot of freckles on her face and a pair of firm, round teats whose nipples were always pointing through her blouse. The younger one, Wetti, sixteen, was short and sturdy, with full breasts that looked like those of Mrs. Reinthaler, and a well-rounded fat fanny that attracted the attention of most men in the street.

Wetti lost her virginity when she was twelve.

A young, door-to-door salesman found her alone at home and she made it quite easy for him to get between her legs. From that day on, her body began to develop all those provocative contours which she knew how to show off.

Wetti, one day, told Schani what that door-to-door salesman had done and she demonstrated all the details to him by making him play the part of the man. He was only nine years old, but he liked the new game, and they often played "door-to-door salesman" together. One day they were caught in the act by the older sister, Rosa. They expected to be bawled out, but Rosa neither bawled them out, nor betrayed them to the mother. She did much better than that. The same night she called Schani to her bed. (The three shared one bedroom.) She proceeded to question him:

"What were you doing with Wetti today?"

"Nothing."

"Nothing . . . ? And just because you did nothing you had taken her teats out of her blouse and put your hands under her skirt?"

"Oh . . . well . . . we were just playing a game."

"Show me right now what that game was."

Schani, standing there beside Rosa's bed in the dark room, didn't know what to do. Wetti was fast asleep in the other bed and he heard his mother snoring in the kitchen. Again Rosa said in a whisper:

"Okay, now show me the game!"

She noticed that the boy was at a loos for what to do next. She encouraged him:

"Come under the blanket with me!" She pulled him in beside her.

He noticed at once that she was quite naked.

118

Instinctively, he touched her firm teats and began to stroke them, while Rosa grabbed his stiff prick and rubbed it gently. He sensed how excited she was and he'd have liked to touch her between her legs, but he was afraid and not quite sure what she expected him to do. He and Wetti had always played the "game" with their clothes on, but here lay his older sister, naked, at his disposal, letting him stroke her big breasts and playing with his prick. What could he do next? he thought. Rosa saved him making a decision all by himself:

"Have you often played this game with Wetti?"

"Yes . . . quite often . . ."

"D' you want me to tell mother . . . ?" she asked while massaging his prick all the time.

"No, don't . . ." Schani whispered.

"First you play with Wetti, and now you are in my bed and play with my teats and let me feel your stiff pencil . . . D'you want mother to know about that . . . ?"

Schani protested: "You won't tell her anything about this, because you called me over here and told me to get in beside you . . ."

"No, I didn't do anything of the kind . . . Mother will believe what I tell her and not you. I'll say you came to my bed and wanted to fuck me. And that you've often fucked Wetti . . ."

Schani tried to get away from her, but she pressed her teats into his hands again and held him firmly by his prick.

"Come on, you idiot . . . I won't say anything . . . but I want you to do it with me, too! D'you hear?"

Schani climbed on top of her and felt how

she pushed his nightshirt up to his chest. Her nude body heightened his horniness to a degree he had not experienced with Wetti. Rosa put his prick between the warm labia of her hairy cunt, but when he tried to enter, he encountered an obstacle: Rosa was still a virgin, though one who was all set to be rid of her virginity. She grabbed his buttocks and pressed him against her, while Schani kept pushing his prick against the hymen which, at last, seemed to yield. Rosa tried to master her pain that made her moan a little, and Schani came as soon as his last trust had blazed the trail which he was to use often in the future.

Rosa seemed satisfied with the mere fact that she was deflowered and sent Schani back to his bed. When he noticed blood spots on his shirt the next morning, he was frightened, but Rosa explained to him that there was always bound to be some blood when a girl loses her virginity.

It didn't take long for Wetti to discover the nightly sex parties of Schani with her older sister, and it seemed quite natural that she should join them in Rosa's bed. The poor boy was obliged to gratify both girls, night after night.

Schani wasn't quite sure how his mother caught on, whether it was his increasing paleness and the dark rings around his eyes that made her suspicious, or whether she overheard some noise at night. After one bout he had fallen asleep in Rosa's bed and their mother suddenly came in and saw him there. She woke all three of them up and ordered Schani back into his own bed.

The next morning, at breakfast, she said to

120

the girls and their brother:

"A growing boy can't sleep with his sisters in the same bed. That's got to stop, once and for all!"

Rosa, who hated to give up the nightly pleasures, protested:

"He was afraid of something. That's why he came to me. That's all!"

"All right," said the mother, "if Schani is afraid of sleeping alone, then he'll sleep with me, from now on. I can't let a growing boy sleep with his young sisters!"

Schani's bed was taken to the kitchen and placed close to his mother's. At night she lay down next to him and, since he was "afraid," she pressed him close to her and let him play with her breasts until he fell asleep. Her breasts were not as firm as those of his sisters, but Schani liked them well enough and continued to play with them, night after night.

After one week, Schani didn't fall asleep any more, but became more and more stimulated. Being rid of the continual demands of his sisters, his vigor had completely returned and playing with his mother's breasts didn't seem enough any more. He began to press himself against her body more closely so that she couldn't help feeling his strong erection. She yielded her breasts to him with more abandon, but didn't go any further.

One night, Schani touched his prick to her nude thigh. She shivered violently and began to breathe faster, but he heard her whisper:

"No! No!"

But she kept pressing her breasts into his hands, exciting him all the more, so that he had trouble falling asleep at last. After another

week of this probing and hesitating there came
the night when his mother didn't push him back
when she again felt his stiff prick on her thigh.
Slowly, very slowly she moved her hand down-
ward until she touched it and closed her fingers around it. Her breathing became heavier
and, suddenly, she straddled the boy, put his
prick into her hole, and pressing her breasts
against his face, she encouraged him:

"Yes, do it! Mother permits it! Push . . .
yes, push it in . . . deeper . . . deeper . . . !"

Schani was now "under contract" to do it
with his mother every night. She showed him
various positions, with her on top, or vice
versa, lying on the side, from the rear, and after
two weeks he was a sexually informed boy. She
induced him to do it several times every night.
In the daytime, his sisters bothered him with
their needs and he had to comply. They had
listened to what had been going on in the kitch-
en with the mother, and now they put aside
all shame and inhibitions. There was no time
of the day, or the night, when his mother or his
sisters didn't use him if they found him alone
in the apartment.

As time went on, the mother didn't mind any
more that her daughters shared in the boy as
long as they didn't weaken him in the daytime
so that she could always be sure to enjoy him
at night. It was a miracle that Schani, being
only thirteen, was able to stand that shameless
sexual exploitation without becoming seriously
ill. When he told me the whole story, he became more and more furious and interrupted
himself with exclamations like:

"Those damned broads! I'm sick of all of
them! If all women are going to be like that . . ."

122

I thought this last remark was an allusion to the fact that I kept playing with his prick while he was talking. Although I was disgusted at hearing about the bestial selfishness of his mother and sisters, I couldn't suppress becoming horny myself. I became more and more stimulated and didn't know what to do about it.

Suddenly we heard the front door being opened and I began to tremble, partly from being startled and partly from horniness and frustration. But it was good old Mr. Eckhardt who came in and I welcomed him as a savior in this situation. I quickly said good-bye to Schani, who was surprised at being shoved out of the door by me so abruptly.

CHAPTER 11

I hurried into the kitchen where Mr. Eckhardt usually sat around when he was at home. I hadn't had anything to do with him since Mr. Horak had given me that wonderful treatment in the cellar, and also since Loisl had made known to me that sex could be more than a momentary climax. I realized that I had neglected Mr. Eckhardt on account of those new experiences and decided to make up for it.

As soon as I was in the kitchen I pounced on him and, without any ceremony, pulled his prick out of his fly and whispered:

"Quick! Quick! Before somebody comes home!"

I saw that he was in the mood, because his tool had become quite hard as soon as I touched it. But he asked, nevertheless:

"What d'you mean . . . quick? What is it?"

I felt that he was at least as horny as I, but that he wanted to see whether I would be frank about it. I was:

"I want to fuck! Come, quick!"

He wasn't expecting so much directness and began to tremble all over. He towered over me and we would have both fallen on the floor, but I didn't want a mere improvisation. I kept holding his prick and dragged him by it to the bedroom where I flopped down on the bed and pulled him over me.

He was so uncontrolled that he'd have forced his prick into me and torn my box apart if I hadn't quickly closed my hand around that long tool so that it moved in it like in a tube. I let only his glans penetrate me and that was enough to make me come at once. He pushed into me with unrestrained force and suddenly I enjoyed it so much that I forgot all the others who had fucked me recently. Mr. Eckhardt had a tremendous orgasm and I was flooded all over my thighs and legs.

I dried myself and then wiped Mr. Eckhardt's moist tool and hoped for a repetition, but he sat in the armchair and seemed quite exhausted. I didn't know what was the matter with me, I just had to feel that prick in me again. As I had seen Clementine do it, I took his soft prick in my mouth and went to work on it. I was soon rewarded for my great efforts. He had a terrific hard-on again. I begged him:

"Please, stick it in all the way, now!"

He didn't understant:

"But . . . but you don't have enough room for all of this . . ."

And in his excitement he probed with his

124

finger in my hole so forcefully that I let out a yell and said:

"No! No, I didn't mean there . . ."

He looked at me, helplessly:

"But how else . . ?"

I quickly turned my back to him and showed him what I had learned from Mr. Horak in the cellar, without, of course, naming my teacher. Soon I felt that long, thin instrument glide into my rectum after he had applied plenty of saliva all over it. Eckhardt's prick seemed even longer than Mr. Horak's and I felt well taken care of. I kept pressing my buttocks together and each time Mr. Eckhardt moaned so wildly that I repeated this little trick merely because hearing him moan increased my pleasure. Unfortunately it also made him ejaculate sooner than I wished, and this time he seemed to be drained of all force.

But the devil must have egged me on and I again tried to give Mr. Eckhardt another erection. He gently pushed me away and said:

"No, kiddo! Let me alone now!"

Schani's story, no matter how unpleasant from a moral point of view — not because of the sex, but on account of the harm to the boy's health — had actually aroused me more than I was aware of. I saw in my mind the naked bodies of his sisters and himself doing it, and asked Mr. Eckhardt now:

"Say, have you ever done it in the nude?"

I'd never been so unashamed and direct in my talks with him.

"You ought to know," he said. "You've been in my bed several times, remember?"

"Yes, I know, but I mean really naked, without any nightshirt!"

He smiled. "Why, have *you* ever done it that way?"

"No, but I sure would like to! Have you?"

"Of course! I was married, you know."

I had never thought of Mr. Eckhardt as being a married man.

"Oh . . . did your wife die?"

"No, she didn't die!"

"What became of her?"

"A whore!"

I winced. Mr. Eckhardt used to call me his "little whore," several times in the heat of fucking, and I wondered now whether he'd meant it as a compliment.

"Tell me, am I a whore, too?"

He laughed and pressed me against him.

"O no! You are my dear little Pepi!"

I immediately made use of being hugged by him and played with his tool again. He still smiled:

"You know, I've never done it with a little girl like you. You are really sold on fucking, aren't you?"

Instead of answering, I put his tool in my mouth and let my tongue play on the glans, but — it remained limp and soft. From time to time, Mr. Eckhardt remarked:

"That feels good!"

"So why doesn't it get hard?"

"You want it that way?"

"Sure! Always!"

"Pepi, Pepi, what would your mother say if she heard you talk like that?"

I didn't know why he suddenly brought that up, but I wanted to show him how "sophisticated" I had become and said:

"Mother would understand. She always wants

father's dick to get hard more often . . ."

Eckhardt was surprised and grabbed me by the shoulders.

"Say, how d'you know that?"

I told him of the scene at night when mother tried to get father to give it to her a second time, because she didn't come before, and how she said she would have to ask other men to do it to her. While telling him this I kept pressing his prick against my slit, still hoping to bring it back to life. He listened with great attention.

"Are you sure your mother said that?" he said at last, while his prick suddenly became firm and hard again. "Are you sure she said she'd have to ask other men to fuck her . . ?"

He took me on his lap and put his prick into me as far as it would go without hurting me and I moved up and down on it excitedly.

"Ah . . . I've come twice already . . . ah, I'm coming again . . ."

But Eckhardt went on questioning me:

"Why doesn't your mother come to me to get a good lay?"

I swung up and down on the tip of his dick and said, absentmindedly:

"I don't know . . . ah . . . I'm coming again . . ."

"Listen, Pepi, I'm going to tell your mother that she can count on me any time, okay . . . ?"

"I don't mind . . . ah, this is wonderful . . . I'm coming all the time . . . fucking is good . . . I want to fuck all the time . . . ah . . ."

Eckhardt was preoccupied with his own problems.

"Tell me, Pepi, do you believe she'd let me fuck her . . ?"

The mere thought seemed to excite him, because he began to push into me very hard.

"Not so deep . . ." I begged. He pushed a little less hard.

"Well . . . would she let me . . .?"

"Perhaps . . . I really don't know . . ."

"Your mother would really have room for my dick, wouldn't she . . ? Wouldn't she . . ?"

"Sure, the whole thing would go in nicely."

"Would you want me to fuck your mother?"

"Sure," I said if only to please him. At that moment he began to ejaculate and I pulled away, but he said angrily:

"Damn it, stay here until I've come. You can't leave me right in the middle of it . . ."

I quickly grabbed his prick and jacked him off and saw the jet of semen spurt into the air as if it would never stop. It had become quite dark outside, and I went into the bedroom, undressed and lay down. Eckhardt also went to bed in the kitchen.

I couldn't fall asleep and began to work on my slit which kept itching in spite of the several lays I had enjoyed that day. I left my bed and ran into the kitchen without my nightshirt. I stood next to Mr. Eckhardt's bed and offered myself again. First he didn't want me there, but soon he began to stroke my small nipples and then he let his fingers work on my slit so that I was just as stimulated as before.

"Try and make it fast," I said.

"Make what fast?"

"Fucking, of course . . . somebody might come home soon now . . ."

"I'll be . . . !" He sat up in bed and put me across his knees, trying to see the expression in my face. "I'll be damned . . . what kind of girl are you . . ? I've never seen such a thing

. . . I've fucked you three times now and you still don't have enough . . . ?"

"Oh . . . now in the nude . . ." I said almost timidly.

"Well, I'll be damned! Your little cunt is quite red from all that fucking tonight . . . and . . ."

"Oh . . . that's not from tonight . . ."

"Is that so? When did it get that way?"

His finger slipped gradually into my hole and I moved against it. My excitement didn't let me find any words at the moment. Eckhardt's face was close to mine.

"Speak up, Pepi! Who have you been fucking around with all these days, eh? You don't seem to be doing anything else, and that's too much for a little kid like you. Come on, speak up!"

His moving finger made it difficult for me to think, but I realized that I had to find a good answer that would not only make sense to him, but which could stimulate him, too. I decided that the time had come to tell about Mr. Horak. After all, all these adults loved to fuck around and so — nobody could blame anybody for doing what he himself was doing.

Eckhardt kept pressing me to talk:

"Well . . . what are you waiting for? Who were the guys you've been screwing with . . . you've got to tell me right now . . . d'you hear?"

"Mr. Horak . . ."

"What? The man who drives the beer wagon? The guy who moves those barrels in and out of our cellar?"

"Yep!"

"That's a nice how d'you do! When did he start doing this to you?"

"Oh, well, it's quite some time ago!"

"What? Before I started doing it with you?"

"No, but right afterwards!"

"But . . . where? Where did he get hold of you?"

"In the cellar . . ."

"And how could he rub you so hard that your box is so red?"

"That's easy! He has a long prick . . ."

"Longer than mine?"

"Yes, much longer, but not so thick!"

"And how often does he fuck you every time?"

"At least five times," I lied. "Always . . . !"

"Come on," Eckhardt sounded quite horny. "Come, you little whore, I'm going to fuck you again right now!"

I promptly slipped underneath him and he pushed his nightshirt up so that his hot body was covering mine. But — nothing doing. His tool was still limp.

"Damn it," he cursed a few times. "Damn it, and I really want to . . ."

"Me, too," I said and raised my belly toward his, squeezing his inanimate tool. Nothing happened.

"I've got an idea," he said. "Why don't you suck it again a little? That'll help!"

I was still trying to give it the hand treatment, without success.

"Come on, Pepi! Put it in your mouth! I'm sure you've been doing it to Horak, too!"

"Sure . . ." I admitted. I knew instinctively that his vanity was hurt and I could egg him on by bragging of other men's virility.

He moved his abdomen over my face until his dick touched my lips. I again had a chance to practice a good blow-job. It requires great skill for the mouth to treat a penis with the same stimulation it usually gets only from the vaginal grip. I did my best to close in on Eckhardt's tool as narrowly as possible and after five minutes it actually began to twitch and become hard again. Now it was too big for my mouth and I made haste to slip upwards against the pillow and grabbed the prick and stuck the glans into my hole. The rest of it that didn't get in was taken care of with my hand, holding it tightly.

Eckhardt moved faster than I'd ever experienced with him. A regular fury of the senses had gripped him and he was panting, gasping and moaning like crazy.

"Ah . . . I wouldn't have believed it . . . I am really fucking you for the fourth time tonight . . . it's incredible!"

"Push faster . . . faster!" I demanded, not paying much attention to his remarks.

"What? Faster? Just wait, kid, I'm going to screw you so that you'll think of it to your dying day!"

He wetted his fingertips and stimulated my nipples with them. A thrill went through my body down to the tips of my toes. I thrust my cunt toward his prick which managed to get in more and more deeply.

Eckhardt was fully aroused. He put his lips to my ear and began to lick it so skillfully that I thought I was going to yell with pleasure. I felt as if I were being laid by six men simultaneously. Eckhardt, panting next to my ear, launched a broadside of furious remarks:

"See? I'm fucking you as you've never been fucked before . . . you horny little brat . . . you whore . . . I'll show you what fucking means . . ."

Although I kept myself from emitting loud shouts, I couldn't avoid talking and gave vent to my feelings:

"Jeez, Mr. Eckhardt . . . that's really good . . . you are the greatest . . . I'll only do it with you . . . nobody else knows how to fuck like that . . . I'm coming . . . this is the third time . . . yes, ram it in some more . . . yes . . . a little deeper . . . yes . . . that's good . . . !"

I loosened my fingers from around the middle part of his prick and let him push it in a little more. It hurt, but I pressed my lips together and made up my mind to put up with a little pain.

He kept licking my ear and whispering between licks:

"Yes, I'll show you . . . I'll show you what a good fuck is . . . you ain't seen nothing yet . . . I'll fuck you like I fucked my wife . . . that bitch . . . I don't mind if I knock you up . . . I don't care . . . ah . . . now you are pushing back . . . you get the idea now . . . that's it . . . keep pushing against me . . . like it now? . . . do you . . . ?"

I was in such a frenzy that I kept talking, trying to compliment him:

"No, Mr. Eckhardt, nobody can fuck like you . . . you're right . . . you're the only one . . . I'll never let Horak fuck me again . . . nobody is going to fuck me from now on . . . only you . . . you alone . . . not Mr. Horak, or Loisl, or Robert, or Franz, or Ferdl . . . only you . . . !"

"What?" Eckhardt exclaimed, "you've had so many pricks fucking you . . . ?"

"Yes," I said, "many pricks, many many more . . . I've been fucked by a whole lot of boys and men . . ."

Eckhardt's prick worked like a piston.

"You are a regular little whore . . . and that's good . . . now I can be sure you won't tattle about me . . ."

"Oh no!!! No, Mr. Eckhardt," I stammered in a state of ecstasy. "I'll never tell anybody about you . . . but you must fuck me every day . . . d'you hear? . . . every day . . your prick feels so good in my cunt . . . ah . . . now I'm coming again . . . yes, keep pushing . . . hard . . . ah . . ."

"If I knock you up . . . you must say it was Horak . . . you understand? . . ."

"Sure . . . but you must fuck me every day . . . d'you hear? . . . every day . . ."

"As much as you like . . . I'll fuck you so often that my whole prick will find room in you . . . and if I've got to do it every hour . . ."

"Oh, that's fine . . ."

But I didn't feel so fine any more. For the past few minutes his prick caused me more and more pain which was not exceeded by pleasure any more. I'd come so often that there was nothing left in me to come, I guess. I lay quite motionless under him and felt my hole getting sorer by the minute.

"Aren't you coming soon . . . ?"

"Not yet!" he panted. "Aren't you coming?"

"Not any more . . . you try to come . . . you're hurting me . . . try to come soon . . ."

He gave one more violent thrust that seemed to split me apart, and then he ejaculated such a tremendous amount of semen that it ran all over me and all over the bedsheet so that it became quite wet. His voice sounded weak from exhaustion when he grunted:

"And now get the hell out of here . . . you fucking brat . . . whore . . . !"

Without answering, I got out of his bed and went back to the room and put on my night-shirt. After I had lain in my bed for a while, I felt how sore my cunt was. Everything in me was burning. I got up again, lit a candle and examined my lower parts in front of the mir-ror. There was no blood and nothing seemed inflamed, but I was startled to see my labia looking limp and half open as if the muscles in that area had become too slack.

I heard my folks outside the front door, and jumped quickly into the bed and pretended to be fast asleep, although I hadn't eaten any din-ner yet. I heard how my parents and brothers ate and then came in to bed. After awhile I fell asleep.

CHAPTER 12

Next morning, Mr. Eckhardt didn't get up and said he was sick. He kept putting cold com-presses on his head and, I believe, also on some other spot. I didn't feel too bad myself, but my cunt was still smarting, especially when I walked. Eckhardt and I avoided each other's eyes, and when I passed his bed in the evening, he hissed at me:

"All this is your fault!"

I became afraid that something was seriously the matter with him and asked my mother in the bedroom whether she knew something about Mr. Eckhardt's sickness. She didn't know and didn't seem to be much interested, but after a while she went to the kitchen and asked him:

"What exactly is wrong with you?"

That frightened me, because I thought he might say now: "It's all Pepi's fault!" But he answered in a whispering tone and I couldn't understand a word. I only heard mother say:

"Aw, come on now! I don't believe it!"

I sneaked to the door and listened. I just had to know what the two were discussing. I heard my mother say in a much softer tone of voice:

"But why do you do such a crazy thing?"

"I couldn't help it," he whispered back, "that broad drove me crazy, that's why. I should have known better . . . I know!"

I still wasn't quite sure he wasn't going to tell on me. Mother said:

"Boy, that sure must have been a horny bitch!"

"No, not quite! She's only a child, not older than your Pepi . . ."

I began to breathe more easily.

But my mother exclaimed now:

"What? And you have the guts to do that to a child? That's rape!"

Eckhardt was laughing now:

"Ha! Rape! Oh, yes, it was rape, but it was me who was raped! That brat just takes my dick from my pants and puts it in her mouth like a piece of candy. There isn't much left to rape, y'know!"

Mother seemed horrified:

"These kids nowadays . . . they're all bad . . . you can't watch them too carefully . . ."

And then her voice became inaudible and I could only guess what she'd said when I heard Eckhardt answer:

"Of course, it didn't get into her completely.

Only a little bit . . . give me your hand and I'll show you . . ."

"No, thank you . . . what d'you take me for?"

"O come now! There's nothing to it!"

Mother interrupted him:

"Say, how many times did you say?"

"Six times," he lied, and I began to enjoy the situation. I knew now why he talked the way he did. My curiosity grew from minute to minute. He was "making" my mother and she didn't know it.

"Six times?" she said. "That's impossible! You tell that to somebody else, not to me . . ."

"I give you my word," he said solemnly, "six times. That's why I had to stay in bed today."

Mother seemed to marvel.

"Six times . . . my God . . . no man could possibly do that . . ."

"Look, Mrs. Mutzenbacher, I'm sure your husband must have made it with you six times, at some time?"

Mother gave out a giggle.

"My husband? That's a laugh . . ."

At that moment somebody came and they had to stop the conversation. I went to bed and was glad that my secret was safe.

Next morning Herr Eckhardt told us he was still sick, but he didn't stay in bed all the time. He put on his underpants and slippers and covered himself with an old overcoat. Mother often made him sit down in the kitchen to keep her company, and I noticed they were still discussing his great feat of virility.

Four or five days later I had no classes after ten in the morning and came home. The kitchen was empty, but I could hear mother and Eckhardt talking in the bedroom. The glass panes in the upper half of the door connecting the kitchen with the bedroom were covered with white chintz curtains and one couldn't see much through them. I decided to listen, because I still wasn't quite sure they might not discuss me, after all.

I suddenly heard my mother say, angrily:

"You haven't heard a damned thing! You're making it up!"

"I'm not making it up! Just try to remember how you told your husband you didn't come and wanted him to try another lay . . . I could hear it quite distinctly from my bed in the kitchen . . ."

Mother laughed now:

"Ha! Another lay! You don't know my husband like I do! I've got to be grateful if he can do it once only!"

"See? I *was* right! But perhaps you're not fair to him. He works hard all day and hasn't got the strength to keep it back long enough . . . that's why he comes so fast!"

Mother said abruptly:

"Other men wouldn't be different!"

"Ah, but that's where you're wrong," said Eckhardt. "Take me, for instance, I can keep it back as long as I want to . . . suppose you want to come three times before I do . . . that's a cinch!"

Mother laughed again:

"Anybody can say that! You're just bragging, I know . . ."

"Bragging?!" He sounded indignant. "Who's bragging? Let me prove it to you, you'll see that I'm not bragging!"

Now I could see a little bit through the curtains. Mother was shaking her head and said:

"No, no, you oughta know I don't do such things!"

Eckhardt grabbed her by her hips.

"Don't be a spoilsport! I'm just in the mood to do it a few times . . ."

They wrestled a bit and mother threatened:

"You'd better let go of me, Mr. Eckhardt, or I'm going to scream!"

He took his hands away, but standing close to her he whispered passionately:

"Why don't you be sensible and let me . . . I've always admired you and liked you . . . you're my type . . ."

Mother stepped away from him and shook her head:

"Leave me alone . . . I'm a respectable woman!"

My mother was about thirty-six, at that time, and still had a good, firm figure. Her face had preserved a certain freshness and was made prettier by her rich, blonde hair.

"Y'know," Eckhardt said to her now, "nobody who sees you would believe you've already had three kids . . ."

Mother didn't answer, and he went on:

"I mean, looking at your face, one doesn't notice anything . . . but . . . in some other place one might see you've had three children . . ."

Mother promptly fell into the trap.

"You're wrong," she protested. "I'm still like I was as a girl . . . everywhere!"

He acted the inceredulous man.

"Aw, you've suckled the kids, haven't you? That must have done something to your teats . . . necessarily . . ."

"You don't know what you're talking about,"

138

she said in a hurt voice. "My breasts haven't changed a bit!"

Eckhardt quickly stepped up to her and wanted to grab her breasts:

"That I've got to see to believe it!"

Mother quickly pushed his hands down.

"You don't have to believe it if you don't want to!"

But he was quicker than she and got hold of one breast which he squeezed gently and then exclaimed repeatedly:

"Well, I'll be blowed! That's unbelievable! You've got a breast like a virgin! . . . Really, that's the first time I've seen such a young breast on a married woman with three kids!"

Mother still tried to keep him away, but with far less energy, and after a while she held still and said with a proud smile:

"See? Now you believe me!"

"You bet, I do!" gushed Eckhardt and took the second breast in his hands. Mother let him this time. He played with the nipples that could be seen quite clearly through the thin blouse and, soon enough, they became quite stiff.

"Y'know," he said huskily, "y'know, you're wasting yourself with wonderful teats like these! A woman whose breasts are like this shouldn't try so hard to make her husband do it better so that she can come. With a woman like you, a man oughta fuck his soul out of his body to let you come, not once, but a dozen times . . . My God, what wouldn't a man give to play with a pair of teats like these . . . !"

"Well . . . I'm just a faithful wife . . . !" said mother, but letting him play with her breasts as before.

"Faithful wife!" Eckhardt chided her. "As long as the husband can satisfy his wife's needs ... yes ... I can see why she's faithful to him. But once he lets her starve, and she can't even fall asleep because he can't take care of her ... I can't see why she should be faithful ... ! Nature must be served, y'know! What you need and want is only too natural ... !"

So saying, he unbuttoned her blouse and soon the firm white breasts were resting in his hot hands.

"You better let go!" she whispered.

Eckhardt quickly bent down and kissed her left nipple. I could see a thrill going through her whole figure and heard her say softly:

"Stop it! Stop it! ... Y'know, somebody might come home!"

She was standing in front of the large double bed, still open from last night, and Eckhardt, with a sudden thrust had thrown her backward so that she lay across the sheets. The next moment he was between her legs. She resisted with her knees, and he had trouble keeping her down.

"Now, stop it," she repeated. "I don't want to. I'm really a good wife ..."

"Aw, don't be like that! I'm sure you must have tasted a strange cock at least once!"

"Never, never! ... Get away from ... or I'll scream ..."

Eckhardt's dick was groping for the opening, and his hands kept stroking her breasts.

"Only once won't do you any harm," he panted.

"Jeez, if somebody comes home, now ..." mother faltered.

"Nobody's going to disturb us," he quieted

her fears and began to push into her forcefully. She lay without moving and only repeated:

"Please, don't . . . please, don't . . . !"

Suddenly she laughed and said:

"You don't even find the right spot!" But after another few trials by Eckhardt, she whispered:

"Wait . . . wait . . . not this way . . . !" Then she sighed deeply. His prick was safely ensconced in her.

Everything was different now, as if the whole atmosphere in the place had crassly changed. And it had, I could feel the change myself. I was well acquainted with Eckhardt's regular thrusts and saw how he applied them now. For a moment I debated with myself whether I shouldn't go down to our cellar and look for Mr. Horak, because staying around here and having to be a mere onlooker, was not very enticing. But I was afraid I could be heard trying to leave the kitchen, and besides, I was too curious not to witness the scene in the bedroom.

Soon my mother was responding to Eckhardt's mighty thrusts, which induced him to praise her:

"Ah . . . you are really good . . . such a warm and tight cunt . . . it's hard to believe . . . and such young teats . . . and how you can give me tit for tat . . . ah . . . that's so good that I won't come at all . . . I'll just stay in you . . ."

He had taken mother's legs over his arms and worked in her with methodical intensity. She had opened her thighs as wide as she could, and her breath came louder and louder.

"Mary and Joseph . . ." she exclaimed, "what a big cock . . . you almost hurt me . . . such a

big cock . . . and so thick . . . ah . . . sweet . . .
so sweet . . . that's different than with my husband . . . yes . . . keep pushing deeper . . . I can
feel it in me up to my teats . . . yes . . . fuck me
. . . fuck me . . . I feel I'll come soon . . . ah
. . . fuck me . . . !"

"Take your time," said Eckhardt moving
like clockwork, "just take your time . . . I won't
come . . . take all the time you want . . . !"

"Ah . . . that's really good." Mother was
ecstatic: "I've never known such pleasure . . .
I've never known what it means to take my
time . . . ah . . . my husband would have come
five minutes ago . . . ah . . . that's wonderful
how you do it . . . push quite deep . . . yes . . .
my husband could never do it this way . . . he
doesn't even know it exists . . ."

"Would you mind if I pulled out now?" Eckhardt asked and slowed up a bit.

Mother gave a shout and hugged him tight
with her arms and legs.

"Not now, for God's sake . . . I'm coming
. . . please . . . please . . . stay . . ."

Eckhardt whipped his hips up and down and
teased her:

"See? Now you let me fuck you! But a while
ago you pushed me away . . ."

"Fuck me, fuck me . . . Oh God, if I'd only
known how good you are . . . how good such a
big cock feels . . . how it feels to be fucked like
that . . . ah . . . now . . . now!"

She started to cry and moan and sob all at
the same time and inhaled in long gasps.

"I've come," she whispered, but Eckhardt
kept moving in her and assured her:

"So what? You'll come another time!"

"Another time? . . . ah . . . you're right . . .

now . . . now . . . I'm really coming again . . . I've never had that happen with my husband . . . ah . . . I'm dying . . . I can feel your cock up to my throat . . . please, play with my teats . . . please, and go on fucking me, please . . ."

Eckhardt drew on his whole repertory of sexual stimulation to please mother. And while he was sucking her breasts and touching her at all the erogenous zones—as they are called now, I've heard—he kept whispering to her:

"Now I can do anything with you, eh? I can suck your teats, and lick you all over, and you don't tell me any more that you are a respectable woman and a faithful wife, eh? Once a good, strong prick is in the cunt, all that nonsense stops . . ."

Her voice reflected her happiness when she replied:

"Yes, you should do everything to me . . . ah . . . just keep your wonderful dick in my cunt and your fingers on my teats . . . that's all I want . . . ah . . . I'm coming again . . . it's the third time . . . it's incredible . . . aw, forget what I said . . . respectable woman . . . good wife . . . for the first time in my life I'm happy . . . go on fucking me . . . I don't care if somebody comes in, now . . ."

Eckhardt outdid himself. He worked on her breasts and stroked the backs of her thighs and legs, and at last, he grunted:

"Now . . . now . . . I'm coming . . ."

"Yes, do come . . ." mother was almost shouting. "I can feel it . . . now, now . . . I can feel that warm semen . . . and you still go on fucking . . . that's incredible . . . you're still coming . . . ah . . . ah . . . I'm coming myself now . . . Jeez . . . you'll make me a child . . .

with all that semen . . . I don't care . . . ah . . .
when my husband comes, he gives two little
squirts and then he stops moving . . . but you
. . . you keep fucking all the time . . . ah . . .
ah . . ."

Both quieted down and didn't move for a
few minutes. Eckhardt got up first so that
mother was able to sit up. Her breasts were
naked and her skirt up over her knees, and her
hair had come loose and hung down over her
shoulders. She put one hand over her eyes in
a gesture of shamefulness, but through her
fingers she looked at Eckhardt and smiled.

He pulled her hand from her face, but she
said:

"Don't laugh at me, I'm really ashamed of
myself."

"Nonsense," he said, "you've got to face up
to facts! You're happy now, and that's the
damned truth!"

She put her hand around his dick and marveled at its size:

"It's really something what such a good
cock can do to make a woman happy . . . I feel
like it's still in me . . ."

With a sudden motion she bent forward and
put the glans between her lips and then shoved
the whole thing into her mouth. There was an
immediate result. That wonder-cock was stiff
again as if it had never been limp.

"Come," invited Eckhardt, pulling it out of
her mouth, and trying to push her onto the bed.
"Come, let's fuck again!"

"What?" Mother opened her eyes wide. "You
mean you can do it again? Now?"

"There's nothing to it! A few more times, if
you want to. Of course, only if nobody comes

in and interrupts us!"

"Jeez, I hope nobody comes . . . I don't know what's happening to me . . . I'm crazy about you and your dick . . ."

"I'll tell you what we'll do," suggested the inventive Eckhardt. "To be quite safe don't let's lie down. I'm going to sit in this chair and you're going to straddle me."

Mother did everything he said, and soon she was swinging up and down on that huge tool which seemed to hold her impaled.

"This is much better," she gasped, "much better than lying down . . . I get it much deeper into me . . . I've never had it so deep in me . . ."

Eckhardt grunted: "See? If you hadn't been so proud all the time, we could've had a good time all these weeks!"

Mother lost all control and began to sob and moan:

"Ah, such a wonderful fuck . . . hold me by the teats . . . please . . . I want to feel you everywhere . . . you do it so good . . . o my God . . . o my God . . . for fifteen years I've been married . . . and I've never been fucked like this . . . a husband just doesn't deserve it . . . ah . . . no, he doesn't deserve it . . . to have a faithful wife . . ."

Eckhardt repeated his artifices holding her breasts, tickling the nipples and sucking at them, and touching her on all the sensitive spots on her body as far as their position permitted it. Mother went plumb crazy:

"Ah . . . I'm coming all the time . . . I didn't know such a thing existed . . . are you sure it's natural . . . ah . . . I'm coming again . . . yes, it must be natural . . . I didn't know what a man can mean to a woman . . . for the first time in my life I'm a woman . . ."

After a few more minutes, Eckhardt came again with long spurts of his inexhaustible semen and mother bit into his shoulder to stifle a scream of wild pleasure. Then both remained quiet in that chair until she got up and repaired her disordered dress. But soon she was kneeling before Eckhardt and put his tool into her mouth, licking and sucking at it with a persistent fury.

"You are sold on it, now, eh?" he said while her treatment sent a pleasant shudder through his body. "Are we going to be together more often now?"

She interrupted her activity and whispered:

"I'm always alone here, in the mornings, you know that."

"Sorry, I've got to attend to my business again from tomorrow on."

Mother saw a solution:

"Why don't I come to you in the kitchen on the nights when my husband is in the tavern?"

"And the children . . . ?"

"Bah, the kids are asleep about that time."

Eckhardt must have thought of me when he said skeptically:

"You can never be quite sure that they're really asleep . . ."

"Don't worry," mother was sure of herself, "my husband always does it with me when they're asleep."

Eckhardt must have thought of me again, but he said: "Are you sure? Well, it's okay with me!"

During this conversation my mother was playing with his tool which looked quite presentable and ready for work.

"Come," Eckhardt suggested, "let's do a quickie before somebody comes home!"

Mother got up from the floor.

"What? Again? How could you do it? I've never known what a real man can do . . . okay . . . but let's hurry . . . it's so late . . ."

She lay down across the bed and lifted her skirts.

"No, not that way," Eckhardt said, "turn around!"

He made her stand in front of the bed and bend forward, with her forehead resting on the blanket, and her fanny raised toward him. He rammed his dick into her and she made a low gurgling sound and started moaning almost immediately:

"I'm coming right now . . . hurry . . . try to come too . . . quick . . . please, try to come . . ."

Eckhardt whispered hoarsely:

"Yes . . . I'm coming now . . . I wish I could have stroked your teats . . . ah . . . now . . . I . . . am . . . coming . . ."

They knew they could not afford to linger like this without risking discovery. My brothers could walk in any moment now. Eckhardt pulled his dick out and dried it with his handkerchief and buttoned his fly. Then he sat down on a chair and wiped the perspiration off his face.

Mother took the china washing bowl from the washstand, filled it with water and put it on the floor. Squatting above it, she washed her cunt very carefully. When she was through she put her skirt back so that it hung neatly down her legs again, but she hesitated to stow away her nude breasts. She held one out to Eckhardt and begged:

"Quick . . . kiss it once more!"

He obliged, kissing and licking both nipples before she buttoned her blouse.

"Maybe I can come out to the kitchen tonight," she ventured.

"Okay with me," he grunted, his voice a little fatigued.

Then mother, without being aware of it, began to talk about me:

"Well, and what are you going to do about that young little bitch you told me about?"

"What d'you mean?" he stalled.

"That young girl who made you fuck her six times, the other day."

"Well, what about her?"

"You still going to fuck her . . . ?"

"Why? You aren't jealous, by any chance . . . ?"

"But I am," she said forcefully. "I want you to fuck me only . . . nobody else . . ."

Eckhardt feigned surprise:

"But you let others fuck you, too . . ."

"What? How can you say that? Who else fucks me?"

"Your husband, of course!"

"Ah, that one! From now on I won't give it to him any more . . ."

"You can't do that! You known damned well he'll want to fuck you . . . and, after all, you're married to him . . . don't forget that . . ."

"Yes, you're right," mother answered slowly, "but he doesn't want it more than once in two or three weeks. And when he does it, he does it quick-quick like a rabbit and comes at once . . . that's all."

"Okay, and I am going to fuck my little girl friend once every two or three weeks, too.

148

What's more, I can't even get completely into her . . . so, we are only fair to each other, you and me . . ."

"Be careful," mother warned him, "you're playing with dynamite! If somebody finds out about it, they'll put you in prison!"

Eckhardt laughed: "Don't you worry, old girl, Eckhardt can't be caught that easily! Don't think you're going to be short-changed on account of that little bitch just because I'm going to fuck her once in a while . . ."

Mother hugged him and said:

"You'd better go into the kitchen now. It's almost noon and the boys will want to eat soon. I wonder why Pepi isn't home by now . . ."

Before I could sneak out the front door, Eckhardt had opened the door coming from the bedroom and saw me. He was startled at first, but when he saw me smirk all over my face, his fear changed to embarrassment, and he couldn't speak for a moment. Then he came close and whispered:

"Did you see something?"

Without answering him, I put my hand under my skirt and played at my slit and kept smiling at him. He quickly replaced my hand with his and said:

"You're not going to talk, eh?" He questioned me while his fingers drummed a tattoo on my slit. I merely shook my head and he seemed assured. He removed his hand because mother might join us any minute.

Ever since that memorable day, I watched every night to see whether mother was going to sneak out into the kitchen. She promptly did so whenever she knew father had gone to the tavern. All I could hear from the bedroom was some subdued panting, now and then. Sometimes I also found them together in the kitchen whenever I came home from school before noon. But they were very careful so that nobody could have suspected anything when seeing them talking quite harmlessly together.

I never permitted Mr. Eckhardt to fuck me, from that time on. I really didn't know what made him undesirable to me, all of a sudden. When he came home one afternoon and found me alone, he grabbed me and wanted me to yield, but I resisted him with all my strength. He pushed me down on the floor and tried to take me by force, but I pressed my knees and thighs together and kicked him in the belly, so that he seemed to have gotten the message. He suddenly let go of me and gave me a long, strange look, but he never tried to touch me again after that.

CHAPTER 13

During the following months I limited myself to Mr. Horak and to Alois. Horak was always delighted when I came down in the cellar and never disappointed me. One day Schani appeared quite unexpectedly and told me that his mother and Rosa were menstruating so that he had to fuck only Wetti, last night. That's how I got to enjoy Schani for the first time. We had a "quickie" stand-up job in the kitchen, because it was never too safe in the afternoon.

It is strange that, although I had wanted to do it with Schani all those months, I can't remember anything special about that "quickie," except that Schani noticed something about my breasts.

"You know," he said, squeezing them, "your teats are beginning to show."

He was right, they were not really full yet, but when I was naked I could see they looked like the halves of two big oranges and were round and very firm to the touch. Once when I was visiting Mr. Horak in the cellar again, I guided his hand under my blouse and when he felt my developing breasts, he was so delighted that his prick became hard at once, no matter that he had just finished fucking me for the second time. I owe it to this lucky circumstance that he laid me a third time, squeezing my breasts all the while.

Franz fucked me a few times in those days, but he kept thinking of Mrs. Reinthaler. Up to then, he had not been able to approach her with his secret wishes. I thought that I was perhaps in a position to act as intermediary. So—one morning I found her up in the attic, or rather the drying-loft, as the place under the roof was called where the women in a tenement building dried their linen after washing it in a special laundry room in the cellar.

I ran down to Franz who was playing in the courtyard and told him of my fortunate discovery, but he was shy and stalled. I told him how she let herself be fucked by Mr. Horak and how much she liked it. I also mentioned her huge, white and firm breasts, but it was in vain. Franz didn't have the guts to go up in the drying-loft and start some diplomatic approach. Being an "experienced woman" now, I offered to come with him and open negotiations. We arrived just when Mrs. Reinthaler had begun to take the dry sheets off the clothes-lines and fold them neatly into the big basket.

I spoke up very politely:

"How are you, Mrs. Reinthaler?"

She turned around quite astonished and said:

"Well . . . hello, you two! What are you doing here?"

"Oh, we are just coming to visit with you," I said as casually as I could.

"Visit with me? I'm very busy as you can see."

"Sure, and we want to help you!"

"No, no, I can do it myself!"

I saw I had to take matters into my own hands, which I did quite literally. Stepping up to Mrs. Reinthaler, I grabbed her breasts and began to stroke them. Franz stared at that majestic bosom and couldn't take his eyes off it.

The fat little woman pressed me against her and inquired:

"What are you doing, Pepi?" she asked again.

"Oh, you've got such a beautiful pair of teats," I flattered her.

She blushed a flaming red and squinted over to where Franz watched her most attentively and gave him a smile. He grinned back stupidly and didn't move. Now I took those impressive globes out of her blouse and went on playing with them. She let me do it, but looked at Franz.

"What are you doing, Pepi?" she asked again.

"You know, Franz would like to . . ." I whispered.

I felt how her nipples became rigid, but she asked nonchalantly:

"Well? What is it that Franz would like to . . . ?"

"You know what I mean," I whispered.

She smiled and let me pull her blouse back on either side so that her breasts were quite free.

"I'm going to stand watch by the door," I announced, and, moving away from her I pushed Franz toward her so firmly that he landed with his face smack between her big teats. I posted myself in front of the entrance to the drying loft and stood guard so that my brother could fuck Mrs. Reinthaler, just as I had stood guard whenever Mr. Horak wanted to fuck her in the cellar.

As far as I can remember, that was the first matchmaking in my life; the law would have named it procuring. On second thought, I had also pandered my mother to Mr. Eckhardt, by telling him of her dissatisfaction with my father's impaired potency. Without this information, Eckhardt would not have found the courage to proceed as he did and offer mother the first chance of being a satisfied woman in all her life.

Franz, that idiot, was still leaning with his face against Mrs. Reinthaler's bosom and didn't move. She put her arm around him and asked:

"Well? What can I do for you, kid?"

He couldn't have answered even if he'd had the gumption to say something, because she had gagged him with one of her large nipples, and he sucked away at it like a thirsty baby yearning for a drop of milk. Beginner though he was, Franz must have done a good job, because the passionate little woman was twitching all over and I knew that the time had come for action instead of yakking.

I found it unnecessary to go on playing watchdog and walked up to Mrs. Reinthaler in order to assist at whatever she decided to do. She lay backward on her laundry-basket full of dry linen, pushed back her skirts and soon exposed her bushy cunt which suddenly seemed so roomy that I was afraid my brother's head might disappear in it entirely. She firmly pulled the boy over her and inserted his little stick into her box that clamped down on it almost audibly.

Franz began to move as fast as the ticking of a watch, and Mrs. Reinthaler burst out laughing:

"Ah . . . that tickles me . . . but it's not bad . . . it's nice being tickled down there . . ."

She was lying without moving herself and asked me:

"Where did he learn to do it so well? Does he do it often?"

"Sure," I said.

"And always so fast . . . ?"

"Yep," I confirmed. "Franz is a fast fucker!"

Since I found there was not enough excitement in the air, I knelt next to Mrs. Reinthaler and began to work my tongue in her ear as I'd learned from Mr. Eckhardt. She purred with pleasure.

"Don't fuck so fast, kiddo," she told Franz. "Give me a chance to push, too . . . wait . . . I'll show you . . . yes . . . you see? . . . it's much better this way . . ."

She regulated the rhythm of Franz' motions and made her fanny move up and down so that the basket made crackling sounds.

"Yes . . . yes . . . that's good . . . I'm going to come now . . . ah, Pepi you drive me nuts

154

with all that licking in my ear . . . oh, go on doing it . . . ah . . . ah . . . I'm coming again . . . what kind of children are you two anyway . . . ah . . . that's wonderful, Franz . . . why don't you take my nipple in your mouth . . . ?"

Franz obediently began to suck at one nipple as if he were dying of thirst.

"Hey, you . . ." Mrs. Reinthaler shouted. "What's the idea? You've stopped fucking . . . I was just about to come . . . yes . . . put it in again . . . and move faster now . . . that's good, now . . . Jeez, now he lets go of my teat . . . why don't you keep sucking my nipples . . . ?"

Franz still hadn't learned to coordinate his caresses, that's why I came to his assistance. I stopped licking Mrs. Heinthaler's ear and worked on her nipples, alternately. As I was standing with my legs on either side of her head, she would reach up and tickle my slit, which was really thoughtful of her. She did an excellent job so that I could easily imagine I was being screwed, too.

We were working in complete harmony now and were moaning in unison. At last we all came simultaneously. Mrs. Reinthaler was enthusiastic:

"Ah . . . ah . . . you're wonderful kids, you two . . . ah . . . Franz . . . I feel your semen spurting into me . . . and you, Pepi, you're getting quite moist in your little hole . . . ah . . . we're having a good time . . . !"

The three of us had collapsed, one on the other, so that we must have looked like a bundle of clothes on that large laundry basket.

Suddenly Mrs. Reinthaler pushed us off her and jumped up. She was blushing now and the reaction set in. She was definitely embarrassed.

"I say . . . these kids today . . . wouldn't have believed it . . ." she murmured and, leaving her laundry basket behind, ran downstairs.

Franz and I sat down on the heap of laundry and I took his prick in my mouth, hoping it would soon be stiff again so that I could enjoy it, too. After all, being an onlooker has its charms, but there's nothing like being fucked in person.

"Come on, Franz," I said, "fuck me now!"

"No," he said, "Mrs. Reinthaler will be back!"

"So what? She knows that we two do it together!"

"I don't want to," he said stubbornly.

"But, why . . . ?"

"Because . . . because . . . you've got no teats!"

"I have, too . . . !" I retorted indignantly and tore my blouse open and exposed my nice round oranges. He began to squeeze them and I, quickly, lay down and, without further ado, put his prick into me and we did a "quickie." It was quite nice, and after we'd finished we left the basket with the laundry where it was and went downstairs.

CHAPTER 14

From then on, Franz always tried to get Mrs. Reinthaler alone. But she didn't want to take any risk of being discovered and took him to her apartment when her husband was at work. There she could train him methodically and to her heart's content. He actually progressed quite satisfactorily. She was quite bold about her interest in my brother. Often she came to our door, and using some excuse like, "Could the boy get me something from the market?" she took him to her place. I always knew what was going on, of course.

Such was the state of things, when my mother died. Nobody told me what her illness was, but since she always looked very healthy, it must have been that severe influenza which she neglected so that it developed into a regular pneumonia.

I was only thirteen and in the middle of puberty. The fact that my breasts grew relatively fast, and that a lot of curly hair soon covered my cunt, gave me great satisfaction. I am quite sure it was the result of my premature sex activities that my body developed so speedily. Up to the day my mother died, I had been having intercourse with about two dozen different men, and, in keeping with my passionate nature, I didn't let one day pass without being fucked, at least twice.

I don't remember many of the men I accosted with my provocative smile and who took immediate advantage of my inviting behavior. Once I was almost strangled by a drunken locksmith who pressed his hands around my throat while he was fucking me, but since he came almost at once, he let go of me. But having had that experience, I was on my guard against similar individuals.

When mother died, we children cried a great deal, because she was a good mother to all of us, while we were more or less afraid of father who could be very abrupt and strict. My older brother, Lorenz, used mother's death to frighten me:

"See?" he said, "that's how God punishes you and Franz for your sinful actions . . ."

His words hit me in a sensitive spot. I had loved my mother very much, even though I discovered that she was just as human as I was, or rather because of it. Therefore, Lorenz' moral pronouncement somehow made sense to me and I believed him.

From the day my mother died, I refrained from any sexual act and made the firm decision not to let any man fuck me any more—at least not for quite some time. I couldn't stand looking at Mr. Eckhardt any more and he also took no notice of my presence. Mother's death must have hit him hard, too, because he seemed quite depressed and didn't talk to any member of our family. One week after the funeral, he gave notice and soon moved to some other part of town. I felt much better when he had left us.

Franz and I were by ourselves far more often now, but I did not encourage him any more, and when he tried to grab my teats one day I slapped his face. He looked at me, quite surprised, but he left me alone from then on.

Mother's death, as I see now, represented a milestone in my young life and perhaps I could have really kept all my good resolutions and led a different sort of life if other, equally incisive impressions, had not pushed me ahead in the direction in which I had started out.

CHAPTER 15

My mother had been dead for two months, and I still kept my resolutions to be a good girl. At school, my teacher had been praising my diligence for the first time and told me that I was a very intelligent girl and could really become a first class student if I continued to improve.

To my own astonishment, I managed to live a chaste existence, not even wishing to see a prick, let alone feeling one between my legs.

It was about that time that confession was becoming obligatory for pupils in Austria, a predominantly Roman Catholic country, and soon a day had been chosen on which I, with all my classmates, had to attend confession at our local church. Although I had no religious streak in me whatever, my mother's death and the stern remark of my brother, Lorenz, had aroused profound guilt feelings in me. Even today I can't explain to myself what I was afraid of unless it was an uneasy conscience that made me believe that I had overdone my sex escapades. I never believed sex in itself to be "sinful" as I've always said, but I do believe today that a child should be permitted to be a "child" in the real sense of the word. Around the turn of this century, it was a known fact that the children of working-class families were unable to develop gradually and normally, because they were forced into too much intimate living among grown-ups. Their parents had no privacy, nor did they themselves. Working hours were long and hard in those days, and most children had to be left to their own devices, while the fathers of families were absent from early morning until late in the evening. By Saturday, which, in most cases, was also a working day, they were ready to get drunk and forget their working-week.

To sum it up, when I decided to "confess my sins," together with all my classmates, it was not from religious conviction, but from a quite irrational belief that my mother would, perhaps, still be alive if I had not been so sex-obsessed and done everything in moderation. It was the "too much" of sex, and not fucking as such, that I thought to be wrong for a young child like myself.

I had made up my mind not only to purify myself by confessing to have "committed fornication," but also the mortal sin of never having confessed my sex bouts before.

On former occasions, when our priest used to ask me, after I had recited the list of my "sins": "Did you break your chastity?" I always replied with a resounding: "No!"

The priest was a dark-haired, young man, very pale in his serious face. He always looked at us very severely so that we were deadly afraid of him. His big nose seemed to point at us like a reprimanding index finger. Nevertheless, I decided to confess everything and leave nothing out.

The church was crowded with schoolchildren and all three confessionals were taken by different priests. I was lucky to be examined by an elderly, fat priest whom I knew by sight only. I had always liked him on account of his round, smiling face. This gave me great encouragement when I knelt down in front of the grilled window.

First I confessed all my "minor sins," but he interrupted me, asking:

"Have you perhaps broken your chastity?"

"Yes," I replied in a trembling voice.

"With whom?"

"With Franz."

"Who is that?"

"My . . . my brother . . ."

"Your brother? Hm! Your brother, eh? And with whom else?"

"Well . . ."

"You did it with somebody else, too, didn't you . . . ?"

"Yes . . ."

"Speak up . . ."

"With Mr. Horak . . ."

"Who is he?"

"The beer delivery man in our building."

"And who else?" he kept asking with a slight tremble in his voice.

I recited the whole list of names as best as I remembered it. Of course, in the case of my "anonymous" sex partners, I merely said, "a soldier," or "a strange boy," and so on.

The priest didn't make any remark until I had finished the long enumeration. Then, after a short pause, he asked:

"And how did you commit the sin of fornication with all those men?"

I didn't know how to reply to that. He growled:

"Just say how you did it with them!"

"With . . . with . . . you know what I have between my legs," I stammered.

I saw how he shook his head impatiently. He

shot me a question without any warning:

"Did you fuck? Yes, or no!"

"Yes," I said, feeling a little more at ease when hearing the familiar term, though it sounded peculiar coming from him.

"And did you take it in your mouth, too?"

"Yes!"

The priest sighed and when he spoke again his voice sounded a little husky:

"God . . . my child . . . those are mortal sins . . . mortal sins . . ."

I became really afraid now and thought he might refuse me absolution, but he said:

"You must tell me everything . . . do you hear? . . . everything . . . God, this is going to be a long confession . . . I can't let the other children wait so long . . . you'll have to come alone and make your confession to me in private . . . that's all I can do for you . . . you understand . . . ?"

"Yes, Father . . ." I stammered.

"This afternoon, around 2 o'clock . . . I'll be expecting you!"

I promised to be punctual, and he added:

"You've time enough, now, to remember every detail, do you hear me? Every detail! Because, unless you confess everything, and I mean *everything*, the absolution won't have any effect at all!"

I sneaked out of the church feeling crushed. I went home and sat down, trying to remember all my adventures, which was not very easy, even at that time. I was very much afraid of that confession in private, which meant I had to visit the Father in his own room in the priests' quarters next to the church. I was also affraid of the kind of penance he would make me do to atone for so many mortal sins.

Shortly before 2 o'clock I was about to leave, and my brother Lorenz asked me where I was going in my only good dress.

"To my Father Confessor," I said proudly to impress my pious brother, "he asked me to confess to him in private."

"Oh . . . ? Is it Father Mayer, perhaps?" Lorenz asked.

"Yes, Father Mayer!"

Lorenz gave me a peculiar look, but I turned around and left.

It was a warm summer day and the cool interior of the rectory was not an unpleasant place to go, I thought, if only I were on a different kind of errand. I stopped at the door that had a sign on it which read "Fr. Mayer," and after a slight hesitation, I knocked gently.

"Who is it?" I heard his big voice.

"Pepi . . . Pepi Mutzenbacher!"

He opened the door from the inside and invited me to step in. He was in his shirt sleeves and his enormous belly threatened to bust his belt at any minute. Seeing him for the first time outside the church and in mufti, I noticed his obesity more than ever. It gave him a ponderous presence which, together with his red, clerical face, overawed me very much. He already knew most of my personal life, and the fear and the shame made me blush.

"Praised be Jesus Christ," I greeted him with the customary formula reserved for priests in Europe.

"In all eternity!" he responded with the proper reply.

I also kissed his big fleshy hand and he told me to sit down. I looked around and saw that

163

the windows looked out on a yard with tall green trees. On one wall hung a large, black crucifix; before it was a nicely upholstered prayer stool. Close to the other wall stood a large iron bed with a nicely embroidered spread. In the middle was a big writing desk with an upholstered armchair in front of it. I sat down on a smaller chair beside the desk.

Father Mayer had put on his cassock and was buttoning it from the collar down to the shoes: it must have had at least twenty buttons.

"Come over here," he said and we both knelt on the prayer stool and recited the Lord's Prayer. Then he made himself comfortable in the big armchair and let me stand in front of him, leaning against the desk.

"Well, you may start," he said.

I found it difficult to begin and looked at the floor. He took my chin and forced me to look at him.

"Listen," he said, "you already know that you have committed mortal sins . . . fornication is a mortal sin . . . and with your own brother . . . incest!"

That was the first time I heard that word, without knowing what it meant. I began to tremble.

"Who knows," he continued, "perhaps you are already beyond salvation . . . if you want me to save your soul, you must tell everything . . . and tell it with genuine repentance."

He talked in a low, hesitant tone which increased my awe. I began to cry.

"Stop bawling!" he growled.

I sobbed only louder.

He became more gentle and patted my arm.

"Now, don't cry, kiddo . . . perhaps we can

find a good solution . . . but you must talk!"

I wiped my tears with the back of my hand, but I still couldn't speak.

"Yes, my child," he said, "the temptations in this world are great . . . you, perhaps, didn't even know that you were committing mortal sins. After all, you are still a child . . . you didn't know what you've been doing is sinful, did you?"

"No," I said, feeling a little better.

"Well, that already sounds much better! Now, let me see, you did not follow your own urge, but you were seduced, hm?"

"O yes, Father," I said eagerly, "I was seduced!"

"That's what I thought," he nodded and looked more friendly now. "If a girl has things like these and men see them," he was touching my breasts, "they become tempted, too. The devil is always waiting to draw us into his snares. And these here are snares . . ."

He again put his palms on my breasts and it comforted me to feel his warm touch. It had been quite some time since a man had touched my breasts, and having a priest touch them seemed harmless enough.

"Yes, my child," he went on, "that is clearly the work of the Devil, the arch-tempter, to give a child such firm round breasts that belong on a mature woman . . ."

With that he took both my teats in his hands and kept holding them.

"These are real women's breasts," he said, giving them a tiny squeeze, "but a God-fearing woman must hide them so as not to tempt men. Teats like that, my child, are instruments of voluptuousness . . . God gave them to women

165

so that they can suckle their babies, but the Devil has turned them into means of pleasure for the fornicators . . . that's why one must hide them carefully!"

I found it quite natural that he kept holding my teats while he said all this, and I listened to him with great attention and, almost, reverence.

"All right my child, now let us get back to you! Begin to tell me about it!"

Again I was unable to comply and I blushed.

"Yes, my child, I can see that you feel shame. It shows that your heart is pure . . . you are ashamed to talk of those things. Aren't you?"

"Yes, Father, that's it!" I said with great feeling.

"I thought so," he said. "Well, I'll respect your shamefulness and make it a little easier for you. I'm going to ask all the questions and you'll answer. And if you're ashamed to describe something with words, you may show me with gestures what you mean, will you?"

"O yes, Father," I assured him and grabbed one of his hands that held my breasts and kissed it gratefully.

"You must know, my child," he explained, "that unless I am informed of all the sorts of fornication you have practiced, I can't give you any absolution . . . now, tell me, you took the prick into your mouth . . . ?"

I merely nodded.

"Often?"

I nodded again.

"And now describe all the things you did with it . . . one after another!"

I looked at him helplessly. I really didn't know what he meant.

"Well, my child, did you caress a prick with your hands?"

I nodded.

"How did you caress it . . . ?"

I was at a loss what he expected me to say.

"Show me exactly what you did, and how," he whispered.

I was more at a loss than ever to guess what he wanted me to do.

He smiled sanctimoniously:

"It's quite all right, my child, for you to use my prick to show me what you did . . . nothing of the ordained priest's body is impure . . . every member of it is pure . . . nothing that he does in the fulfillment of his sacred duty is sinful . . ."

I was greatly frightened and remained motionless.

He took my hand and put it next to the fly of his trousers, still whispering:

"You may take out my penis and use it to show me all the sins you committed. I let you use my sanctified body so that you can purify yourself by using it for demonstration."

He unbuttoned his fly and put my trembling hand inside where I felt some warm pulsating stiffness. A short, thick prick burst out, hard and ready as any I'd ever seen.

"Now show me, my child, how did you caress it?"

I was awfully embarrassed, but I closed my fingers around that dick and moved them awkwardly up and down a couple of times.

Father Mayer's face was serious.

"Was that all you did? Don't try to keep anything from me . . . if you want to be absolved . . ."

I massaged his prick a few times more.

"What else did you do with it?"

I remembered what I had learned from Clementine, that ugly, fat little governess of Alois', and took the priest's prick between my thumb and middle-finger and tickled his glans with my index so that the foreskin retreated completely around it.

He leaned back in the armchair.

"What other sinful artifices did you do?"

I was afraid to go ahead with my demonstrations, and let go of his prick.

"I . . . I put it in my mouth," I lisped.

He began to breathe audibly.

"And how . . . how did you do that?"

I looked at him questioningly, but he gave me a serious look full of dignity and said:

"Don't you want to show your gratitude for the mercy I am showing you? Know, my child, that you are already half purified by touching me the way you touched your lovers, those fornicators . . ."

Somehow I thought this made sense and I was overjoyed to be given a chance to deserve my absolution. I quickly knelt before him and put his thick, short specimen into my mouth.

"What?" he asked, "only the tip?"

I obediently put the whole thing in my mouth.

"Is that all . . . ?"

I began to lick and suck it, and the more my tongue touched that velvety glans the less shy I became, until I noticed that I was actually excited as if all this were not part and parcel of my confession. I heard Father Mayer moan:

"Ah . . . ah . . . such carryings on . . . ah . . . what a sin . . . ah . . ."

I didn't want him to suffer any longer and

took his prick from my mouth and dried it carefully with my handkerchief. When I looked up I saw that his face had become almost purple. He grabbed my hand:

"And what else did you do . . . with all those pricks . . . those sinful pricks . . . what else did you do with them . . . ?"

"I committed fornication, Father," I whispered, using the new term I had learned.

"I know that," he gasped, "I know that. You have shown me now three kinds of fornication and by doing so you have become purified from these three kinds of mortal sin. But you have done various other kinds . . . with all those pricks . . . do you deny it . . . ?"

"O no, Father!"

"Then speak up! What else did you do?"

"I did a lot of fucking, Father!"

"How did you . . . er . . . fuck?"

I looked surprised.

"Well . . . fucking is fucking, after all."

"That doesn't tell me anything," he said, becoming angry, "you've got to show me how you did it!"

I had reached another impasse. I didn't dare to lift up my skirts and put his prick into my cunt.

"All right, child . . . do you want me to show you what you possibly did?" he asked, "shall I show you myself?"

"Please, do!" I said. I was quite curious about what was going to happen now. After all, it was for the sake of becoming absolved from my sins. I hadn't had a prick in my mouth, or in any part of my body, for quite some time, and if it was possible to have a little sex with a holy man to have my body purified, I didn't see why I shouldn't let him push it right into my hole.

He got up and led me to the large bed.

"Now show me," he said, "how you did it."

"Oh, Father, you know," I said.

"Don't give me that, child. I know nothing at all. You must tell me everything. Now . . . did you lie below, or on top of your fornicator?"

I lay down across the bedspread and let my legs dangle over the edge.

"That's the way you were lying?"

"Yes, Father!"

"You can't possibly sin this way. The devilish tempter can't do anything to you if you just lie like this. You must have done something else . . . or . . . did he perhaps lift up your skirt?"

"Yes, Father!"

"This way . . . ?" He had pushed my skirt quickly above my belly so that my nude thighs and the slit bordered by curly blonde hair lay exposed.

"Was it this way?"

"Yes, Father!"

"And like this . . . ?" He parted my knees.

"Yes . . ."

He stepped between my thighs and his fat belly rested on me, though he was still standing.

"And your fornicator's prick entered you in this way to rouse sinful fleshly lusts in you . . . ?"

I thought it unnecessary to reply, because he was shoving his sanctified candle into me. It felt nice and warm between my labia. He penetrated me very slowly and carefully. I couldn't see his face, but I heard him grunt and groan when I pinched his prick with my labia. I was

170

glad to be fucked again, for a change, and all the more so as it was not only no sin, but, on the contrary, it was a fuck that was going to absolve me from all my previous fucks. This fuck was going to make me as pure as an angel in heaven.

Father Mayer began to move in and out, and I was tasting again, after so many months of abstention, the immense joy of having a good, sturdy prick in my cunt. I felt a mixture of surprise, delight and happiness, but gradually something began to dawn on me, and all my former misgivings disappeared in a flash. I knew now that the Reverend Father Mayer was nothing but a horny hypocrite, playing a "sinful" comedy in order to get a piece of ass without appearing to be a sinner.

I made up my hind to play my assigned part in this comedy and let him believe that I thought he could actually purify me with his sanctified body by giving me a good fucking. And, besides, what did I know? Maybe a priest like him *had* the power to absolve me from my sins. I didn't worry about it any more, and since I heard him groan on me, more and more, I began to swing my fanny up and down, making him groan and sigh like anybody enjoying a good lay.

Suddenly I had an idea. The Reverend Father had insisted on my showing him quite exactly how I had fornicated. I decided to become exactitude itself.

"Father . . . Father . . ." I whispered.

"What is it . . . ?" he asked, gasping.

"You're not doing it correctly!"

"What . . . what do you mean . . . ?"

"My fornicator moved in and out very firmly

and with great force and he stuck his prick into me as far as he could."

He actually increased his speed and pushed into me like a pump handle.

"Yes . . ." I said again, "yes, Father . . . now you've got the right idea . . . ah . . . you're doing it fine . . . faster now . . . faster . . . ah . . ."

"You're a good girl," he panted heavily on me, "you're a good girl . . . tell me everything that you can remember . . . tell me everything . . ."

He couldn't go on talking because he needed all of his breath to work on me. But I didn't need any further encouragement.

"That's it, Father . . . now you're on to it . . . I'm coming soon . . . Father . . . try to come at the same time . . . at the same time . . . ah . . . I'm coming now . . . I'm sorry to be so fast . . . what can I do? . . . your prick feels so good . . . you have a wonderful prick . . . Father . . ."

He was supporting himself with his hands on either side of me as best he could and tried to bend over me as much as his fat belly would let him. His face was a bluish red and he looked at me like a dying calf, but he kept working with a frenzy that was astonishing considering his great obesity and his shortness of breath.

"I'm coming soon," he panted, "let my penis be an instrument of divine mercy to you, my child . . . it will do you only good . . . only good . . . now I'm going to anoint your vagina with my semen . . . it will purify your whole body . . . ah . . . I'm coming now . . . soon . . ."

But he took his time and I wanted him to give me more pleasure by stroking my breasts.

"Father," I interrupted him, "I have also

sinned with my breasts . . ."

He glanced at me stupidly: "How . . . ?"

"Because . . . ah . . . ah . . . I'm coming again
. . . ah . . . because when somebody fucked me,
I let him also caress my teats and suck my
nipples . . ."

I noticed at once that his big belly would not
permit him to absolve me from that special
sin, too.

"Later . . . my child . . . later I'll purify your
teats . . . yes . . . move your sweet little cunt
. . . it feels great . . . you are a good girl . . .
you know what to do . . . now . . . now . . . I'm
coming . . . ah . . . ah . . . sweet . . . sweet . . ."

He discharged a flood of semen into me and
kept sighing:

"Ah . . . this is it . . . ah . . . ah . . ." and with
his last thrust, ". . . ah . . . what a sin!"

When he had finished, he suddenly said with
great dignity:

"You have heard my words, my child . . . I've
imitated the kind of talk made by the tempter
when he roused in you the lusts of the flesh
. . . I had to do that, because repeating the acts
your fornicator committed with you, and repeating the words, the shameless words he
moaned over you . . . all this takes away the
curse of the sinful actions you committed in
the past. To repeat all this with a man ordained
to the priesthood purifies you truly!"

I sat on the edge of the bed, trying to dry
all the moisture off me. I knew now that what
he told me was nothing but a shrewd trick
aimed at what he thought was my credulity,
the credulity of a girl coming to confess her
sins. But I let sleeping dogs lie, so to speak.
A lay is a lay, and Father Mayer meant to me

now what Mr. Horak and Mr. Eckhardt had meant to me in the past. But I liked him better because he was an educated man and I needed his good will as a priest.

The benevolent savior of my sinful body and my pure soul was sitting down in the armchair. He was still panting heavily as if he had done some exhausting work, which he had.

"Come now, Pepi," he called me over to him. "Now I'll take care of your sinful teats, so that your purification will be complete."

He unbuttoned my dress and, with great care, he brought out my breasts which, in those days, were really an appetizing pair. Round and very firm, with nipples that looked like ripe strawberries against the milky white of my skin, they aroused the erotic zeal of Father Mayer to no small degree. He began to lick them, first the nipples, then the surrounding area, with his fat, though skillful tongue. After he had done that for a few minutes, he inquired:

"Is this the way your various fornicators have attempted to rouse your lusts?"

"Yes, Father, you have guessed it!"

"Good! But were you just looking on without doing anything yourself? Didn't you perhaps play with their pricks at the same time?"

Now I knew what he would like me to do and I began to work on his limp tool.

"Sit on top of the desk!" he ordered.

I complied and placed my fanny on the large blotter on the desk and let my feet rest on his knees.

"Now comes the best part of it," he said, and then correcting himself, he added, ". . . I mean, the most important part of the purification."

I didn't quite know what he was going to do

and smiled at him noncommittally.

"Yes, my daughter," he said, breathing heavily, "now I'll undertake to purify you quite thoroughly so that nothing of that sinful influence will remain in your body."

He lifted my dress and folded it securely over my thighs, then he put my legs over his shoulders so that I had to support myself on my elbows in a reclining position.

He brought his thick lips to the lips of my little box and I could feel his hot breath there. Suddenly his warm tongue performed a thorough lick down the length of my cunt and I felt a most delightful sensation. Up to then it had been my male partners who had had to be serviced in this way. None of them had ever applied his tongue to my cunt. Had I known what extreme pleasure can be gotten that way, I would have insisted that the various enjoyers of my body had done it to me.

I almost began to feel affectionate toward Father Mayer who took the purification rite so seriously. I began to move my fanny and noticed an involuntary twitching in my cunt.

"Are you enjoying it?" he asked, interrupting his labor for a moment.

"O yes, Father, it is most enjoyable, I am very grateful to you!"

"Has any of your tempters done that to you?"

I was in a dilemma. He might not continue this delightful activity if I denied it, according to what was true. Because he had mentioned that he had to imitate everything that was done to me in order to purify me by that repetition, this time performed by a man of God. But I counted on his need to continue satisfying his own greed and risked telling him the truth.

"No, Father, this is my first experience..."
and I lifted my fanny so that my wet grotto
lay invitingly open before him.

I had not miscalculated, because he nodded
and said:

"In that case my doing it will sanctify your
misused body by applying my tongue to the
most sensitive part of it. My lips that are pro-
nouncing the holy words during worship are
touching you now and will wash away any
trace of sin in you."

I was eager to make him continue and ventured to push his large red face down toward
my cunt again. He did not resent my taking
such a liberty with his holy person and began
to concentrate on my clitoris which roused in
me an unknown kind of bliss that could never
be achieved by the most skilled finger technique.

Today, at the end of my career, I have come
to the conclusion that only few men are familiar
with the supreme role that the clitoris plays
in the sex life of women. It is all the more sad
as those men who call themselves "solid citi-
zens," take inexperienced girls for wives without knowing the most primitive things about
the sexual constitution of their mates, who
enter marriage with a lot of romantic ideas
and no knowledge of the sexual part at all. It
is a case of the blind trying to lead the blind,
and, in dire contrast to the contention of mor-
alists that a marriage is chiefly based on mu-
tual respect of the partners, I maintain that
all the respect in the world is not sufficient to
compensate a husband, or a wife, for having
to lead a poor sex life.

Father Mayer, a professional celibate, knew

more about women than most of the married men I encountered in my own profession. It may be that hearing so many diversified confessions of both sexes had given him an education that is sorely missing in the lives of non-celibate people.

But these thoughts did not occur to me at the moment when my ambitious confessor was giving my clitoris a masterly workout. Although I had thought I had become superior to the situation in which that strange private confession had placed me, I suddenly became immersed in the most voluptuous mood I'd ever known. That thick, though quick and elastic, tongue seemed to control my whole nervous system and I felt the room whirl all around me as if I were riding a merry-go-round. I closed my eyes and gave myself unrestrainedly to this bliss.

Without the slightest shame I mouthed my intense feelings:

"Ah ... Father ... you're sure the most holy man I've ever met ... I'm going to be a pious girl from now on ... I promise ... I'll always come to you to confess ... ah ... there's nothing like being purified by you ... ah ... you sure have the grace of God in you ... ah ... I'm coming all the time ..."

Without answering, Father Mayer now let his tongue enter quite deep in my cunt and that gave me the sensation of being fucked by a new kind of prick, a regular miracle prick that could do what no other prick had ever done to me before. I was losing my head and kept murmuring like mad:

"Ah ... Father ... you darling ... you are so sweet ... you are my savior ... my sweetheart . . . nobody does it better than you . . . it must be God's grace that gives you such power . . . ah . . . I'm coming again . . . I'm going crazy . . . I . . . I . . . want to do something for you . . . give me your holy prick . . . put it into my cunt . . . fuck me . . . or, no! . . . stay where you are . . . it's too sweet to stop . . . I've got to yell . . . I can't stand so much bliss . . . heavenly bliss . . ."

He suddenly stopped and I saw his purple face and his foaming mouth over me. He grabbed my hips and made me sit up straight.

"Yes . . ." he panted with great effort, "yes . . . I'm going to insert my penis into your sweet little cunt again . . . come . . . sit down on my knees . . ."

He leaned back in the armchair and I began a wild ride, impaled by his stiff candle, or rather only its tip, because his big belly didn't permit more of it to slip into me. I had to grab the arms of the chair to keep my balance and all the good will that the ministrations of his tongue had awakened in me went into the speed with which I swung up and down until we both came at the same time, and I could see that my Father Confessor didn't enjoy it any less than I did.

He let me slide down from his lap and got up to give me a towel to dry myself.

"I guess you want to make water now," he said and brought a big chamber pot from the adjoining closet.

I sat down on it and urinated without any shame. My bladder needed that release and, besides, all the holy oil that he had injected into me was running out of me, too.

Father Mayer was standing next to me and

buttoned up his trousers and the cassock over it. I got up and rearranged my wrinkled dress so that it looked not too bad and would not arouse any curiosity when I came home. But before I had buttoned my dress completely, Father Mayer had to pat my breasts affectionately as a kind of leave-taking. I was waiting for what he was going to do next. But I was disappointed.

He had assumed his dignified bearing again and gave me his hand to be kissed, saying:

"Go home, now, my daughter. The devil will have no more power over you. Pray often until tomorrow morning when you must come to church to confess any undue thoughts that may arise in your still unformed mind!"

I obediently kissed his thick hand and took my leave. Before I had reached the door, there was a knock on the outside. He opened it and I saw a girl from my class on the threshold.

"I've no more time today," he told her rather abruptly. "You'd better come tomorrow afternoon . . ."

CHAPTER 16

The girl and I left together and walked next to each other without talking for a while. Her name was Melanie. She was the daughter of a well-to-do restaurant owner and although she was only thirteen, her body was so much developed that one would take her for the wife of the owner. She was very fat so that she had to keep her legs apart to be able to walk without rubbing her thighs against each other. Her huge behind and her large breasts were quite conspicuous. She could not possibly look at her navel without using a mirror. I had always thought Mrs. Reinthaler had the biggest teats, but regarding Melanie I had to revise my opinion.

After some minutes of walking silently, she suddenly said:

"What were you doing there, at the rectory?"

"I might just as well ask you what *you* were going to do there," I shot back.

"I asked you first . . ." said Melanie.

I didn't answer.

"You don't have to tell me," she continued. "I have a good idea what you were doing there . . ."

"If you're so smart, why don't you tell me what it was . . . ?"

She glanced at me sideways.

"Perhaps one of those confessions about fornication, eh? . . ."

I burst out laughing, but didn't say anything.

"Was this the first of its kind?" she asked.

"Yes, today was the first time . . . and what about yourself . . . ?"

"Oh . . . I am used to it. I've confessed to him about twenty times. And not only myself, but also some of the other girls, like Grossbauer, Klein, Ferdinger, Schurl, yes and Hauser, too . . ."

She kept enumerating several other classmates of ours. I was baffled, to say the least.

Melanie asked me now:

"Did he do a blow-job on you, too . . . ?"

"Did . . . did he do it to you . . . ?" I asked, probing.

"Of course!" she said. "Father Mayer takes his priestly duties very seriously. He always puts his tongue into me . . . he does it to the

180

other girls, too . . . it's got something to do with purification . . . he really does it awfully well . . . don't you think so . . . ?"

"Yes," I admitted. "Awfully well!"

"Has anybody else ever done a blow-job on you?"

"No, today was the first time . . ."

She began to brag:

"I've known about this for quite some time. Our headwaiter is an expert at it . . . he does it to me whenever I want him to . . . all I've got to do is to look for him in the bunkroom where our waiters and busboys sleep . . ."

"But what do all the others in the bunkroom say to that?"

"Nothing! They know about it and never come in when we do it together . . ."

"What? They all know about it . . . ?"

"Sure, why not? Any of them will fuck me whenever I want it . . ."

I kept my mouth open for a while. Melanie did not pay any attention to my surprise, but went on giving me all the details:

"We have one headwaiter, two waiters, one barman, one busboy and then, our coachman, who is also taking care of the horses . . ."

"How old are they . . . ?"

"They're all young men and very strong. The busboy, of course, is only fourteen . . . just a shrimp!"

"How did it start . . . I mean with those men . . . ?"

"It began with the coachman. About two years ago he had to drive me to the eleventh district in town, and when we were on our way home it began to get dark. We were just crossing over a field when Johann—that's the

coachman's name—put his hand on my teats.
I was sitting on the driver's seat, right next
to him. My teats were already big when I was
only eleven.

" 'What are you doing, Johann?' I asked him.
He didn't answer but made the horse stop and
stuck his hand right into my blouse and grabbed
my naked teat. Again I asked:

" 'What are you doing, Johann?'

"No answer, but he lifted my skirt and
touched my cunt. I repeated the question.

" 'What are you doing, Johann?'

"Of course, I had a good idea what he wanted.
You know Lini Ferdinger in our class? She,
too, has big teats. It was she who told me all
that's necessary, what goes on between men
and women, but I was still without any experience myself.

"I kept asking the coachman: 'What are you
doing, Johann?'

"He acted as if he were hard of hearing. He
let go of me and stepped down from the car-
riage. Suddenly he'd found his speech again:

" 'Come, Miss Melanie . . . ?' he said and lifted
me down from the seat. Without any ceremony
he laid me down in the grass right next to the
narrow road, and I thought now I was going
to find out whether all that fat Ferdinger
had told me was true. The next moment Johann
was lying on top of me and made me open my
knees. He held me by my teats, and all of a
sudden I felt his dick push into me. I let out
a big yell, but he put his hand over my mouth
and went on to move in and out. Soon the
pain gave way to a pleasant feeling and when
he saw that I had relaxed, he took his hand
from my mouth. Again I asked him:

" 'What are you doing, Johann?'

"He didn't answer, but sprayed his semen into me and grunted a little. Then we both got up and he helped me to get back on the driver's seat. After a while he said to me:

" 'You've got to wash up the blood stains when we get home, so that nobody notices anything!'

" 'What blood stains?' I asked.

" 'Well . . . you were still a virgin . . . that's why! . . . You know . . .'

"I didn't, but I'd have liked to look at my cunt to see what he meant. I also would have liked to get a good look at that thing he stuck into me and wondered what it would feel like if I touched it with my hand. But I was too shy, in spite of everything.

"After we had driven for a while, he turned to me and said:

" 'Miss Melanie isn't going to talk about it, I hope? . . .'

"That gave me courage. I cuddled against him and put my hand on his fly. He immediately gave me his dick and I kept playing with it without either of us saying anything all the way home. When we were close to our restaurant, Johann suddenly said:

" 'That Peter is a damned liar!'

" '(Peter is our barman.)

" 'Why d'you say that, Johann?'

"He hesitated for a moment.

" 'Tell me, Johann, I want to know!'

"He smiled sheepishly:

" 'Y'know, that boy told me he'd fucked you . . .'

" 'What? How could he say such a thing . . . ?'

"I became quite angry and assured Johann

that nobody had ever touched me before.

" 'I know, now,' he said. 'That's why you've got to wash off the blood from your pussy. You were really a virgin!'

"A few days after that, I went to our stables and Johann put me on one of the feed-boxes and gave me another taste of his prick. It still didn't go in completely the way it does today, of course . . ."

"You mean to say," I interrupted her, "the prick of a grown-up gets all the way into your cunt . . . . ?"

Melanie laughed.

"Of course, stupid! Our headwaiter has one like a stallion and he can put it into me up to his balls. And Father Mayer's prick, too . . ." she added proudly.

"I can't believe that . . ." I said, moved by sheer jealousy.

"If you can't believe it, just don't," she pouted.

After a while she suggested:

"You know what? You can see for yourself if you come with me to our place now. I'll go to the boys' bunkroom because Father Mayer didn't give it to me today, and I'll look for Leopold. If we find him, you can watch and see how his huge prick goes right into me. Lini Ferdinger didn't believe me either and I made her see for herself . . . She saw how Leopold fucked me!"

"That's fine," I said. "I'll come with you then!"

I was really anxious to see how this fat girl with the enormous teats was getting laid, and I hoped to get a chance to play with her nipples when things got going.

Women's breasts have always interested me, somehow or other. I guess, one doesn't have to be an outright lesbian to be a little stimulated by a woman's figure. But I don't want to go into that now. My sexual appetite was whetted, and having been made "pure" by my Father Confessor, I thought I could permit myself to taste a little of that well-known pleasure again. If that Leopold was such a stallion as Melanie said, he might have something left over for me.

Melanie continued her story:

"A few days after that second lay, I went again to the bunkroom, but I found only Peter, the barman, there. When I saw him I remembered what Johann had told me and I shouted at him:

" 'You damned liar! How could you tell such lies about me, huh?'

"He laughed: "What's biting you, Miss Melanie?'

"His laughter only increased my anger.

" 'How dare you tell Johann that you've fucked me, you shameless liar, you! Johann knows it isn't true . . .'

"I saw that I had betrayed myself now . . . Peter would know when I said this that Johann had already fucked me. Naturally he knew at once. He kept smiling at me and said:

" 'Johann is the liar, not me! I never said I fucked Miss Melanie. I only said I'd like to fuck her . . . There's no harm done, is there . . . ? I just couldn't help myself . . . because Miss Melanie is so beautiful . . . you see, you can't be mad at me for admiring you . . .'

"He came over to me and stroked my breast. My anger disappeared immediately. I had come to be laid, and when Peter said now: 'Do let me, Miss Melanie, please!' I told him to bolt the door. He did it with alacrity. Well . . . and then I lay down in one of the bunks and he fucked me very slowly so that I really enjoyed it."

"D'you fuck with the busboy, too?" I asked.

"With Maxl?" she laughed. "Of course!"

"Who made the first approach, you or he?" I wanted to know.

"Approach? That's a good one! That impertinent shrimp! He watched me secretly doing it with Peter, one day, and the next afternoon he surprised me in the toilet where I'd forgotten to bolt the door. He said he knew why I always came to the bunkroom and I should let him, too. So, in God's name, I let him. We had a quick standing-up party. It was quite nice."

"And what about Leopold, the headwaiter?" I wanted to know.

"Oh, that one! Maxl told me about how he always bragged to the other boys he had the longest prick of them all. So I became quite curious. Leopold always works until very late at night and can afford to sleep until noon. One morning I went to see him in the bunkroom, knowing he'd be alone. He was still asleep. I bolted the door and he woke up from the noise I was making and yawned and said: 'What's up?' 'Why don't you get up, you lazy bum,' I said, but he didn't want to. 'Let me stay in bed for a while,' he said. I began to tickle him and he grabbed my teats and held them, looking at me steadily. I didn't move and returned his look. Suddenly he pulled me down to him and when I was lying next to him, he put his prick into my hand. Boy, I was almost frightened when I felt that big

186

thing. A horse would be proud to have that.

"In a jiffy he was over me and began to shove that monstrous dick into me, but suddenly he pulled it out again and said:

" 'No, Miss Melanie! I'm afraid that's still too big for you. You might get hurt. I'm going to do something else instead.' He put his head between my legs and gave me a workout with his tongue that was really something! I had to bite into a corner of the blanket to keep from yelling. I came perhaps three or four times. Then he said now he could think of himself, and he put his prick between my teats, pressed them together, and in a few minutes he squirted his juice right into my face . . ."

"What?" I said, "the headwaiter fucks you only between the teats . . . ?"

"O no, that was only in the beginning, two years ago, when I was only eleven . . . Now he fucks me quite regularly . . . I told you you can come with me and see how he does it . . ."

We had arrived at her house and walked through the restaurant. Leopold saw us and looked up from the table he was setting.

"Is father here?" Melanie asked him.

"No, he's at the coffeehouse!"

"And mother . . . ?"

"She's still sleeping . . ."

"And where's Johann . . . ?"

Leopold laughed: "He's gone to the market downtown!"

"Well," said Melanie, "what are we waiting for?"

Leopold's face darkened with excitement and he whispered:

"Okay, I'll come in a little while . . . go ahead . . ."

He was a little guy with a clean-shaven, pale face, not very attractive at all. But I was curious to see that phenomenal tool he was supposed to have.

Melanie and I went to the bunkroom, a large room with white-washed walls and four iron beds in each corner. Leopold appeared almost immediately. He didn't quite know what to make of me, but Melanie threw herself on a bed that must have been his and called him over to her. He gave me an appreciative glance and asked:

"Perhaps the young lady would like to get fucked a little . . . ?"

Then he knelt by the bed and buried his head between Melanie's thighs. I sat down next to her head and saw her eyes were already turned up in the throes of pleasure.

"I'm going to be good to you, too . . ." I told her and opened her blouse. Her overgrown teats were really something to see. Firm and well-shaped, with small pink nipples like two strawberries inviting to be tasted. No matter how I squeezed, those teats always jumped back into place like elastic rubber balls. It was a real pleasure to play with them and to suck at those strawberry nipples.

Leopold's eager tongue, caressing her clitoris, and my efforts on her teats, made Melanie rear up her whole body and screech with delight:

". . . That's too much . . . I've never had it so good . . . yes . . . yes . . . suck my teats . . . suck my teats . . . it's so good what you're doing . . . I wish I could do something for you, too . . . ah . . . ah . . . if I could only get my tongue on your cunt . . . I'd do it to you like Leopold does it to me . . . ah . . . ah . . . ahh . . ."

She let out a scream so that I let go of her breasts. I was afraid she could be heard by somebody. But Leopold assured me:

"There's nobody around here who could hear anything. In a minute she's going to yell even louder!"

He prepared to mount her.

"Look at his prick . . . !" Melanie said.

I slid down the edge of the bed and Leopold lifted his belly from Melanie's so that I could see that rare specimen of a prick. It measured at least eight inches and was curved like a bologna sausage. I couldn't resist taking its large tip into my mouth.

Leopold didn't let on what I was doing, but started playing with Melanie's breasts. His prick was twitching so violently that it nearly forced my jaws apart. When I applied my fingers to it, I marveled at the distance between the glans and the root of that terrific stem growing from a thicket of black hair.

"Okay," I heard Melanie say, "let him fuck me now . . ."

I had to release that wonderful tool and watched with fascination how it disappeared bit by bit into Melanie's moist hole.

"Look . . . !" she said. "See how the whole thing goes into me . . . ?"

There wasn't much that I could see, but I probed with my hand and felt that thunderbolt disappear into Melanie's cunt until my fingers touched only the enormous balls.

Melanie started to let out a few loud yells: "Haaah . . . hah . . . hah . . ."

Then she inhaled deeply and said:

"It's only when Leopold fucks me that I can't help yelling like that . . . it's because I'm

coming all the time . . . all the t . . . ahhhh . . .
ahhhh . . ."

Leopold fucked her with the violence of a
bull in heat and since she hugged him with her
legs, she moved up and down with him so that
the bed squeaked and began to move on the
floor with little jerks.

I felt a familiar itching in my cunt and
jumped on the bed, sitting down on the pillow
above Melanie's head. Almost mechanically I
threw back my skirt so that my cunt was
exposed and Melanie, who'd noticed it, said to
Leopold:

"You can lick her, can't you?"

He stopped sucking her nipples and approached my grotto. His tongue surrounded my
clitoris like the body of a snake and I was soon
in the same state of excitement as Melanie.
Then he made his tongue as stiff as a prick
and stuck it into my hole so that I mixed my
moans with Melanie's. All three of us came
together.

Leopold put his giant machine back into his
pants and disappeared. He couldn't afford to be
missed in the restaurant too long. Melanie and
I had to take quite some time to come down
to earth again and make ourselves presentable
before we left the bunkroom.

CHAPTER 17

The next morning I had to go to church again
to continue my confession just as Father Mayer
had requested.

It was a strange feeling to kneel before the
confessional and tell the priest the kind of

things that are usually not discussed in a church.

He asked me with great dignity:

"So you have committed the sin of fornication . . . ?"

"Yes, I have."

"You let yourself be fucked?"

"Yes!"

"By many men . . . ?

"Yes!"

"You've also put the male genitals into your mouth . . . ?"

"Yes . . ."

"You also manipulated them with your hand . . . ?"

"Yes . . . !"

"You did something else with them, too . . . ?"

"Yes!"

"What was it . . . ?"

"I was fucked from the rear, too . . ."

"From the rear, you say . . . ?"

"Yes, Father . . ."

"But not in the rectum . . . ?

"I'm sorry to say . . . yes . . ."

"You didn't mention that yesterday . . ."

"Sorry, you didn't ask me . . ."

He thought for a minute:

"Yes, you're right. I forgot that . . . well, did you fornicate in any other form . . . ?"

"Yes!"

"What else could there be . . . ?"

"Oh, I had my cunt licked . . ."

Father Mayer said angrily: "You don't have to confess that . . . that was no sin . . ."

"I didn't mean you, Father . . . it was also somebody else . . ."

"What? When? Who?"

191

"Yesterday afternoon . . . Leopold did it . . ."

"Who is Leopold . . . ?

"The headwaiter in Melanie's restaurant . . ."

"My God! How did that happen?"

I confessed the whole interlude. He shook his head in wonderment.

"You certainly didn't lose any time! Did you do anything else . . . ? Did you perhaps play with any female genitals . . . ?

"Yes . . . with Melanie's teats . . . also with the teats of other girls . . ."

"And you committed incest with your brother?"

"Yes," I said to appease him, because I still didn't quite know what the word meant.

That was all. He gave me a strange look and then told me what penance I must do.

"You'll pray every day, my child, fifty repetitions of the Lord's Prayer, then fifty Ave Marias and fifty repetitions of the Creed. And now go and sin no more! Your sins are forgiven! But if the devil should again win out over you, don't hesitate to come at once to me so that I can purify you again. But if you should tell anybody of the sacred relationship that you have with your Father Confessor, everything is lost and your soul will be condemned for all eternity! Now, go, my child!"

I left the confessional with a much lighter heart than when I had entered it. The penance was stiff, but I figured it was still better than not being saved at all.

Nowadays I do wonder how little I reflected about that incident. I suppose our superstition is never so strong as when we feel guilty. Even the "enlightened" people are not quite free of superstition, I discovered.

During the weeks following that memorable confession, it seemed to me that Father Mayer was watching me closely in class. He always looked at me so peculiarly that I thought he was carrying a grudge of some sort, though I had no idea what it could be.

But soon I saw that his attention sprang from other motives than anger. One day when he was walking up and down between the rows of our desks, he stopped next to me and gave me a friendly pat on my head and stroked my back a few times. During this demonstration of affection he kept talking to the class as if nothing special were happening. He told us that he would give us a lot of homework as preparation for the strict examination he was going to hold, the following week.

Such examinations were conducted according to a routine that was Father Mayer's very own. First he dicatated to us all the questions and then he summoned one pupil after another to come up to his desk on the platform and write some of the answers on the blackboard. The whole class had to copy those answers in their notebooks.

I was the first girl that was called up to the platform.

"I'm sure you've studied everything well," Father Mayer said, making me stand between his knees, with my back against his desk. The back of the desk reached down to the floor so nobody could see how he grabbed one of my hands and pressed it against his fly. I could distinctly feel his erection. When he released my hand I did not pull it away. He gave me a meaningful look and turning to the class, he said:

"All of you write down very neatly what I'm going to dictate!"

While he dictated some episode from the Bible, he opened his fly and let me hold his thick, curved prick. I was very proud of being thus "chosen" and duly rubbed his stick until I heard his breath coming faster and faster. I stopped from fear I might make him come then and there, but he put my hand back, and he himself slipped his hand under my skirt and began to tickle me on my slit while looking me straight in the eyes. I returned his look and he smiled almost unperceptibly. We understood each other. At last he sent me back to my desk and asked another girl to come up to him. He had been dictating all this time at a slow pace.

I could see from my desk how that girl was also standing between Father Mayer's legs and from her awkward movements it was easy to infer that she was going through the same experience I had.

After five minutes the girl was dismissed and Father Mayer called my name.

"Bring your notebook and pencil with you," he added.

This time he made me face the desk and asked me to write what he continued to dictate to the class. I wondered what he was going to do this time. When he lifted my skirt in the back I knew what he wanted. Soon I felt his hot prick trying to enter my hole from behind and since he pressed his hands on the front of my thighs I understood that I should sit down. Soon he was neatly within me and I feigned bending over my notebook one moment and then sitting back again. This way I kept my hole moving around the prick and saved Father Mayer the risky business of making any movements himself.

Today, in retrospect, I can't help marveling at the enormous boldness of that voluptuous priest who fucked me in front of the whole class while dictating some pious epistle from the Bible. I remember how excited I was and how I tried hard to control my facial muscles when I suddenly came. I felt Father Mayer come without noticing any change in the monotonous manner of his dictation. I came a second time and was hard put to pretend that all my concentration was focused on what I was supposed to be writing. Father Mayer couldn't expect anything but the zig-zag scrawl I produced with my pencil while he was giving me the business. When he had come, he pulled out of me and smoothed my skirt down before he told me to go back to my desk. Soon after that the bell announced the end of the lesson.

On the way home, Melanie and the girl who had also been "examined" by Father Mayer, came up to me.

"Could you see it?" I asked.

"He fucked you, today," said Melanie.

The other girl, Ferdinger, laughed:

"Yes and no . . ."

"We know the procedure . . ." added Melanie.

"He's never fucked me," said Ferdinger as if complaining. "I only jack him off on such occasions."

I wasn't surprised at that. She was a lean, ugly creature and had nothing to show except a pair of pointed teats that stood out provocatively against her thin blouse.

Melanie boasted: "Oh, he fucks me all right.

He's been doing it since last year. He hasn't asked me lately, though."

If Father Mayer was neglecting Melanie, it was, definitely, on my account. He concentrated his attention on me. "As long as you are touching my sanctified body," he explained, "you'll not fall into the clutches of sinful fornicators, and if it should happen, you'll come to me for purification."

From then on, he kept me after class about three times a week. In the empty classroom we could be quite at ease and go through all the "purification rites" at our leisure. He, usually, let me ride on his prick and squeezed my teats while I was straddling him. It never took longer than ten minutes so I could always be home on time.

When all is said and done I must admit that I really liked Father Mayer, no matter that he was, plainly speaking, a hypocrite and a corrupter of girls, as the phrase goes. Celibacy is a task for a saint and in all my life I have never met one.

Of course, it is one thing for a priest to relieve tensions by having clandestine sex relations with adult women, and another to choose for this purpose young girls at a school where he teaches religion. And yet, although I don't condone the actions of Father Mayer, I felt sorry for him when he, at last, became a victim of his uncontrolled sex drive and his lack of responsibility.

He was so careless as to seduce a girl in the third grade who didn't know what it was all about and consequently talked about it. She was a little beauty, only eight years old, rather pudgy with the rudiments of breasts that looked

196

quite promising for the future. When Father Mayer played the same sex-games with her, protected by the wall of his desk, as he did with us older girls, she seemed to have actually believed it was a new kind of game and told her mother about it. The woman not only reported it to her husband, a construction worker, but did a great deal of hell-raising of her own. Both parents went to the police who had Father Mayer arrested and set a date for a general hearing on the case.

My father received a summons to report to the police court and bring me along. When we arrived there, we found the whole first floor full of parents and children. There were fifteen girls of my class and about a dozen from lower grades. They looked sheepish and kept silent, giving each other embarrassed smiles. The parents talked quite loudly about the case, complaining to each other and cursing the unfortunate priest who had "debauched their innocent daughters," as they said, not realizing that most of us were not so innocent any more and had had several sexual experiences before Father Mayer took it upon himself to "purify" us during confession and play sexual games with us behind his desk.

My father was quite unprepared for what he heard from other parents and asked me whether all this was true. I was too ashamed to answer and he gave me a long, searching look, but didn't question me any further.

Melanie, who had also come with her father, was the only girl who behaved with great self-assurance and didn't mind discussing the event with adults. As a matter of fact, she enjoyed being questioned by some of the people, but every time she wanted to elaborate, her father told her to shut up. Otherwise he was quite calm and didn't participate in the excited gossip going on all around him. People, sizing up Melanie's huge teats and broad fanny, shook their heads and said:

"That one is no child any longer. It's not surprising that he did it with her. Look at those teats and that broad ass!"

Some of the fathers accompanied their remarks with appreciative glances that betrayed anything but indifference to Melanie's abundant charms.

At last it was my father's and my turn to appear before the police magistrate. He was a very handsome young man who tried hard to hide his amusement at the often peculiar answers and comments he had to listen to. Next to him sat an older man who was the police physician as we found out later.

"Well, my child," asked the magistrate, "has your priest done anything to you . . . ?"

I was trembling with fear.

"No, sir . . . he hasn't done anything to me . . ."

"I mean, has he touched you in any way . . . ? You know what I mean, don't you . . . ?"

"Yes . . ."

"And where did he touch you . . . ?"

I pointed silently to the spot between my legs.

"What else did he do . . . ?"

"Nothing . . ."

"Didn't he put something in your hand . . . ?"

"Well . . . yes . . ."

"And what was it . . . ?"

I didn't answer.

"All right . . . we know what it was. And now, tell us . . . did he perhaps put that thing there in that spot you showed us . . . ?"

"Yes . . ."

"Did he put it in the whole way . . . ?"

"No . . . not the whole way . . ."

"Only a little bit . . . ?"

"Yes . . . perhaps half of it . . ."

The magistrate laughed and the doctor at his side smiled broadly. My father gave me a strange look and kept silent.

"Where else did he touch you . . . ?" continued the young magistrate.

"Here . . ." I pointed to my breasts.

Since my thick woolen dress covered my chest quite chastely, the magistrate looked at the doctor questioningly who got up and groped quite businesslike around my teats and said dryly:

"O yes, there's quite enough to touch . . ."

That was a surprise for my father, who looked curiously at my bosom whose development was new to him.

"And now tell us . . . what is your name . . . ?" the magistrate looked down at a list in front of him. "O yes, Pepi . . . Now, Pepi, didn't you resist at all when the priest touched you that way . . . ?"

"Resist . . . ? What do you mean . . . ?"

"I mean, didn't you push his hand away . . . ?"

"No, sir . . ."

"And why did you touch his . . . I mean that thing of his at all . . . ?"

"Because Father Mayer wanted me to . . ."

"Because he wanted you to . . . ? But he didn't force you, did he . . . ?"

I hesitated, because the question might lead

to complications:

"Well . . . no . . ."

"If he didn't force you, why did you let him do all those things to you . . . ?"

"Just because he wanted to . . ."

There was a moment of silence during which the doctor and the magistrate glanced at each other.

"Now, listen Pepi," continued the magistrate, "why didn't you simply tell Father Mayer that you didn't want to do this, or that . . . ?"

"Because I was afraid . . ."

"Afraid? Of what . . . ?"

"Oh . . . because . . . because . . ."

"Because he is your teacher of religion . . . ?"

"Well . . . I just was afraid . . ."

"You mean to say . . . it was real fear . . . ?"

I decided to stick to that:

"Yes . . . fear . . . just fear . . . !"

But the magistrate was not convinced:

"Tell me, Pepi . . . are you quite sure you didn't make it easy for him . . . ? Hm? Did you never let him know, somehow, you liked to do it? Or did you look and smile at him in a certain way . . . ?"

The young magistrate imitated the "come-on" look and smile used by streetwalkers trying to acquisition male customers. I had to smile in spite of my fear.

"No, sir . . . I didn't do that . . ."

"All right, Pepi . . . but now tell us one more thing! And you must tell us the full truth, do you hear? The whole truth, d'you understand?"

"Yes sir . . ."

"Were the things that Father Mayer did to you agreeable . . . ?"

I looked at him questioningly.

"What I mean is this: Did you like what he did to you . . . ? Did you get some pleasure out of it . . . ?"

I was too afraid to answer that.

"Listen, Pepi, did you like touching his thing and playing with it . . . ?"

"O no . . . I didn't . . ."

"You didn't? All right, but—and tell the truth now—did you like it when he put that thing into you . . . ? Or did it hurt . . . ?"

"Well . . . sometimes it did hurt . . ."

"But . . . not always . . . ?"

"Not always . . ."

The magistrate was looking at me searchingly now:

"In other words . . . it was pleasant . . . sometimes . . . ?"

"O yes, sometimes . . ." I admitted, but quickly added: "But only rarely . . . !"

The magistrate and the doctor smiled, and my father looked furious.

"Now we're getting somewhere . . ." the magistrate went on, "and now repeat it, Pepi . . . it was pleasant and you liked it . . . eh?"

Being afraid of my father, who looked angrier by the minute, I said:

"No, sir . . . I didn't like doing it . . .!"

"But you said yourself that it was agreeable . . ."

"I can't help it . . . it wasn't me who did anything . . . I just felt . . . I mean it didn't feel too bad when his thing moved in me . . ."

The magistrate interrupted me quickly:

"All right . . . all right . . . In other words, you didn't like doing it, but it felt good without your wanting it to feel good. Is that it . . . ?"

"O yes . . . that's it . . . !"

He turned to the doctor:

"Would you mind examining the child so that we may be quite sure . . . ?"

Before I knew what was happening to me, the doctor had lifted me up on a tall chair and stuck something hard into my cunt after probing first with his finger. Then he pulled that instrument out and said to the magistrate:

"Yes, it's true. The child's had intercourse with him."

I got down from the high chair, feeling embarrassed.

The magistrate turned to me again:

"Now tell us, Pepi, do you know whether Father Mayer did the same thing to some other girls, too . . .?"

"Well, there are so many of them waiting outside . . ."

He laughed and said:

"Yes, I know that, Pepi . . . I only want to know whether you know something . . . or perhaps saw something . . . ?"

"Yes . . . Melanie Hofer and Ferdinger have told me so themselves . . ."

"And he's done the same things with them as he did with you . . . ?"

"No . . . he didn't fuck the other one . . . I mean he didn't fuck Ferdinger . . ."

There was a moment's silence. My father looked surprised.

"Tell me," said the magistrate, "where did you hear that word? Did Father Mayer use it . . . ?

"No . . ."

"Well . . . where did you hear it first . . . ?"

"Oh . . . you know . . . at school . . . the kids

talk a lot . . ."

"Did Hofer or Ferdinger teach you the word . . . ?"

"I don't think so . . ."

"Well . . . who did . . . ?"

"I can't remember . . ."

There was a pause during which the magistrate leafed through the papers in front of him. Then he said:

"Now you said he didn't fuck Ferdinger . . . is that right . . . ?"

"Yes, he only played with her . . ."

"But he did it with the Hofer girl . . . ?"

"O yes . . . he fucked her quite often . . ."

"Have you ever seen it . . . ?"

"Yes, I saw it . . . once . . ."

"And the other times . . ."

"She told me about it . . ."

The magistrate turned to my father and said in a solemn tone:

"We are very sorry, Mr. Mutzenbacher, that you had to listen to such a sad testimony from your child. It is, of course, deplorable that an irresponsible and sex-obsessed priest deflowered your daughter, but take heart, the girl is so very young that she won't necessarily suffer any bad consequences from it, provided she is properly supervised from now on. And rest assured, the whole affair will be kept secret so that your name and that of your daughter are protected from any publicity."

CHAPTER 18

My father and I went home without exchanging a word. At that moment I was really convinced that Father Mayer had de-flowered me. He received a stiff sentence be-cause his victims were so young.

I can't help feeling sorry for him because he certainly didn't "corrupt" me, or Melanie. We both had been pushovers for anybody who tried to get us. But today I realize that the affair with Father Mayer was quite decisive for my future life, because if my own father hadn't heard of it, I still might have changed like my classmate, Melanie, who became a good wife and the mother of six children. Most of the other girls who were involved at school, underwent a similar change and forgot those early adventures.

Around fifteen and sixteen, those girls be-gan to use their brains and realized that they didn't want to be saddled with an illegitimate child and ruin their chances of a good marriage. They controlled their sex drive and got in-terested in all sorts of things that didn't offer them any temptations. The men they married didn't have any idea that their wives were not innocent any more, and even if some of them were not always faithful, like my late mother, they didn't overdo it and didn't become whores, which, unfortunately, was my own fate.

I want to make it quite clear that what had happened to me up to the examination by the police magistrate, did not contribute to my becoming a prostitute. It was rather what hap-pened *after* that fateful day that ruined all my chances of staying away from a professional sex-life. I have already said that I don't regret having become what I am, but I do regret what caused it. The reader will soon understand what I mean.

204

My two brothers had begun to earn their own keep. Lorenz, the older, worked in the same shop as my father, and Franz was apprentice to a bookbinder who, according to the custom in those days, had taken him into his home, thus providing for his board and room. Franz told me on Sunday afternoon when he came to visit us that he could have as much sex as he wanted to, because his master's servant girl, a healthy young country wench, let him sleep with her every night.

We still rented the iron bed in the kitchen, but the "sleeper" who had been with us for some time was an old man who left early in the morning and returned late at night, when I was already asleep on the sofa in the bedroom. Father slept alone in the large double-bed.

When we had come home from the hearing at police headquarters, father kept an ominous silence that frightened me more than a severe bawling out would have done. A few days later, after we'd eaten our dinner, he growled:

"I really should put you over my knee and give you a good beating until your ass becomes black and blue . . . you shameless bitch . . ."

I became afraid since this was the first remark he'd made regarding the affair. I stammered:

"But . . . you know . . . it wasn't my fault . . ."

"Okay . . . so it wasn't your fault . . . but that guy is a no good sonofabitch . . ."

He muttered something under his breath and then grunted:

"What's done is done . . . but from now on I'm going to keep my eye on you . . . you're not going anyplace without my permission . . . d'you hear? And . . . and . . ."

He began to stammer and suddenly he yelled at me:

". . . And from tonight on . . . you're going to sleep right here . . . !"

He pointed to the doublebed he used to share with my mother. When he saw my surprised look, he added:

"We've always got some 'sleeper' in the kitchen . . . you never can tell . . . we've got to be careful . . . and I'm going to keep my eyes open . . ."

I couldn't say anything and while my father left for a few beers at the tavern, I lay down on the side of the bed where mother used to sleep. When father came home it must have been close to midnight. I was already asleep, but I woke up when I became aware of his voice:

"Are you here, Pepi . . . are you here . . . ?"

"Yes, father . . ." I answered sleepily.

"Where are you . . . ?"

"Here . . . father . . ."

He groped for me.

"Ah . . . here you are . . ."

I felt his hand on my chest, but when he took one of my teats in his hand I lay like paralyzed.

"That's it . . ." he stammered . . . "that's where that damned priest touched you . . . ?"

"Yes . . . father . . ."

"And here, too . . . ?"

He had grabbed my other breast.

"Yes, father . . ."

"What a goddamned sonofabitch . . . a no good bastard . . . to do such a thing . . ."

He kept my breast in his hand and began to play with the nipple.

"How did he do it . . . that bastard . . . ?"

"The way you're doing it . . ." I whispered.

He slid his other hand under my shirt and touched my cunt. His fingers combed my pubic hair.

"Pepi . . ." his voice was quite husky.

"Yes . . . father . . . ?"

I was so frightened that I couldn't move a limb.

"Pepi . . . did . . . did he . . . touch you here, too . . . ?"

"Yes . . ."

"Perhaps with his . . . his prick . . . ?"

I couldn't understand all these questions. My father knew exactly what had happened with Father Mayer. What was his purpose?

"Answer me . . . did he put his prick there . . . ?"

"Yes . . . father . . ."

"Did he put it inside . . . ?"

His finger tried to open my slit, but I pushed his hand away.

"But . . . father . . ." I protested.

"I damned well want to know it . . ." he hissed.

"But . . . father . . . what are you doing . . . ?"

His finger was in my cunt.

"Father . . . father . . . stop it . . . stop it . . . you know he was in there . . . stop it now . . ."

"Did he fuck you . . . ?"

His finger went in deeper.

"Yes . . . he fucked me . . . but it wasn't my fault . . . why don't you leave me alone . . . I didn't want him to do it . . ."

"I hope it's true . . ." he growled. Then he took his hands off me, turned around and went to sleep.

The next few nights nothing happened and I almost forgot the incident. When I'd tried to explain my father's strange behavior to myself I thought he was not only drunk, but also quite furious about what had happened to me.

A week later, on a Saturday, we had dinner at the tavern and when we came home we went at once to bed. Suddenly my father put his hand on my breast and whispered:

"Pepi . . ."

I pretended to be asleep.

"Hey . . . Pepi . . ."

"Yes, father . . ."

"How . . . how often did that priest fuck you . . . ?"

"I don't remember . . ."

"Tell me . . . how often . . . ?"

"I really don't know any more . . ."

"Hey, you . . . I want to know . . . !"

He squeezed my breast so hard that I cried out.

"Don't . . . father . . . it hurts . . ."

"Answer my question . . . how often . . . ?"

"Perhaps ten times . . ."

"What? Ten times? That pig . . ."

He played with my nipple which became quite stiff.

"Ten times? You mean . . . in one day . . . ?"

I couldn't help smiling.

"No, father . . . on ten different days . . ."

"I'll be damned . . . ten times . . . !"

He kept fingering my nipple. The stimulation began to affect me more and more. It was a strange mixture of curiosity, well-being, horniness and fear. It was the fear which made me push his hand away.

208

"Stop that, father . . . what are you doing . . . ?"

"Nothing . . ." he muttered and took his hand off me.

He left me in peace for another week. I always tried to fall asleep before he came home. I didn't exactly understand why he behaved that way and thought it might still be his fury against Father Mayer that upset him whenever he thought of it.

But one night he started all over again. We had gone to bed rather early and I felt his hand groping for me in the dark.

"What've you been doing all day . . . ?"

His hand slid into the opening of my nightshirt at my neck and closed over my breast.

"Oh . . . nothing much . . . father . . ."

I pushed his hand away and tried to protect my breasts by pressing my palms against them. He tried nevertheless to get hold of them while he talked:

"You been in school . . . ?"

"Yes . . ."

"You got a new priest there teaching religion . . . ?"

"Yes, father . . ."

"Does he also play with your teat like that . . . ?"

He had gotten hold of one breast and fondled it.

"No . . . father . . ."

"And what about the teacher . . . ?"

"It's a woman, father . . ."

"And you're quite sure that the priest doesn't do anything . . . ?"

I tried to push his hand away.

"No, father . . . nothing . . . nothing at all . . ."

He let go of my breast and, with a quick movement, his hand was between my legs before I could press them together. His fingers closed over my cunt with a firm grip. I struggled:

"Please, father . . . father . . ." I felt quite uneasy and all the more so because that warm hand woke up all the familiar desires. "Please, father . . . don't . . ."

"Listen, Pepi . . ." his voice was husky again. "Listen . . . if the new priest should try to do this to you . . ." His fingers played a tatoo on my cunt.

"Yes . . . ?"

He tried to insert a finger into my hole.

"If that new man tries to do things like this . . . don't let him . . . d'you hear . . . ? don't let him . . ."

"No, I won't father . . . but now stop it . . ."

I quickly closed my legs and jerked my fanny sideways and was free of his hand. He grunted:

"Okay . . . okay . . . now go to sleep like a good girl . . . !"

I obediently turned on my side, but I couldn't sleep. What was going on in my father's mind? I couldn't figure it out, mainly because I was too stimulated to be able to think clearly. I still didn't suspect his motives, but I was greatly afraid of myself and my reactions. When I felt his hand in my cunt and on my teats I almost forgot who touched me and I wanted to be fucked. I caught myself wishing to touch his prick and feared he'd kill me if I ever forgot myself that far. I became more and more convinced my father was doing all this touching and playing merely to test me, to see whether

I'd give in to temptation.

Although I had learned the word, *incest*, from Father Mayer, I thought he used it to describe the sin of fornicating with my brother. It didn't occur to me that its meaning could go any further.

One night when I'd been fast asleep, I woke up feeling father's hands all over my body. He touched me very gently and got me terribly excited, but I pretended to be still asleep. I had made up my mind to find out what he actually wanted of me and decided not to let him notice that I was awake no matter how far he would go.

He tickled my nipples and began to take them into his mouth . . . first one and then the other. It became more and more difficult for me to hide my excitement. I heaved a big sigh and then went on to breathe regularly, still feigning deep sleep.

I still believed he did all this to test me. When a new touch of his tongue on my nipples made me twitch, he stopped to see whether I was awake, but I began to snore so convincingly that he seemed assured.

Suddenly he lifted the blanket off me and raised my nightshirt up to my belly. My horniness made me almost burst, but I still feared that my father did all this to find out how I'd react so that he'd know whether I'd be a push-over for other men. Now he slowly pushed my legs apart and squatted over me, supporting himself on his hands. When his hot prick tickled my slit I twitched wildly and he stopped momentarily. I felt him watching me. I pretended to feel all this in my sleep and to react merely automatically to exterior stimulation. When his prick pushed against my cunt, my fanny began to move imperceptibly up and down while I didn't stop my snoring. Now I suddenly realized what my father wanted. Since my mother's death he hadn't had a woman.

Although the memory of it has become anything but pleasant for me, today, I didn't resent the situation when it happened. I managed to feign being asleep even when my father rubbed his prick against my grotto and I was tempted to grab it and stick it in myself. Fortunately he came instantly and I felt his hot semen flood my belly. He wiped it carefully off with his nightshirt and seemed relieved that I was not awake. After a while I heard him snore on his side of the bed.

This experience took away all fear from me. My father, after all, was a weak mortal like other men, and he desired a female body even though it was the body of his daughter. Today I know that incest is not limited to the lower strata of society, although poor living conditions offer easy temptations. I also know that when my father had ordered me to sleep next to him in the marital bed, he was following an instinct of which he himself wasn't aware. He really believed it was to be better able to watch out for me and to protect me against some possible attempts of our "sleeper" to lure me to his bed in the kitchen. If I had known in those days what I have come to know in my older age, I'd perhaps have been able to resist not only my father's blind urge, but, above all, my own. But I was young and ignorant and prematurely obsessed with sex.

The following night I stayed awake until my father came home, but pretended to sleep when he entered the bedroom. When he heard my imitation of snoring, he was less careful than the previous night. He lay down quite close to me and pushed his and my shirt way up to our hips and then pressed his body close against mine. I felt his stiff tool twitch against my thigh and decided to play the game to the end, this time.

My father shoved my shirt up to my throat so that his lips had free access to my nipples, which he began to suck, alternately, so that I was soon wishing he'd go on to more important things. He didn't make me wait for it and soon squatted between my open thighs. I let my fanny dance like the night before when his prick touched me in my center. My movements made him bold and he tried to enter me slowly. While I kept on snoring I moved slowly in order to make his entrance easy, and soon enough he ventured a forceful thrust so that he penetrated me almost completely.

Now I knew I could afford to let him know I was aware of what was going on. I sighed aloud and opened my eyes and exclaimed:

"Father . . . what . . . what are you doing . . . ?"

At the same time I was moving my hips obligingly.

I noticed he was startled, but also too excited to stop. I had to save face somehow without discouraging him. While I continued to move my hips, I whispered:

"For God's sake . . . what are you doing? . . . stop . . . you mustn't do that . . ."

My hips moved stronger and faster. I heard my father whisper hoarsely:

"I . . . I . . . don't know . . . I must have been

dreaming something . . ."

"Dreaming? But we aren't dreaming now . . . what are we doing . . . ?"

"I . . . I didn't know it was you . . . I thought . . ."

"Yes, it's me, father . . . it's me, Pepi . . . it's me . . ."

And I made my fanny dance in an ever increasing rhythm.

"Father . . . father . . . you . . . you are fucking me . . ."

I embraced him firmly and gave up all pretense. He was poking me now with sharp thrusts and grabbed my teats without answering me.

"This is a sin, father . . . I'm afraid . . . ah . . . faster . . . faster . . . that's good . . . but I'm afraid . . ."

"Nonsense," he spoke at last, "nobody'll know about it . . ."

"No . . ." I assured him, "I'm not going to tell a soul . . ."

He was increasing his speed, and murmured:

"Good girl . . . good girl . . ."

I lost all inhibitions now.

"You enjoying it, father . . . ?" I asked bluntly.

"Yes . . . o yes . . ." His mouth groped for my nipples.

"You can always fuck me, father . . . if you want to . . ."

"Shut up now . . . yes . . . I want to . . ."

"Ah . . . father . . . I'll come soon . . . push faster . . ."

I was happy I needn't pretend anymore. Father was like Mr. Horak, or Mr. Eckhardt. Everything seemed to be permitted now.

"Are you coming, too . . . ?"

"Ahh . . . yes . . . now . . . now . . . ah . . . that's good . . . !"

We both came at the same time and then fell asleep in each other's arms.

The next day father seemed very shy and avoided looking at me. When he talked to me he was almost inaudible and never turned in my direction. I addressed him as little as possible and waited for the night.

When we both were lying in bed again, I took his hand and put it on my bosom.

"Father . . . are you mad at me . . . ?"

"No . . . I'm not mad at you . . ."

"I just thought . . . because you didn't talk much today . . ."

"I was thinking a lot . . . that's why . . ."

"What were you thinking about . . . ?"

He began to stroke my breasts.

"I was thinking . . . if that bastard of a priest was doing it with you . . . why, it's all the same anyway . . . I mean . . . I don't feel so bad about us doing it now . . ."

I put my hand under the blanket and grabbed his prick that became hard at once.

"Father . . . if you feel like it . . . let's . . ."

"In God's name . . . let's do it . . ." he said quite huskily.

This time I mounted him and planted his stick into me while he held me by my teats. We both came after a few minutes.

From then on my father was very nice to me during the day. Whenever we passed each other he took me by the breast and I quickly knocked my fingers against his fly. He began to tell me of things that happened at his workshop and of his money problems, and we both tried to budget our household so that we could save a little, every week. He also bought me new dresses as often as he could afford it, and he delegated me to collect the rent from our "sleeper." In brief, he treated me like an adult and it gave me a lot of self-confidence.

One night I said to him:

"Do you remember what I did to Father Mayer, sometimes?"

We had just finished a good number and father's prick was limp again.

"No," he said, "what was that?"

"You want me to show you . . . ?"

"Yes . . . I'd like to know . . ."

I began to work on his tool with my lips and tongue.

"D'you like it, father . . . ?"

"Yes . . . ah . . . that feels good . . ."

I worked on him with all the artistry I had acquired and soon enough his joystick was rigid and ready again.

"Father . . ." I said now. "Father Mayer put his tongue in my pussy, too . . ."

"Do you want me to do it . . . ?"

"O yes . . . please . . ."

He pushed me on my back and stuck his head between my thighs. He was quite adept at it, and suddenly he interrupted the pleasant activity and decided to fuck me. I liked either treatment and soon we both finished with great satisfaction.

CHAPTER 19

About this time we lost our "sleeper," who had been accepted in a home for the aged that was managed by the municipality. His place was taken by the headwaiter of a small coffee-house in our district, a more or less shabby place, frequented by streetwalkers, pimps and the likes. He never came home before three in the morning and then slept until noon the next day. Then he left at once for work.

Rudolf — that was his name — was a thin man with a pale complexion, almost yellow, and the mere hint of a mustache, if the few short hairs on his upper lip could be called that.

I didn't like the looks of him and when he tried to grab my breast on the second day, I slapped his hand. He gave me an ugly look and let go of me.

But a few days later he tried a new maneuver while I had something to do in the kitchen. He hugged me from behind and started in on my teats as if he were beating a tattoo on a drum. I was afraid my nipples would get stiff and I began kicking my legs in all directions so that he had to release me. He said quite angrily:

"Well, well . . . I suppose you are a great lady who may be touched only by priests . . ."

That startled me, and I yelled at him:

"Shut up this minute!"

"Okay . . . okay . . . I see, you permit only a member of the clergy to fuck you . . ."

He must have heard something about it from some of the other tenants in the building. Head-waiters collect all the gossip of a neighborhood like barbers.

"Listen," I said severely, "if you won't leave me alone, I'll go to the police . . ."

That stopped him, but he became quite furious and kicked his things around in the suit-case under his bed. He put his hat on and was about to leave, but came up to me and hissed:

"You're threatening me with the police . . . YOU . . . I'll show you . . . you little whore . . . you'll soon go down on your knees and beg me to fuck you . . . !"

I laughed at him and be banged the door behind him.

But I had misjudged him and it was he who had the last laugh.

One morning when my father was about to leave I was still in my shirt and father quickly touched my teats as an affectionate good-bye gesture. At that moment the door from the kitchen opened and Rudolf's face appeared just as father pulled back his hand.

"Excuse me," Rudolf said politely, "could I have my breakfast a little earlier this morning? I've got to go to the magistrate before going to work . . ."

We thought he hadn't seen anything and father left.

But when I went in the kitchen to prepare the coffee, Rudolf grinned all over his face and said:

"Aha, now I know . . . your father has your permission to play with your teats, eh . . . ?"

"You're lying . . . !" I said, but felt how red my face had become.

"Lying? Ha! I've got good eyes in my head. I saw it just a while ago . . ."

"You didn't see a damned thing! Father just told me to wash more carefully . . . that's all . . ."

He laughed and stepped in front of his washbasin, and without any sign of embarrassment pulled his prick from his pants and began to wash it. When I ran into the bedroom, he called after me:

"I've got to wash better, too . . . !"

Then he came after me into the bedroom and said:

"Yes, I've got to wash better, because very soon your ladyship is going to beg me to fuck her . . ."

This time I didn't say anything.

Several weeks passed without Rudolf speaking to me. We tried to ignore each other as best we could. Father and I continued to give pleasure to each other, not every night, but often enough to try out all the tricks I had learned from others. Having this new relationship with my father had a peculiar effect on me. I avoided meeting any boys and men, and minded my own business.

I did go to confession twice and discovered that the new priest had the same idea of giving absolution as his fat predecessor. But he was careful enough to limit his acts of purification only to licking the cunts of his female devotees with his skilled tongue. I, being older than his usual charges, and also more reliable, was purified with a few good lays.

When I visited him the second time, I decided to find out how far his power of absolving people would go. I confessed to him my relationship with my father. He threw up his arms and exclaimed:

"O God, you are lost . . . !"

I wasn't fooled by his clerical cant and told him I was ready "to do anything" to get absolution from him.

"I'll do severe penance . . ." I assured him.

"Penance . . . ? What kind of penance . . . ?"

I knelt in front of him, and after pulling his

aspergil from his pants, I began to lick it so that he let out a loud groan.

"Come . . ." he said, and made me bend over the bed and then purified me with his stick from the rear. I felt he was very conscientious about it. When he had deposited his liquid in me, I again went to work on his tool with my lips and made him fuck me a second time.

He let me go only after I had promised to stay away from my father. I promised, and he gave me absolution. I knew that he would forgive me if I had to break my promise.

After several weeks of my new relationship with father, our sex activities were gradually limited to Sundays before getting up. I discovered that most workingmen were so tired all week that they had to save up their energies for the weekend. There was an exception, now and then, but only if I took the initiative and got my father turned on. Nevertheless, every morning he liked to fondle my breasts while he and I got dressed. It put him in a good mood before going to work.

One Thursday morning he was quite horny, because, for some reason or other, we hadn't done anything the previous Sunday. After fondling my breasts for a minute, he suddenly pushed me backward on the bed and was just about to enter me, when the door opened and we heard Rudolf exclaim:

"Oh . . . pardon me . . ."

We immediately jumped up as if a bomb had exploded next to us. Father went to the kitchen and I heard him say to Rudolf:

"That lazy girl has to be pulled out of bed by force . . . she doesn't like to get up otherwise . . ."

Rudolf laughed, and when my father came back to the room, I looked at him questioningly.

"Don't worry," he said, "he didn't see anything."

I didn't answer, but I was not convinced. As soon as father had left, Rudolf burst into the room.

"Well, what was it this morning? Did father tell you again to wash yourself more carefully . . . ?"

Since I was still in my shirt, I held a towel in front of my breast, but he pulled it away and said:

"Cut out that nonsense, Pepi . . ."

He didn't call me Miss Mutzenbacher any more. I didn't like this impertinent familiarity and told him so.

"Ha!" he laughed raucously, "perhaps I should apologize to a whore like you that fucks her own father, eh?"

"We didn't fuck . . ." I said truthfully. He had interrupted us before we were able to do anything.

"You shut your filthy mouth!" he yelled. "Perhaps you're going to tell me again that I didn't see anything this time."

"You didn't . . . !"

"Is that so . . . ? Perhaps he wasn't lying on you? And you didn't have your shirt up to your belly, eh?"

"No, I didn't . . . !"

My voice had become less firm. Rudolf stepped close to me and hissed:

"Before I opened the door, I looked through the curtains over the panes. You know one can see quite nicely. You should put up thicker curtains . . ."

I remembered that that was exactly how I could observe my mother and Mr. Eckhardt. It seemed a long time ago.

"And you know what I saw . . . ?" Rudolf said with an ugly grin. "First, I saw how your father played with your teats. Then, you pulled his prick from his pants . . . and then he pushed you on the bed . . ."

I looked at the floor.

"Well . . . ?" Rudolf grabbed my chin and made me look at him. "Is that not true . . . ?"

I couldn't say anything and looked again at the floor.

"And now," he went on, "because you were always so fresh with me, I'm going to report the whole thing to the police."

I didn't expect that and began to be very much afraid. He gloated over my anxious expression and tried to scare me even more.

"Both of you are going to prison . . ."

"No . . . !" I yelled.

"No? We are going to see about that! I can testify under oath, if necessary . . . !"

He moved toward the front door.

I pulled him back and begged:

"Please . . . don't . . ."

"It's too late now . . ." He grabbed the door knob. I didn't let go of his sleeve.

"Please . . . please . . ."

"Please, what . . . ?" he asked sarcastically.

"Please . . . forgive me for being the way I was . . ."

"Aha! . . . now all of a sudden?"

"Please, don't go to the police . . . please . . ."

"It's too late for all that please-business . . . I'm going to the police right now . . . !"

I began to cry:

"Please, don't do it . . . it wasn't my fault . . ."

"What wasn't your fault . . . ?"

"Well . . . that my father . . ."

"Oh? I see! And it wasn't your fault either that you pushed me away when I wanted to touch you a little, eh?"

He put his hand on my breast and looked at me.

"I'll not act that way again . . ." I promised.

"So . . . now you let me play with your teats . . . ?"

"Yes . . . Rudolf . . ."

He tore the shirt off me and began to tickle my nipples with his long fingers.

"Now you let me do this . . . ?" he laughed.

"Yes . . . Rudolf . . ."

He rubbed his fly against my cunt and asked:

"And this . . . ? You'd let me do it, too . . . ?"

"Yes . . . Rudolf . . ." I seemed to have lost all willpower.

"That's interesting . . . the great lady would like me to fuck her now, eh . . . ?"

I saw that I had no other way out.

"Yes . . . Rudolf . . ."

He laughed. "But I don't want to fuck you. I want to report you and your father to the police . . . ?"

I began to sob again. Rudolf took me by the chin.

"If you want me to fuck you . . . you'll have to ask me very nicely to do you this favor . . ."

"Please, Mr. Rudolf," I begged, "do me the favor and fuck me, please . . ."

His sadistic needs seemed to be satisfied. He told me to follow him to the large bed.

"Lie down and open your legs . . ."

He looked me all over and then ordered:

"Open my fly . . . !"

When I had done what he ordered, his stiff prick burst from his pants. It was thin and pale and I touched it shyly. Rudolf climbed over me and said:

"You must stick it in yourself."

When I felt him in me, I heaved a sigh of relief. I wasn't sure whether it was the feel of his prick in me, or the knowledge that he wouldn't go to the police now.

"And now, you must say: 'Please, Mr. Rudolf, do fuck me!' "

I didn't mind saying that. He took one of my breasts and began to play with it, while his thin prick was working within me. I hated the man with all my heart and would have liked to kill him, but soon my excitement got the better of me and I concentrated on the pleasure that was beginning to make itself felt.

Rudolf had a special way of fucking. He pulled his prick out almost completely and then pushed it in with one sharp thrust. After he'd done that about ten times, my fanny began to dance, and I didn't understand why I had defended myself so strongly against Rudolf's advances in the first place.

"Ah . . . ah . . ." he exclaimed. "I can see that Pepi would like me to fuck her more often, eh . . . ?"

"Yes, Rudolf . . . faster . . . I'm about to come . . . yes . . . you must fuck me often . . . yes . . ."

"Fine . . . that way we'll get along . . ."

"Ah . . . I'm coming, Rudolf, try to come, too . . ."

"I'm taking my time . . ." he said.

Suddenly, without stopping his even, slow

thrusts, he asked:

"You're doing it often with your father . . . ?"

"No . . ." I lied. "Today he tried for the first time . . ."

"Don't lie to me . . ." he hissed.

"Ah . . . I'm coming again . . ."

"Tell the truth . . ." he commanded.

"Yes . . . yes . . ." I stammered.

"So your father fucks you often . . . ?"

"Yes . . . I'm coming now . . . faster . . ."

"When? When does he usually fuck you . . ."

"At night . . ."

"How long has this been going on . . . ?"

"About half a year . . ."

"Every night . . . ?"

"No . . ."

"How is he? . . . good . . . ?"

"Yes . . ."

"Better than me . . . ?"

"No . . . no . . ." I tried to flatter him. "Ah . . . I'm coming again . . ."

"You doing a blow-job, too . . . ?"

"Yes . . ."

"For me, too . . . ?"

"Sure . . ." I promised.

"And does he eat your pussy, too . . . ?"

"Yes . . ."

"You like that . . . ?"

"Yes . . ."

"D'you want me to do it, too . . . ?"

"Yes . . . Rudolf . . ."

It was really incredible. He fucked me for half an hour and I had hardly any juice left to come with. At last he gasped:

"I'm coming . . . now . . . now . . ."

His semen squirted into me with such force that it felt like an injection from a water hose.

225

Afterwards he lay next to me and played with my breasts.

"When I met you I knew I was going to fuck you . . ." he said.

"How could you know that . . . ?"

"It was easy. I heard about that affair with the priest . . . I also noticed you were sleeping in the same bed with your father . . ."

"He asked me to . . ."

"I believe that . . ." he said laughingly.

I took it as a compliment.

"You're not going to tell anybody, are you . . . ?"

"No . . . provided you let me fuck you . . ."

"O yes . . . you can fuck me as often as you like . . ."

"And, by the way . . ." he smiled, "I've known about it for some time . . ."

"What . . . ?"

"Your doing it with your father!"

"But . . . how could you . . . ?"

"Because I watched you two . . . several times . . ."

I was still frightened, even though Rudolf had promised not to tell anybody. Father and I had been too careless, it seemed.

"When did you see us . . . ?" I asked.

"Oh . . . usually on Sunday mornings . . ."

"Really . . . ?"

"Want me to prove it . . . ? Okay, last Sunday, for instance, you were lying on top of him. Then you took his dick in your mouth to make it hard again . . . and when he was ready for the second number, he was lying on you . . . correct . . . ?"

"Yes . . . I remember . . ." It was just before sunrise and it was sufficiently light to let anybody watching us through the thin curtains over the glass panes in the door, make out what was going on in the bedroom.

Rudolf got up and made ready to leave.

"Okay, now you are my second mistress . . ."

"Your second . . . ?"

"Sure! I've already got one . . . and you are the new acquisition . . . It's nice to have two mistresses . . ."

"Who is the other one . . . ?"

"You'll meet her soon . . ."

He had to leave for work then. Every morning after father had left, he questioned me about what had happened at night. He also wanted to know if I'd fucked with other men, but I was smart enough to deny that. Nor did I tell him of the new Father Confessor. Rudolf didn't fuck me every morning. Sometimes he only played with my teats, or rubbed my slit with his finger, and sometimes he said quite frankly:

"No fucking today . . . my other mistress took everything out of me last night . . ."

I still didn't go all out for Rudolf, except when he was fucking me, but, on the other hand, I didn't hate him any more. I couldn't help seeing that he was very clever and respected him for it.

CHAPTER 20

Every other week I went to confession, but that new priest was quite different from Father Mayer. He didn't keep up all the holy talk about purification and damnation. As soon as I entered his room, he took my clothes off, then his own, and we went through a series of remarkable lays. It was gratifying to see what an enthusiastic pussy-eater that man was. He made it very easy for me by making me forget his clerical status. He always called things by their real names and told me many dirty jokes. After a while I became quite familiar with him, even calling him by his first name.

Rudolf had become quite nice to me, which made our relationship tolerable. He didn't watch father and me any more, because I had admitted what was going on.

When father and I were groping and fondling each other early in the morning, I was quite free and uninhibited, knowing that I had nothing to fear from Rudolf who usually slept right through until noon, unless I felt like waking him sooner. I even began to say jokingly:

"Well, this morning you really could have seen something if you'd watched again . . ."

He laughed and then inquired:

"Oh . . . you two been fucking again . . . ?"

"No . . . but we played around quite a bit . . ."

"Okay, play as much as you want to . . . I won't be watching any more . . . I need my sleep . . ."

He said that quite often and I believed him. I became so overconfident that I even poo-pooed father's warning every time we seemed to be too loud.

"Don't worry," I said, "Rudolf is sound asleep."

One morning my father was very horny and after sucking my nipples for a few minutes he wanted to do the regular stuff.

"Be careful," I said, "Rudolf might hear us . . ."

"Aw, don't worry," father repeated my own phrase, "he's sound asleep . . . !"

We started a standing-up number. I didn't want to be caught doing it in bed, in case Rudolf woke up and wanted to embarrass us.

"Quick . . . father . . ." I hurried him. "Try to come soon . . ."

"But then you won't get anything out of it . . ." he protested.

"Never mind . . . it's not necessary . . ."

I knew I could get Rudolf to fuck me later on so that it was easy to take an unselfish attitude, if only to make father finish soon. But he didn't like that and insisted on being generous.

"No . . ." he said, "I want you to enjoy it . . ."

Against my better judgment I let him push me across the unmade bed and he really went to town on me.

"Ah . . . it's especially good today . . ." he gasped.

"Yes . . . I'll be coming soon . . ." I admitted.

"Ah . . . me, too . . . in a few seconds . . ."

Just when I felt his first squirt of semen splash into me, the door opened and Rudolf's voice said, quite calmly:

"Well, well . . . neighbor! What are you doing there . . . ?"

Father was so completely taken by surprise that he quickly finished his last few thrusts and completed his ejaculation.

Again the voice of Rudolf sounded:

"Oh . . . don't let me disturb you, neighbor . . ."

Now my father straightened up and just stood there panting, pale as death. Rudolf kept his eyes on him like a snake hypnotizing a bird. I was still lying on the bed and didn't know what to do or say.

"Well, let's cover up the girl first," Rudolf said and pulled my nightshirt down over my legs. Then he put a pillow on my chest and said:

"Keep those teats covered. They excite me . . ."

Father was still standing there, speechless. Rudolf turned to him:

"Well, neighbor . . . lost your speech . . . ? What were you doing with the girl, eh . . . ?"

Father began to stammer:

"Mr. Rudolf . . . you . . . you're not going to ruin me . . . ?"

Rudolf laughed:

"Ruin you . . . ? But why? It's nobody's business if you want to fuck your daughter . . . after all, you made her, didn't you? Without you she wouldn't be here . . ."

"Mr. Rudolf . . ." father was still stammering, "you know . . . I'm a widower . . . and . . . and I'm not so old yet . . . and I have no money to . . . to . . . you know what I mean . . . and, after all, I can't just sweat it out of my system . . . a man has got to . . ."

"Sure . . . sure . . ." Rudolf interrupted him, but father's face was full of fear.

"Mr. Rudolf," he pleaded, "you must swear a holy oath that you will not tell anybody . . ."

Rudolf laughed:

"I won't swear a damned thing . . . it's not necessary . . . but get dressed and come into the kitchen . . . we're going to have a long talk now . . ."

Father got dressed in haste, but when we

both went into the kitchen, Rudolf had already left. Now I was frightened, too. Father had to go to work and left soon. I tried to get through the day somehow or other, and at night when father and I went to bed, we both were too depressed to talk. Before falling asleep I heard father mumble:

"If that bastard reports me . . . I'm going to kill him! . . . I don't care . . ."

I couldn't blame him for feeling like that and thought that I, for my part, would not take it lying down if Rudolf actually turned out to be a traitor. I'd implicate him in every way.

We both fell asleep, but woke up again. We wanted to hear when Rudolf came home. At last we heard the squeaking of the front door; it must have been three in the morning.

"He's here now . . ." said father, who knew I was awake, too. "Shall I talk to him now . . . ?"

"You can try . . ." I said.

Before he could get up, the door opened and Rudolf addressed the darkened room:

"Hey, neighbor . . . are you asleep . . . ?"

"No, no . . ." father assured him. "What can I do for you, Mr. Rudolf . . . ?"

"That's easy . . . tell Pepi to come to me in the kitchen . . ."

"What? What did you say . . . ?" Father sounded upset.

Rudolf's calm voice repeated:

"Just tell Pepi to keep me company for a while . . . I'm sure you have no objections . . . or do you . . . ?"

My father understood that threatening question and kept silent. Rudolf was waiting in the door. At last father whispered to me:

"Okay, Pepi . . . go to him . . . there's nothing

we can do about it . . . you'd better go to him . . ."

Father's voice sounded sad and low.

I quickly jumped out of bed and walked to the door where Rudolf took me by the arm and then shut the door.

"Come," he said, "lie down in my bed with me . . ."

We were soon resting in his narrow iron bed, and he began to giggle, and cuddled against me:

"Fine! And now listen to me: You're going to stay here for . . . say, half an hour . . . and then you go back to him and tell him I fucked you, okay . . . ?"

"I don't dare . . ." I whispered.

"Don't be silly! He won't do anything to you. First, he knows he's lost the right to talk like a father, and second, he told you himself to come to me . . . so what can you lose . . . ?"

We were lying in silence and I was waiting for him to speak again.

"You're going to tell him I fucked you, okay . . . ?"

"But . . . aren't you going to . . . ?" I asked, surprised.

"Nope . . . I've just fucked my girl friend twice . . . and I'm all played out . . ."

"Aw, come on, Rudolf . . . you're a pessimist . . ." and I touched his joy-stick, "don't give up so easily . . ."

He seemed astonished and groped for my breasts.

"Say, Pepi . . . you really want to . . . ?"

"Try me . . ." I challenged him.

"Okay, I'll try . . ."

"D'you want me to put it in my mouth . . . ?"

"Wait . . . I'm going to show you something

so that you'll get something out of it, too . . ."

With that he mounted me, but he put his head between my thighs while I put his prick in my mouth. It was my first acquaintance with what the French call the sixty-nine position as symbolized by the two figures "69."

Rudolf's tongue gave me plenty of pleasure, but his tool remained inactive. I tried not to moan too loud on account of my father's presence in the next room; but when Rudolf noticed my excitement, he got into the mood and his prick soon became as hard as can be. I quickly turned around so that our genitals met the way they should, and we both controlled our panting as much as possible. Although Rudolf had a sadistic streak, he instinctively shrank from hurting my father where it was not necessary. When he came, he lifted my abdomen so high that he nearly pushed me out of the bed. His orgasm overwhelmed him so much that he did something he'd never done before: he kissed me.

"Go back now," he said when he had calmed down.

"I'm afraid . . ." I said and I spoke the truth.

"Nonsense, Pepi! If there's something he doesn't like, tell him to come out here and talk to me. Remind him that it was he who agreed to let you come to me . . ."

I sneaked back to the bedroom. Father didn't move and I thought he had dozed off, but when I got into bed, he said:

"Well . . . what did he want . . . ?"

"Nothing . . ."

"He wanted something, didn't he . . . ?"

I hesitated. "You . . . you can guess . . ."

"What? You mean he fucked you . . . ?"

"You sent me to him yourself . . ."

"He really fucked you . . . ?"

"It wasn't my fault . . ."

"You come over here, at once . . . !" he ordered.

I crawled to his side and he pounced on me violently, pulling up my nightshirt at the same time, and spreading my legs apart. I'd never felt his prick as hard as this time.

"Don't worry," I told him, "it doesn't change anything between us . . . and I'll never let that guy do it to me again . . ."

"Shut up, you whore . . . !" he hissed. "That's what you are . . . let's face it . . . !"

He rammed his tool into me so that I thought it touched my stomach inside. He began to push like a wild bull. I'd never known him to be that way. It was a mixture of anger, horniness and jealousy.

"Sonofabitch! . . . Now that guy fucked you, too . . . !"

"Father . . . I'm coming . . . you do it so good . . ." I flattered him.

"Shut up, you whore . . . did you perhaps blow him, too . . . ?"

"Yes . . . he put his prick in every hole in my body . . . he also licked my pussy . . . it was good . . . now . . . faster . . . faster . . . I'm coming soon . . ."

I knew father wanted to hear what Rudolf did to me, because it excited him.

"That bastard . . . did he make you come . . . ?"

"Yes . . . of course . . . several times . . ."

I'd hardly finished saying it when I felt his semen shoot into me. He slumped down on me and groaned in deep satisfaction. We soon fell asleep.

There was a holiday a few days later and father could stay at home. He had not exchanged a word with Rudolf after that fateful night. He always left when Rudolf was still snoring and was already sleeping himself whenever Rudolf returned from work late at night. That holiday evening I had cooked a good dinner and when we'd eaten, father lit his pipe and read the newspaper.

At 9 o'clock Rudolf came home, which was an unusual thing for him to do. He was quite friendly and put two bottles of wine on the table.

"Hi'ya, neighbor!" he greeted my father. "How about having some good wine with me . . . ?"

Father, who never refused a drink, accepted with alacrity, and when Rudolf said, meaningfully, "No hard feelings, I hope?" he understood and said:

"Hard feelings . . . ? Oh, you mean about Pepi . . . ? No . . . there are no hard feelings . . ."

"Neighbor, you are a regular guy . . . let's have a good time. From tonight I'll have lots of free time. After a while I might look for another job, but in the meantime I'm going to live, for a change. Would you mind if my girl friend joined us?"

"Your girl friend . . . ?" Father was surprised.

"Yes, I left her outside . . . should I tell her to come in . . . ?"

"Sure . . ." father said, "you shouldn't have made her wait . . ."

Rudolf went out to the staircase and came back with a very lean girl of about fifteen. She had a snub-nose and a wide mouth and her eyes had a certain provocative look peculiar to street-walkers. The only redeeming feature was her overdeveloped bosom. It was quite firm and trembled slightly when she walked.

We all began to drink and Rudolf told one joke after another. His girl, Zenzi, laughed at everything he said. Whether she did it to play up to him, or whether she actually found him to be a good comedian was not certain.

Father soon became high and also laughed often and heartily. After a while Zenzi and I began to feel the effect of the dry wine.

Rudolf lifted one of Zenzi's breasts and said to father:

"Look at this, neighbor . . . this is firm and hard like a rock!"

Zenzi laughed and father squinted at the big teat in Rudolf's hand.

"Touch it, neighbor," Rudolf encouraged him, "don't be shy . . . I'm not the jealous type . . ."

Father didn't follow the invitation, and Rudolf came over to where I was sitting.

"Yes, Pepi also has nice teats . . . very nice teats . . . just as nice as Zenzi's . . . but they're not so big and more round . . ."

He fondled my breasts, looking all the while at father who didn't move a limb. Rudolf ordered Zenzi to move closer to father:

"Hey, Zenzi, be a good girl and show Pepi's father your teats . . . !"

She laughed again and obediently opened her blouse so that one big globe burst out of it. It was really a well-formed teat, with large pointed nipples of a dark-red hue. I was hardly aware that Rudolf had his hand inside my blouse and was playing with my breasts. He addressed father again:

236

"Well . . . neighbor . . . how'd you like it . . . ?"

"Yes . . . very pretty . . . very pretty . . ."

Father couldn't resist and began to fondle Zenzi's teats. She laughed and thought it great fun.

"Why don't you give me tit for tat, neighbor . . . ?" Rudolf asked laughingly. And then to Zenzi:

"Entertain the gentleman, Zenzi . . . !"

She opened my father's fly and pulled out his dick and his balls. She began to caress them gently while looking at father with a smiling face.

"Go ahead, neighbor . . ." Rudolf laughed, "if you want to fuck Zenzi . . . don't let me detain you . . ."

Father let Zenzi massage his prick and din't say anything.

"Zenzi . . ." ordered Rudolf now, "you are going to let the gentleman fuck you now, okay . . . ?"

Zenzi immediately lifted her skirt and was about to straddle my father's knees, but Rudolf cut her short:

"Zenzi . . . !" he sounded severe, "you forget what a good girl has to do first . . ."

She knelt in front of father and took his prick into her mouth.

"Stop sucking . . . !" Rudolf told her after a few minutes, "and do the next thing that has to be done!"

Father couldn't control himself any longer. He pushed the girl on the bed and dropped on her, while she skillfully inserted his dick into her hole. He began to work in her furiously so that Rudolf and I didn't wait any longer and flopped down on the other half of the double-bed.

The bed was soon squeaking and groaning under the concerted motions of the four of us. Zenzi kept exclaiming:

"That's so good . . . Rudolf, Pepi's father is a good fucker . . . yes . . . that's a good fuck . . . suck my teats . . . bite my nipples . . . ah . . ."

But Rudolf was too busy giving me a passionate workout to pay much attention to his girl friend. Soon we all came and lay back exhausted.

Then Rudolf told Zenzi to get up and said:

"I'm taking Zenzi into the kitchen to my bed. We're going to do the second number with our own girls, eh?"

He and Zenzi disappeared in the kitchen and father began to play with my breasts while I tried to revive his dick with my lips. I was successful and just when I was slipping under father's belly to install him within me, we heard Zenzi's voice from the kitchen:

"Ah, Rudi . . . fuck me . . . fuck me . . . so many guys have fucked me, but you are the best . . . go on fucking me . . . I do everything you want . . ."

Rudolf grunted:

"Aw, shut up . . . silly girl . . . open up and let me fuck you . . . you talk too much . . ."

Father had began to poke me and I asked:

"Is she really that good . . . ?"

"Yes . . . very good . . ."

"Is she better than me . . . ?" I asked jealously.

"No . . . no . . . you're better . . . yes . . . yes . . . wiggle your ass like that . . . that's

238

good . . ."

And I seemed to have learned something from Zenzi, because I muttered:

"Ah . . . fuck me . . . fuck me . . . you're the best . . . !"

CHAPTER 21

After that crazy night, Zenzi moved in with us and slept with Rudolf in the kitchen. I didn't exactly like her, but she was always friendly and did what she was told so that I soon got used to her being around. Father and Rudolf exchanged partners frequently, but Rudolf got the better end of the deal because he wasn't working and could stay at home whenever he liked, and he often fucked Zenzi and me alternately the same afternoon.

One day, when I came back from the store with some groceries, I saw Zenzi standing with Mr. Horak near the entrance. She greeted me cheerfully, but Horak didn't seem to know me. I was mad and when I found Rudolf upstairs I decided to take my revenge.

"Didn't you see Zenzi someplace . . . ?" he asked.

"Sure . . . down by the entrance . . ."

"Doing what?"

"Mr. Horak had her by the teats when I walked by . . ."

To my surprise Rudolf laughed:

"Ha! The beer man? That's okay if he likes doing that . . ."

When Zenzi joined us after more than an hour, Rudolf talked with her in the kitchen. I expected him to give her a good bawling out.

"Where were you for so long . . . ?"

She laughed: "He fucked me . . . at last . . ."

"What? Already? Where . . . ?"

"Down in the cellar!"

"And what's the result . . . ?"

"Here! Two guilders! See? Solid silver . . . !"

Rudolf laughed aloud and told her to use the money to buy him cigarettes and then give him back the change.

I wasn't too surprised at that, because Horak used to give me some money, too, once in a while, but Rudolf's behavior seemed odd.

A few days after this, Zenzi appeared with a man at the front door. It was already twilight and I couldn't see the man distinctly. Rudolf pulled me into the bedroom and said:

"We've got to stay here for a while. Zenzi has a customer!"

Customer? It took me awhile to get the idea. We heard the bed squeak in the kitchen and then Zenzi began her customary exclamations:

"Yes . . . fuck me . . . fuck me good . . ."

But the man interrupted her:

"Just shut up . . . I can't stand any yakking when I'm fucking . . . just let me fuck you and keep quiet . . . !"

"Bastard!" whispered Rudolf close to me.

Listening to the goings-on outside stimulated me and I touched Rudolf's fly, but he pushed my hand away and hissed:

"Not now . . . this is business! Don't you understand . . . ?"

At last we heard Zenzi's shrill giggle:

"Finished . . . ! It was good!"

We heard the jingling of coins and then the opening and closing of the front door. Zenzi joined us soon. She was in the nude and handed

Rudolf the money.

"Three guilders! He was a real gentleman!"

Rudolf pocketed the money.

"Now get dressed, quick!"

While she was slipping into her dress, she told us what a small prick the man had and how quickly he moved.

"Don't talk so much, Zenzi, and get going. Bring us some wine and cigarettes. And make it snappy!"

When she had left, he turned to me:

"How about a quickie now . . . ?"

He didn't wait for my answer, but pushed me against the wall and did a quick standing-up job. I was so stimulated by what had gone on in the kitchen that I came before he was finished.

"Tonight you're going to sleep with me . . ." he declared, "and then we're really going to do a good job!"

Zenzi came back with the wine and the cigarettes and father came home soon afterwards. We all started in on the wine and Rudolf and father were soon quite drunk.

Father put his hand under Zenzi's dress and Rudolf told her at once to undress.

"And you, too . . . !" father said to me.

In a minute Zenzi and I were stark-naked and went over to the men who were sitting on the sofa. When Rudolf was about to touch me, father protested:

"No! No stranger is going to fuck my daughter . . . it's me who's going to do it . . ."

Rudolf wanted to say something nasty, but Zenzi had already straddled him and buried his prick between her thighs. I was riding on my father's dick and soon the entertainment ended in a general chorus of moans and sighs.

We were so tired that we lay down all four of us, on the large bed. The men were snoring, but Zenzi and I were still awake. We hadn't drunk much and felt cheated by the fact that our men had gone to sleep so fast.

"Want to get fucked . . . ?" asked Zenzi.

"Sure . . . but you can't get them awake now!"

"That's not necessary . . ." she laughed. "I'll show you how to go about it. Every time that Rudi is drunk, I can still get fucked. Just watch . . ."

She grabbed Rudolf's prick, that became immediately hard. I got hold of father's dick and wanted to put it in my mouth, but Zenzi held my arm.

"No, don't do it now! You can do that only if a guy isn't drunk. When he's drunk he'll shoot the whole load into your mouth."

Soon both pricks were standing up like candles.

"Which one do you like?" I asked.

"I don't want any . . . I've fucked enough for today!"

"But . . . but what are we going to do . . . ?"

"That's easy . . . you'll take on both of them . . . !"

She told me to start with father and to straddle him with my face toward his feet. Zenzi tickled my clitoris, and soon I was moving up and down and enjoying it to the utmost. Father began to moan in his sleep. Zenzi also sucked my nipples so cleverly that I came at once and when I felt father's load spray into me I came a second time. His dick became soft and limp, and Zenzi suggested:

"Quick, now take Rudi's prick . . . !"

I moved over and squatted in the same manner over Rudolf's middle, and Zenzi repeated her kind ministrations so that I was soon moaning again:

"Jeez, I'm coming . . . ah . . ."

"Rudi's prick is good . . ." Zenzi laughed, "you can't help coming soon whether you want it or not . . ."

I bent forward and took her nipple in my mouth as if following some blind instinct. It increased my pleasure and opened up the sluice-gates for all my secretions. Soon I sank forward and sighed:

"I'm finished . . . help me get off him . . ."

But Zenzi propped me up firmly and said:

"No, you must go on until Rudi comes . . . that's the decent thing to do . . . !"

I was grateful when I felt his liquid splash into me after a few seconds and then both Zenzi and I slumped down between the two men and fell asleep.

After about and hour I woke up and found Zenzi trying to revive my father's limp dick.

"Now I feel like doing it . . ." she explained to me when she noticed I was awake.

But no matter how she tried, father's tool was not usable any more.

"Come on," I said, "try Rudi's . . ."

But even Rudolf's reliable machine was on strike and Zenzi, in desperation, licked it furiously so that it began to twitch after a while and seemed to get hard.

"O my God . . ." I heard Zenzi whimper. "He's coming already . . ."

She coughed and pulled the prick out of her mouth and the rest of the semen was shooting into the air like a fountain. Zenzi spat out the portion she had received in her mouth into her handkerchief and yammered:

"O God . . . O God . . . all that work for nothing . . . and now I'm more horny than before . . . all that sucking has made me more horny . . . what can I do now . . . ?"

I laughed, but she was angry:

"Yes, you can laugh . . . you could get it when you wanted it . . I was stupid . . . I shouldn't have said no . . . !"

She suddenly pulled my hand between her legs and begged:

"You do it to me . . ."

"But how . . . ?"

"I'll show you . . . come . . . lie on top of me . . ."

I did as she told me and she began to rub her cunt against mine, then she said:

"Put your finger into my hole . . ."

I drilled my index finger into her and kept moving it like a prick. She yelled:

"Yes . . . that's it . . . that's it . . . move faster . . ."

I played with her nipple, using my free hand, and put my lips to her other teat. Suddenly she gasped:

"You did it . . . now . . . now . . . I'm coming . . ."

I kept poking my finger in her and sucking her nipple until she collapsed with her last twitch. Then, at long last, we were both tired enough to sleep peacefully until morning.

I felt really friendly toward Zenzi from that night on, and whenever we were alone and horny, I repeated the pseudofuck of the other night to her great satisfaction.

She kept earning money by bringing men to the apartment from time to time, and I could learn many things about people by listening in the bedroom.

Once Rudi and I were in the bedroom together when we heard Zenzi appear in the kitchen with a man whose quavering voice marked him as at least sixty years old.

Zenzi was laughing:

"Gee, what a little thing you have . . ."

"Never mind . . . once it's stiff it is quite big . . ."

"But it isn't stiff . . ." remarked Zenzi.

"Put it in your mouth, then!"

"How much are you going to give me . . . ?"

"What am I going to give you . . . ? Okay, let's make it ten guilders . . . !"

Rudolf, sitting next to me, gave a start and hissed:

"Jeez! Ten guilders! That guy sure has dough!

After a while we heard Zenzi say:

"It's hard, now . . . quick . . . let's do it . . ."

We heard the bed squeak, but after a while Zenzi was laughing:

"It's soft again . . . o God . . ."

The old man was whispering something and soon we heard the two rolling around in the bed. Suddenly Zenzi began:

"Yes . . . that's good . . . go on . . . faster . . ."

Rudolf explained: "I bet he's eating her pussy now . . . !"

"Oh, now you've got a hard-on again . . ." Zenzi exclaimed, "come . . . let's try it now . . ."

But soon Zenzi laughed again:

"Bang . . . it's collapsed . . . it's no use . . ."

"That's not true . . ." the old guy hissed,

"just put it in and don't talk . . ."

The bed was squeaking and Zenzi exclaimed:
"But you don't have it in . . . !"

"Never mind! I'll do it . . ."

The bed kept squeaking and, at last, Zenzi started to moan:

"Thank God . . . now . . . at last . . . fuck me . . . faster . . . what? . . . that's all? . . . o boy . . . !"

We heard them get up and walk around and then Zenzi said:

"Thanks a lot! Come again soon!"

The front door banged and Zenzi came running to the bedroom.

"Look!" she shouted and gave Rudolf a ten guilder note which was soon converted into food and lots of wine and cigarettes. Naturally, we had a big celebration that night and we got so soused that I couldn't remember what happened before we fell asleep. It was the second time that my father didn't wake up in time to go to work and when he came home in the evening he told us he'd been fired.

Rudolf comforted him and said:

"Don't worry! You'll soon find another job."

But father couldn't see it that way and said the boss had no right to do that after using his skill for over a dozen years.

"Don't be silly!" Rudolf said. "It will do you good to be able to sleep in the mornings for a week. And then you'll feel good and can look around for a new job. After all, a skilled journeyman like you doesn't have to worry to find work."

Father agreed, at last, and got used to sleeping late in the morning. He stayed at home a great deal and passed the time playing cards with Rudolf and playing around with Zenzi and myself. There was always enough wine to keep him nicely drunk.

One day he was still at home when Zenzi brought a customer up and father joined Rudolf and me behind the door where we were eagerly listening to the goings on in the kitchen. When Zenzi came in, afterwards, and gave Rudolf three guilders, father made big eyes. He hadn't realized that Rudolf was able to live on his girl friend's earnings, and became quite thoughtful.

A few days later, the manager came up and told Rudolf very politely that he was sorry, but the landlord had got wind of what was going on and sent word that we would have to move out unless Zenzi stopped bringing strange men home.

After the manager left, Rudolf had a big conference with Zenzi in the kitchen. They didn't join us but went straight to bed. From then on Zenzi was seldom at home during the day and returned only very late in the night, sometimes even the following morning. When she handed her earnings to Rudolf, father showed great interest in the amounts she made.

Zenzi being away most of the time, I had to satisfy both father and Rudolf whenever they needed me. It kept me quite busy running from one bed to the other during the night, or in the morning.

Father was in a rut now and forgot that he ought to be looking for work. He had borrowed money from Rudolf several times who had complied without saying anything. But after a few weeks of that, Rudolf replied to another of father's requests for a loan:

"Why don't you let Pepi earn some dough . . . ?"

"Pepi . . . ?" Father looked astonished. "What d'you mean . . . ?"

"I mean she could earn just as much as my Zenzi . . ." My father stiffened.

"What? Pepi should become a whore . . . a prostitute . . . ?"

"Aw, neighbor . . . that's just a word! Thousands of girls are earning money that way . . . and she's been fucking with us anyway . . ."

"But that . . ." father hedged, "that isn't the same thing! What she's doing here remains in the family . . ."

Rudolf laughed:

"The world is a big family! Don't take on, my friend! Do you think if you, her own father, fucks her it's more virtuous than a stranger fucking her? And what's more, I trained Zenzi to get only the better kind of customers. That way she always makes good money. None of her customers is such a dirty bastard as that Father Mayer who fucked Pepi without giving her a cent! That dirty old bastard . . ."

"Yes, he's a dirty old bastard," father echoed, his anger at the priest being aroused again.

"See?" Rudolf went on, "and it wouldn't do Pepi any harm to earn some money for her father, would it? You've been slaving for many years to earn some dough to keep your kids alive. Let them reciprocate for a change!"

Father weakened: "Yes . . . it's true what you say . . . !"

"Now you're talking . . ." said Rudolf. "Why don't you let Pepi go with Zenzi until she's learned how to go about it . . . ? She's a pretty girl, Pepi is, and I bet she'd come home with at least three guilders every day . . . that's more than you earned . . ."

I felt quite flattered at his words, but father said anxiously:

"That sounds okay . . . but . . . what about the police . . . ?"

"Forget the police . . ." Rudi said contemptuously. "Have I, or Zenzi, ever gotten into trouble with the police . . . ? Let Pepi learn from Zenzi! She can show her how to stay clear of the law!"

"But . . ." father stammered, "but . . . if it should happen one day . . . ?"

"Okay! Suppose something does happen, one day . . . you can always tell the police that the girl does it on her own and you didn't know a damned thing . . . I'm sure Pepi will cooperate and protect her old man . . ."

This was the first time I learned that I had to be careful about the police. I'd kept silent while the men were discussing me and nobody seemed interested in what I'd have to say to all this.

Father tried to make up his mind, but at last he said:

"I don't want the girl to be a whore . . . not that . . ."

And he kept repeating it over and over, until Rudolf interrupted him:

"But . . . for Christ's sake . . . who the hell says she has to spend her life that way . . .? The whole thing serves only to make it easier for you until you've found some work again! As soon as you can make money again, Pepi can stop looking for customers and do whatever she likes . . . marry a respectable man . . ."

This seemed to convince my father and he lost

all his doubts when Rudolf added:

"Why d'you think I let Zenzi earn money that way? It's only for the time being because I have no job now. She'll have to stop it when I work in some coffeehouse again . . . then she'll have to be a good girl again!"

CHAPTER 22

The next day I accompanied Zenzi to the inner districts of the city. She had told me never to wear a shirt under my blouse or dress, so that my breasts could be noticed. We were heading for the center of old Vienna, the St. Stephen's Square. From here radiated the main avenues and streets in all directions.

Zenzi was in her element and smiled whenever men passed us. I couldn't bring myself to do it—yet. When I had been a mere amateur, it was great fun to smile provocatively and see the effect it had on boys and men of all ages, but now I was supposed to be a professional and it would take a little time to get used to my new status. Besides, my father's misgivings about the police were still in the back of my mind.

Zenzi took me to the little furnished room that Rudolf had rented for her in an old, cheerless building near St. Stephen's Square. An old toothless hag opened when Zenzi knocked at the door of a fourth-floor apartment.

The room we stepped into was the kitchen —as in all of the older, cheap tenement buildings—and through an open door, at one end of it, I saw a very small room whose one window offered no other view than the dirty wall of a light-shaft.

The old woman looked at me suspiciously when Zenzi introduced me as her "best friend."

"Is she fourteen?" she asked.

"More than that," lied Zenzi, "she's not very tall for her age, that's all."

"Okay," the woman said in an unfriendly tone, "you know that you've got to give me one guilder every time you come with a customer. And never after eight in the evening! That's the rule!"

We went back to the street.

"Don't mind that old bitch," Zenzi advised. "She has a one-track mind. Money is all she cares for. Now, remember: never accost a man when a cop is near, and, second, always ask a customer for the money before you let him do it!"

We were slowly walking from St. Stephen's Square toward the Opera. It was in Kaerntner Street, the most elegant section of the inner city, and all around us costly jeweled ladies and elegant men were walking in either direction.

"Don't turn around, now," Zenzi warned me. "A very elegant fellow is following us. He's going to pass us soon to see how we react. If he turns his head you've got to smile. You know what I mean . . ."

It happened exactly as Zenzi predicted. When we smiled, the man slowed down and smiled back at us.

"We have to turn into this small street, now," Zenzi said, "he won't talk to us otherwise."

We had gone a few steps down the narrow Dorothea Street when the man followed us. Zenzi drew me into a large building entrance and we waited. Soon the man looked in and said:

"Hello . . . how are you . . . ?"

"Fine . . . !" Zenzi answered. "Would you perhaps like to come with us? I've got a room pretty close . . ."

"No . . ." he said, "I don't have much time . . ."

"We can stay here on the staircase. It's an old office building and nobody is here these days."

The man kept looking at me and asked:

"Would you like to . . . ?"

"Sure . . ." I said. He carried a cane with a knob of ivory and silver, and the watch chain on his vest was of sparkling gold.

We went up to the first floor and stopped on the landing. Zensi said:

"I'm going to stand watch. Take all the time you need . . ."

She went to the banister and looked down, with her back to us. The man put his hand on my blouse.

"Open your blouse a little . . ."

He was visibly glad to see that I wore no shirt and started to caress my breast very gently. His breath became audible.

"Come . . . let's do it . . ." he whispered and took his dick out of his fly.

I lifted my skirt because I thought he wanted to do a standing-up number, but he said:

"No, no . . . not here . . . it's not safe enough . . ."

He continued to play with my breasts while I jacked him off. He pulled a silken handkerchief from his pocket and gave it to me. I held it over the tip of his prick so the semen would spurt into it. He soon came and I noticed how his legs trembled a little. I had to dry my hand, too, which received a few drops of the white fluid. When I handed the handkerchief back to him, he gave me two guilders and left without a word and without looking back. He wanted to get out of the building as quickly as possible.

I was happy to have earned two guilders, but Zenzi reminded me severely that I should not have let the man touch me without asking for the money first.

"If you were not a beginner, you might have waited until it was over, because your experience would have told you that he was a gentleman and would pay anyhow. But you never can tell. Be careful!"

When we were back at St. Stephen's Square an old man approached us and I was a little scared when he addressed me with a serious face:

"You know a place we can go to . . . ?"

Zenzi poked her elbow in my ribs and I quickly said:

"Sure . . . we've got a room . . ."

"All right, then . . . you walk ahead and I'll follow you . . . !"

Zenzi left me discreetly, but not without giving me a knowing wink. I started walking to the old building where Zenzi's room was. The old hag let us in and soon I was alone with the old man in that dark little room.

"Get your clothes off . . ." he commanded.

While I got undressed I watched him. He had a clean-shaven face and an almost toothless mouth. There were a few white hairs on his otherwise bald head. He was extremely thin and didn't seem to be in condition to do much

253

good for a woman.

I remembered that I should have asked him for the money, but somehow I was still too shy to be so open about it. He made the impression of a cultured, well-to-do man and I had to trust my luck. He was sitting down on the big leather sofa and told me to stand in front of him. I thought I had to take the initiative and wanted to unbutton his fly, but he slapped my hand away.

"Just wait . . . wait until I tell you what to do . . . and don't fidget . . ."

I was somewhat startled and didn't quite know how the situation was going to develop. He began to caress my breasts and my belly, then he grabbed his cane and poked it between my legs to force them apart.

"Now, come . . ." he said, and lay back on the sofa.

I was about to join him, but he again slapped at me and growled:

"Stay where you are . . . always wait until I tell you what to do . . ."

He made me open his fly and take out what used to be a prick when he was younger, I suppose. Now it was a tiny something, all wrinkled and shrunken to the size of a pencil-point. I couldn't believe that all my finger-work would ever make it stiff again.

"*Minette* . . . !" he ordered.

I didn't know what he meant and looked at him.

"What are you waiting for? Do some *minette* . . . !"

He became angry when he noticed my helpless stare.

"Damn it, girl . . . I told you to do some

minette on me . . . now, how long will I have to wait . . . ?"

I wasn't familiar with the French term for a blow-job in those early days of my career and I stammered:

"Excuse me, sir . . . I really don't know what that is . . . *minette* . . . ?"

He didn't see the humor of the situation and merely snarled:

"Stupid broad . . . it means you should take it in your mouth . . . !"

I at once did as I was told and since I was afraid of him, my tongue and lips combined to do an extra good job. But to my amazement his wrinkled little thing came to life after my tongue had licked it only a few times.

A veritable miracle happened before my eyes, or rather, in my mouth. That thing began to grow and grow until it became too large for my mouth and I had to let it go. It snapped back against his belly like a steel spring and he panted:

"Now . . . quick . . . you do the fucking . . . quick, I said . . . you should have it in you by now . . ."

He stayed on his back and, thanks to my preliminary "studies," I knew what he wanted. I quickly mounted him and, to tell the truth, it was not simple to lodge that revived miracle-prick in my hole. Once I was firmly established in my seat I bent forward to give him a chance to touch my breasts, but he pushed me back and growled:

"Stay where you are . . . ! Sit up straight . . . !"

He began to raise and lower his hips and soon was fucking me like a man thirty years younger. He suddenly became talkative:

255

"I can still fuck any girl as well as my grandson who's twenty . . . I'm just as good if not better . . . you thought an old man can't do anything, eh . . . ? I'll show you what I can do . . . see . . . ?"

His thrusts became more and more powerful until he, at last, came. But then he collapsed and could hardly move a limb. He told me to run downstairs and buy him some wine. When I came back he lay there like one dead and I was so scared that I called the old woman to ask her what I should do. She sprinkled some cold water on him and said:

"I know him . . . he's too old for all that nonsense, but he's too stubborn to let go . . . just wait, he'll soon come to . . ."

She was right. He opened his eyes and didn't quite realize where he was, but when he noticed the glass of wine I held, he grabbed it and emptied it with one long gulp. Immediately his strength came back and he got up, adjusted his clothes and looked at me with a grouchy face. Then he pulled out his wallet and gave me five guilders and left without a greeting.

Five guilders! For only half an hour's "work." I danced around the small room and vowed to become a good professional who's well aware of what that thing between her legs can achieve if she uses it in combination with her brains. My decision was made: I'd never again do it for nothing!

Thinking of the idiosyncrasies of that old man I realized that no two customers were alike and that I could not afford to be simple-minded about it any more. I'd also have to learn a lot of technical terms like "minette" for instance. It was perhaps on that day that

I dimly understood that becoming a good prostitute required far more than merely spreading my legs. The two customers I'd had so far were better class people and they needed sex, as I saw, just as badly as men from my own class, the poor day laborers and trades people. And they were willing to pay good money for it, too.

I sat down in that dismal dark room and began to think. I wondered whether Zenzi could remain my teacher for long and whether she herself had any ambition to be more than a streetwalker. Of course, it was clear to me that I had a prettier face and a better figure than she had, but I also knew by now that her experience and shrewdness gave her every advantage over me. Zenzi would be able to teach me many things I needed to learn to become even a simple streetwalker before I could try to aspire to higher things, like becoming the mistress of some rich man.

It also became clear to me that I would have to watch my own need for sexual pleasure and learn to control it if I wanted to make a lot of money. I couldn't afford to be as greedy as men who were always willing to pay for it. It is just the opposite with a woman: she is the one who has to make men pay. It was thus that I learned quite early a prostitute's most important lesson.

After spending an hour of deep reflection about my past, present and possible future, I decided to look for Zenzi in the street. I met her on the stairs with a tall young man and she whispered to me:

"Wait a minute . . ."

And turning to her companion she asked:

"Would you like my friend to come with us . . ."

"Oh . . . please . . . yes . . . by all means!" he said in a curiously shy manner.

Back in the room I was formally introduced.

"This is my good friend, Josephine."

I was surprised at Zenzi's formal tone and even more at the young man's reaction. He bowed very deeply before me and kissed my hand as if I were a real lady. I couldn't help laughing, but Zenzi nudged me and hissed:

"No laughing now . . . be serious . . . !"

The young man had a bashful, pale face that was framed by a black beard. His dark eyes were infinitely sad.

He looked at me and whispered:

"The young lady is very strict, I bet . . ."

"Shut up . . . you!" Zenzi yelled at him.

He looked frightened and stammered:

"Oh . . . I am sorry . . . !"

"I said, shut up! You open your mouth only if I ask you something . . . !"

That was a new Zenzi to me, stern and almost cruel.

"And now get out of your clothes . . . !"

"Not yet . . ." he interrupted her, but in a normal voice without that exaggerated shyness.

Zenzi seemed embarrassed, like an actress who got her cues mixed up.

"Oh . . . what comes next . . . ?"

"First comes the questioning, remember . . . ?" he whispered like a prompter.

"You're right . . . !" Zenzi tapped her forehead and seemed to reflect. Suddenly her face assumed a forbidding expression again and she yelled at him:

258

"You no good bastard! You stinking dog . . . !
I bet you were thinking of me again . . . what?"

He stammered fearfully:

"Pardon me, countess, but I couldn't help
it . . ."

"Tell me this instant what kind of thoughts
you had about me . . . ?"

"Oh, countess, you can imagine . . ."

"You despicable pig, you! I know . . . you
were thinking of my cunt . . . of my teats . . .
you shameless fucker . . . confess now . . ."

"Yes . . . I admit it . . ."

"And what's more . . ." she continued merci-
lessly, "you thought how you are going to lie
on top of me, eh? How I'm going to spread
my legs and how you'll put your prick into
me . . . you jerk, you . . . and how you are
going to fuck me . . . and play with my teats
. . . you son of a bitch . . ."

"Yes, my good countess . . . I confess everything . . . !"

"Have you no shame at all . . . ? Admitting
all this before the princess here . . . ?" She
pointed at me. I was so astonished by what
was going on that I didn't marvel at my sudden
promotion to princess.

"Oh . . . yes, I am ashamed . . . !"

"Kneel, you dog!" thundered Zenzi.

He fell at once on his knees and begged:

"Forgive me, dear countess . . . and you,
too, beautiful princess . . ."

"No . . ." hissed Zenzi, "no forgiving . . . not
yet . . . there will be punishment, first!"

He blushed and nodded:

"Yes . . . punishment first . . ."

"Now, get out of your clothes . . . !" commanded Zenzi.

259

He was undressed in a minute and stood there trembling like a dog waiting to be beaten. His body was almost white and soft like a woman's. He stepped in the narrow spot between the sofa and the clothes chest as if observing a ritual.

Zenzi undressed herself and I followed her example when she winked at me meaningfully.

"I'll show you . . . you bastard . . . you'll look at us and admire us . . . but that's all . . . you'll see me and the princess in all our nakedness . . . and don't you dare to move . . ."

Her eyes gleamed when she went to him and I could see that she began to be horny. She rubbed her enormous teats against his body and asked me to do the same. His skin was soft as velvet, but when I rubbed my pubic hair against his center, his dick didn't show any sign of life.

I wondered what all this business meant and when we were going to get laid at last, because I, too, began to be horny and wanted some real action.

But Zenzi pulled me away from his hot body and told him:

"And now you'll be punished . . . you jerk . . . !"

He followed her with feverish eyes when she took two birch rods from the clothes chest.

"You know what these are, you dog . . . ?" she asked.

"Yes . . . dear countess . . . !" he swallowed hard.

"And you know what is going to happen now, you son of a bitch . . . ?"

"Yes . . . you'll punish me, dear countess . . . yes, you must punish me . . . I deserve it! And

you must punish me, too, dear princess . . ."
he had turned to me and lifted his hands like
a beggar.

Zenzi handed me one birch rod and said:
"Hit him hard . . . don't hold back . . . !"

He approached her slowly and her birch rod
smacked right across his chest so that a red
stripe appeared there at once. He jumped and
—o wonder—his prick was suddenly rigid.

Zenzi began to work on him with her rod
as if he were her enemy and accompanied every
stroke with a new burst of abuse:

"D'you feel that . . . you no good pussy-eater
. . . you dirty thief . . . you criminal . . . d'you
feel it . . . ?"

His chest and belly were already covered
with red welts. He panted:

"Yes . . . countess . . . dear countess . . .
thank you for the punishment . . . beat me
more . . . but why doesn't the gracious princess
beat me, too . . . ?"

"Go ahead and beat him . . ." Zenzi ordered
me and threatened me with her rod so that
I was frightened for a second. I beat him rather
gently. He turned to me and remonstrated:

"Please, gracious princess . . . do beat me
harder . . . or don't you want to punish me . . . ?
I know I'm not worthy to be punished by you
. . . but have mercy on me and do beat me
very hard . . . please . . ."

I hit him pretty hard this time and, to my
great surprise, I felt I liked it.

"Oh . . . thank you . . . thank you so much
. . ." he stammered.

"Shut up, you dog . . ." Zenzi yelled at him,
"or I'll kill you . . . !"

We had it nicely organized by now: Zenzi

261

beat him on his chest, belly and thighs and I on his back and buttocks. The more he was beaten the more he seemed to enjoy it, but we, too, began to become quite excited. He lifted his hands in a plaintive gesture:

"Oh . . . pardon me . . . countess . . . I won't ever think of your beautiful teats any more . . . pardon me, princess . . . you are good to me . . . oh, it hurts, it hurts very much . . . I'm learning my lesson now . . . I won't think of your cunt any more, countess . . . you know . . . I dreamed I was taking your virginity, countess . . . but I know now one must not do that . . . and I also thought that I was fucking you, my dear princess . . . that was not right . . . I know . . . you must pardon me for that . . ."

Zenzi ordered him now to kneel down and to work on her clitoris for a while and then on mine. I became exceedingly horny and wondered when the actual fucking was going to start.

At last the young man begged:

"Stop now, countess . . . I beg of you . . . you, too, princess . . . forgive me and let me finish . . ."

I didn't know what he meant, or what was supposed to be done now, but Zenzi turned to me and demonstrated:

"Here . . . take him by the balls and squeeze them . . . but be careful, not on the sides, but behind them where his cock begins . . . and with your other hand you keep beating him on the thighs and wherever you can reach . . ."

I did as she suggested and while I was doing my part, Zenzi beat his buttocks like mad so that he began to sob and groan like somebody in agony. But suddenly he ejaculated a flood of semen that hit me right in the face.

"Ah . . . countess . . . princess . . ." he gasped.

When he had finished, Zenzi threw the rod on the floor and dropped on the sofa quite exhausted. I squatted on the floor to wipe my face clean. I still hoped that strange man would fuck Zenzi or me, but nothing of the kind happened. He stared in front of him for a while and then he began to dress quickly without looking at either of us. Before he left, he stepped into the corner and put something on the broken-down armchair that stood there. There was no sound from him when he walked out of the door.

As soon as the door was shut, Zenzi ran to that armchair and triumphantly showed me two bills of ten guilders each that the young man had put there for us. She held them high above her head and danced joyfully around the room.

"How d'you like that . . . ? That's good pay I'd say . . . !"

She gave me one bill and tucked the other behind her elastic garter. I had to admit it was easy money, and yet, not quite so easy. I didn't quite know what to think of men who have to be beaten black and blue until they could ejaculate at last. Sex was not so simple as I had been led to believe, I thought. I knew I wouldn't like to be beaten myself and also that I had to overcome some initial revulsion to use the birch rod on that sad young man, but, at the same time, I remembered that I began to like it after a while and that it actually excited me. Did I know myself as well as I thought I did?

I had no time to meditate on that because

Zenzi reminded me that we should hunt up some more business. She suggested that we should separate and try our luck each by herself.

"Just remember what I told you, Pepi! Watch out for the cops and always ask for the money first."

We first had a snack at a small restaurant and then went our separate ways.

"See you at home!" said Zenzi. "You've made more than enough money for the first day, but . . . if you see somebody who looks promising . . . try him anyway. And . . . watch out!"

CHAPTER 23

I was so elated from my successful "premiere" that I decided not to hurry home yet, but to investigate the terrain on my own.

About three in the afternoon, I was sauntering along on Kaerntner Street when I noticed a man was following me. He looked like an Italian, black eyes and hair and olive-colored complexion. Like many Italians and Frenchmen of that period, he was clad in a dark velvet suit. That, and a black goatee, gave him a bohemian-like appearance. I turned into the same small street where the old, uninhabited building was to which Zenzi and I had taken our first customer. I waited about two minutes in the house entrance when the "Italian" walked in and, without much further ado, touched my breasts, but not to play with them. He seemed to test them as a horse dealer feels an animal all over to see whether it was a good buy. We said almost simultaneously:

"Well? Would you like to . . ."

It's the standard question for buyer and seller alike. I added:

"D'you want me to walk ahead? It's close by . . ."

"Where?"

"On Dorothea Street . . ."

"But I don't want to come to your place . . ."

"Okay," I consented, "if you prefer, we can stay right here . . ."

"Here . . . ?" He was astonished.

"Sure . . . on the staircase! There's nobody in this building . . . we'll be quite undisturbed . . ."

He didn't like that either.

"I'll tell you what . . . why don't you come to my place . . . ?"

I became cautious. "Is it far from here . . . ?"

"No, but we'll take a cab anyhow . . ."

"What's in if for me . . . ?"

"Don't worry your little head off . . ." he said with a grand gesture, "you'll be very well paid . . . as a matter of fact . . . I pay better prices than anybody else . . . !"

I was impressed by his self-assurance, but I wanted to play it safe.

"That's fine, but I've got to get the money first . . . !"

He became urgent:

"You'll get it soon . . . ! As soon as we enter my place I'll pay you!"

We walked back toward Kaerntner Street and he hailed a cab. When it began to move toward the address he'd given the driver, he said smilingly:

"You think, of course, that I want to fuck you . . ."

I smiled coquettishly:

"Well, don't you . . . ?"

"No," he said, making a mysterious face, "I want something else . . ."

"Aha! I know . . ."

"Can you guess . . . ?"

"*Minette* . . . ?" I was showing off my recently acquired knowledge of the term.

"No . . . !" he laughed, "try again . . . !"

"Perhaps . . . from behind . . . ?"

He shook his head.

"Ah, I know . . . you want me to beat you . . . ?"

"Boy, you *are* familiar with all sorts of things. But no, not even that . . . !"

"All right . . . I give up . . ."

"I want to take pictures of you . . . photos . . . you know . . . ?"

"Phot . . . ?" That was a new word again.

"Yes, photographs! Never heard of it? I want to photograph you in the nude . . . in all kinds of positions . . ."

I laughed. I'd never been photographed before and thought it was wonderful to get some nice pictures of myself.

After a fifteen minute ride the cab stopped in front of a newly built bungalow that was enclosed by a large garden. It was a nice place consisting of several rooms and a large studio in back. We were received by a blowzy blonde in a red robe, her eyes heavily mascaraed. She nodded to me and exclaimed:

"Yes, I believe she will do fine . . ."

"Okay, but let's hurry," the photographer said, "we must take advantage of the light . . ."

"Do you want me to get Albert . . . ?" she asked.

"What a question! You know we can't start without him . . . !"

She was about to leave, when he stopped her:

"I'd better get him myself . . . you stay here. The two of you ought to be ready when I come back . . . !"

He walked toward a tenement house next to the garden, and she turned to me:

"He's too damned jealous to let me alone with Albert even for a minute . . . !"

She led the way to the studio which had a glass ceiling and tall windows. After moving a chest, she opened a hidden door in the wall behind it. It opened into a very small room lighted only by a small window near the ceiling.

"You'd better get undressed," she said.

I was surprised to see her take off her robe, too. She looked at me:

"Undress completely, take off everything except the shoes and stockings. . . you know you'll be photographed in the nude . . ."

She was standing in her light shirt and waited until I was undressed. She examined my body and asked:

"How old are you . . . ? Fourteen . . . ?"

"Not quite . . . !"

"My husband must have told you what he needs you for . . ."

"Yes, he did . . ."

She slid off her shirt and smiled at me:

"Fine! You'll see what it's all about and how it's done . . ."

I was surprised to see her naked, too.

"Oh . . . is he going to make pictures of you, too . . . ?"

"Of course . . ." she laughed. "Up to now I was his only model. We couldn't find a suitable girl, and what's more we have to be very careful about our choice . . . Then, most of the professional models ask for too much money . . ."

"How much am I going to get . . . ?"

"You needn't worry . . . you'll be satisfied . . . !"

I liked the friendly way she said that.

I smiled: "Okay, then I won't worry . . . !"

"Since he has me, he wouldn't have looked for another model, but this time he needs a young girl like yourself . . . he has a special order from a customer . . ."

"But you are also young . . ." I wanted to pay her that compliment.

"Thanks . . ." she laughed, "my teats are, thank God, still firm, see . . . ?"

She was weighing her large breasts in her hands.

"They are beautiful . . . !" I said.

"Want to feel them . . . ?"

I tested them and found them to be really hard and elastic. She touched her belly:

"Only here I'm a little too fat . . ."

"I wouldn't say that . . ." I flattered her.

She slapped her mighty thighs.

"And look at these two columns . . . when Albert looks at them he's horny in a jiffy . . ."

"Well, that's natural . . . !"

"But it makes my husband mad . . . on the other hand, how could he make any good pictures if Albert doesn't get a hard-on . . . ?"

I began to understand what this was all about. Her husband came back and called us:

"Come out here to the studio . . ."

Next to him stood a boy of about eighteen, nicely dressed and of an athletic build. He had a sun-tanned face, small, thick ears and a broad, red nose. I liked his slim and yet sturdy figure. He must have been a messenger boy, or apprentice of a sort.

"All right, Albert," said Mr. Capuzzi (that was the photographer's name), "go to the room in the back and get your clothes off. And hurry . . !"

Then he turned to me and looked me over:

"Not bad, eh . . ?" he said to his wife.

"Yes, just what you needed . . ."

"These little teats are nice . . . like a virgin's . . ."

"Yes . . . they're still growing! And so is the whole girl . . ."

"Lean hips, like a boy . . ." he said.

"And not much hair on her pussy . . ."

Both seemed to be quite satisfied with me and Mr. Capuzzi said I was going to be satisfied, too. He moved his large camera into place and, covering his head with a black cloth, he looked at us. It was the first time I saw a photographer at work.

Now Albert came back from the dressing room and gloried in his virile nakedness. His joy-stick stood at attention and I liked the big smile he gave me when he noticed my fascinated stare.

Mrs. Capuzzi laughed:

"Ha! Good boy! He's got a wonderful hard-on . . !"

Mr. Capuzzi muttered angrily:

"Just mind your own business . . !"

Albert was a well-built youth, his arms, legs and thighs swelling with pure muscle, a concave belly and — what I appreciated most — the extremely well developed "muscle" standing up straight and hard from his pubic hair.

Mr. Capuzzi called us to order.

"What's your name . . ?" he asked me.

"Pepi . . ."

"All right Pepi . . . pay attention now . . !"

He pushed a low bench, covered with a small rug, toward the center of the room.

"Albert . . . you sit down, right in the middle . . . Melanie, you sit on his right . . . and you, Pepi, on his left . . ."

We did as we were told.

"Now, girls . . . each of you put your fingers around his cock . . . yes, that's it . . . and you, Albert, put your arms around the shoulders of each girl . . . good! And now . . . hold still . . ."

He disappeared behind the black cloth.

"That's good . . ." his voice sounded muffled, "don't move . . . both of you girls look at Albert . . . good . . . and you, Albert, turn up your eyes like being overcome by pleasure . . . that's it . . ."

Albert's prick was so big that our combined hands couldn't cover it completely. The tip was still visible.

Mr. Capuzzi counted: "One . . . two . . . three . . . four . . . five . . . six . . . okay!"

We got up to stretch ourselves, but Capuzzi ordered:

"Now another position . . !"

"Which one . . ?" asked Melanie.

"Albert, you lie down . . ." said Capuzzi.

Albert lay down the length of the narrow bench and let his legs dangle on the floor.

"Now . . . you, Melanie . . . stand over him with a leg on each side . . . wait . . . I'll put a cushion under your feet so that you're taller . . ."

Without the cushions Melanie's short rump

would have rested on Albert's thighs.

"And now bend forward and support your arms on the sides of the bench, so that your teats almost touch Albert's face."

"I remember . . . we've done that before . . ."

"No . . . not the way I'm going to arrange it now . . ." Capuzzi said.

"Albert, you take Melanie's teats in your hands . . ."

The boy obeyed only too willingly and immediately began to play with the nipples. Melanie complained:

"He's turning me on again . . ."

"Hey, Albert . . ." shouted Capuzzi, "you keep your hands still, or else . . . !"

Albert's hands didn't move, but now it was Melanie who tried to move her breasts in his palms.

"See . . . ?" Albert said. "She's doing it herself . . ."

"Melanie . . . behave yourself . . . !"

"I can't help it . . . I'm too excited . . ."

He ignored her and turned to me:

"Pepi, you take Albert's cock and put it into her hole, but don't take your hand off it . . . !"

Melanie didn't wait for my assistance and had the boy's stick in her cunt in no time at all. She sighed:

"O God . . . all this posing . . . it's torture . . ."

"Melanie . . . !" he yelled at her, "don't put it in all the way . . . Pepi's hand can't be seen . . ."

She lifted her fanny so that only Albert's glans was in her. She asked plaintively:

"Now . . . is it better this way . . . ?"

"That's fine, now . . ." he agreed.

271

"No, no . . . !" Melanie protested, "it's going to slip out this way . . ."

She promptly lowered her hips so that only my hand prevented her cunt from swallowing up that cock down to its root.

"Hell's bells, Melanie!" Capuzzi cursed her, "you pull back the way you were . . . we're trying to get a good photo, d'you hear me . . . ? Just control yourself . . . !"

She made a face and raised her hips a little, but suddenly she pushed down on the cock again so that it disappeared from view.

"Why don't you like it this way?" she commented. "It looks good, too . . ."

Capuzzi came over and whacked her fat behind.

"Who are you trying to fool . . . you bitch? You want to fuck . . . we've got to take a photo now . . . keep still . . . !"

"Once I got the cock in me it's fucking, anyway . . ." she argued. "You're splitting hairs . . . !"

"The hell I am . . . !" he said angrily. "How often do I have to explain to you the difference between feigning and the real thing, eh . . . ? We are merely simulating various positions so that it looks like the real thing, but we're not doing it! My wife is not going to be fucked by anybody but myself! And don't you forget it!"

In those days I was gullible enough to believe in the subtle difference that Capuzzi tried to define for us. Today I can't help smiling at the strange code of honor of that jealous husband.

The pulsating of Albert's prick excited me and I slid my hand a little upward so that I touched Melanie's labia. I felt how she contracted them every second so that Albert became more and more horny. Melanie sighed:

"How much longer will it take . . . ?"

"It's over soon . . . just smile and look at the camera . . . that's it . . . you, too, Pepi . . . one . . . two . . . three . . . four . . . five . . . click!"

Melanie got off Albert's cock and whined:

"One more minute and I'd go out of my mind! What a torture for a healthy woman . . . !"

Albert lay on the bench without moving. Capuzzi ordered:

"Now Pepi plays Melanie's part and you, Melanie, put Albert's cock into Pepi's hole . . . quick . . . !"

"D'you want me to hold Pepi's teats?" asked Albert.

"Go ahead . . ." Capuzzi encouraged him.

Albert smiled at me and played with my teats. When Melanie inserted his stick into me, he began to move it up and down so that Melanie had to pull her hand back. She complained to her husband:

"You don't say anything this time . . . !"

"Hold still, kids!" Capuzzi said and began to count while Melanie touched Albert's cock to give the impression she was assisting us.

"One . . . two . . . three . . . finished!"

Now Albert and I started to fuck with enthusiasm.

"Will you stop this minute . . . !" yelled Capuzzi. "First we've got to take all the pictures. You can fuck later, if you want to . . . !"

During the next position Albert remained where he was and Melanie knelt before him and took his tool in her mouth.

"Only the tip . . . Melanie! It's mere make-believe . . . !"

I had to stand over Albert's head and offer my grotto to his mouth. He demonstrated his skill by letting his tongue beat a tattoo on my clitoris, but after a few seconds of this he stopped and merely feigned. Melanie squinted over to her husband who had disappeared behind the black cloth and from the working of her cheeks I could see she was sucking away like crazy.

"One . . . two . . . three . . ." we heard Capuzzi intoning, "and . . . done!"

Albert quickly gave me a few licks before I straightened up. Capuzzi called:

"Girls you change positions now . . . !"

When I closed my lips around Albert's tool I showed him that I was no novice at the art. He was so excited by now that he didn't feign eating Melanie's pussy, but moved his tongue on her clitoris quite realistically. She began to pant and tried to hide her excitement and was grateful when her husband called from behind the black cloth:

"Melanie . . . try to caress your own teats . . . kiss your nipples, or something . . . !"

Now she could hide her emotions by burying her face in her breasts, which she could comfortably lift up to it. Suddenly she moved her hips so that Albert's tongue missed and gave a smacking sound. Capuzzi came running:

"Albert . . . you no good bastard . . . you're actually licking her pussy . . . !"

"No . . . not really . . ." Albert's voice was muffled under the weight of Melanie's body.

"I hope you're not lying . . ." Capuzzi stooped to examine the situation.

"Don't be ridiculous . . ." shouted Melanie,

274

"he doesn't do a damned thing . . . !"

"Is that so? Your face is quite red . . . and you're breathing to beat hell . . ."

Melanie faced him angrily:

"What d'you expect . . . ? Naturally I get excited every time I have to do this . . . I'm a human being of flesh and blood . . . not a piece of wood! Just let's get it over with!"

While her husband crawled back under his black cloth, she quickly rubbed her slit against Albert's tongue which reacted accordingly, but Capuzzi was hurrying now:

"One . . . two . . . three . . . and . . . finished!"

We jumped up and looked at Capuzzi. Melanie was trembling all over and her nipples stood up stiff and hard.

"What next . . . ?" she queried.

Capuzzi reflected for a moment, then:

"Now Albert will lie on top of you and Pepi will offer you her pussy . . ."

"No, I don't want to eat her pussy . . ."

"But, jeez, you don't have to . . . you just feign it . . ."

"No, I don't want it . . . period!" Melanie said energetically.

"Okay . . ." Capuzzi agreed, "then Pepi will lie down and pretend to eat you pussy . . ."

"I know something better . . ." she interrupted, not wanting to lose the opportunity of getting Albert's prick into her. "Why can't Pepi just play with my teats . . ? It looks much better that way . . . not so perverse, you know . . ."

He gave in because he wanted to take all the pictures before the sun got any lower. I knelt on the floor next to the bench and began to work on Melanie's teats while Albert tried to keep his prick in her hole without moving. But my tongue excited her too much and she moved her hips violently so that Albert's stick moved in and out of her cunt. Capuzzi noticed it, came over and slapped her face soundly.

"I told you not to fuck, you bitch . . ."

"I didn't do anything . . ." Melanie panted.

"You did, too . . . you always do . . . I know you!"

"You rude bastard! Pepi was sucking my teats and that made me move . . . I couldn't help it . . ."

"Pepi, you stop sucking . . ." he ordered, then he yelled again at Melanie:

"You're using all sorts of excuses every time . . . don't you think I know you want Albert to fuck you? You ain't fooling anybody . . ."

"Leave me alone . . . I told you I'm not a stone . . . getting such a big prick into me I should pretend I don't feel it, eh? What miracles d'you expect of a woman . . . ?"

Capuzzi became conciliatory:

"You know I'm going to fuck you later on . . . can't you wait another hour or so . . . ?"

He went to the camera, counted up to three and clicked.

"Now I've got to go to the darkroom . . . if you won't behave until I come back . . . I'll break every limb of yours . . !"

He disappeared into another room.

"Jeez, what I've got to go through every time . . ." Melanie sighed, and Albert remarked:

"I wouldn't mind shooting my gun off soon either . . ."

"Albert, dear, wouldn't you like to fuck me just once . . ?" Melanie drooled.

"Sure," he said, "but it can't be done . . . you

know . . ."

Melanie carried on like a bitch in heat. She turned to me:

"You have no idea how I like that boy! I'd give anything to be fucked by him only once . . . O God . . . !"

"But why don't you do it . . . ?"

"Because . . ." she pointed to the door through which Capuzzi had disappeared.

"Can't you do it right now . . . a quickie . . . ?" I asked.

"No, he'd see it at once."

"But how? He's in the other room . . ."

She pointed to the yellow glass panes in the door:

"Through that he can see everything that goes on here!"

She turned to Albert and moaned:

"We've been working together for two months, now, haven't we, Albert . . . ?" Then to me:

"For two months I've been feeling his huge prick all over my body, in my hand, between my teats, in my cunt, in my ass, in my mouth, in my armpit . . . anyplace . . . and all he's permitted to give me is the tip, never the whole thing . . . it just drives me nuts . . ."

Albert concurred:

"She's right . . . if he doesn't want me to do it to his wife, he shouldn't offer her to me in all those positions . . . I'm not made of stone either . . ."

"Yes, that's mean . . ." I said.

"You said it . . ." pouted Albert, "I see her naked and he makes me grab her teats . . . and I know her cunt like I fucked her sixty times . . . but he never lets me do it . . . that's not fair . . ."

I sympathized with him:

"Well, how do you shoot off your gun, after all?"

He blushed.

Melanie laughed: "The Italian way!"

"How's that . . . ?"

Melanie laughed again:

"Maybe you'll see it if my husband makes him do it for another picture . . . he needs new photos like that pretty often . . ."

Capuzzi came in, scowling:

"The last position didn't come out right . . . we've got to do it again . . . and that's your fault . . ." he pointed an accusing finger at his wife. "You kept wiggling your ass all the time . . ."

We went into the same position again. Albert dipped the tip of his prick into Melanie's cunt, I took her by the teats and Capuzzi clicked. Albert kept lying on Melanie and moved his prick in her cunt so forcefully that she exclaimed:

"Ah . . . Jesus and Mary . . . ah . . ."

With one forceful jerk Capuzzi pulled the boy off her, who muttered under his breath:

"Never mind . . . some day I'll fuck her, but good . . . !"

"Over my dead body!" yelled Capuzzi.

Melanie was too aroused to stay quiet and shouted at her husband:

"If you don't want him to do it then do it yourself now . . . I can't stand it any longer . . ."

Capuzzi was furious:

"How am I to do this work if you can't wait . . . no, I won't do it now . . . just because you are such a bitch . . . !"

Melanie worked on her slit with her finger.

"You come to me this minute, or I'll call Albert . . . !"

Capuzzi turned to the boy and myself:

"Get the hell out of here . . . I'll call you when I need you . . ."

We didn't have to be told twice and ran to the small dressing room. I flopped down on the floor and Albert was immediately mounting me. It was good to feel his giant-sized cock in me. He whispered:

"Ah . . . I'm so glad you are here . . . at last I get a decent fuck . . . I'll hold back for a while . . . because you have such a nice and tight little cunt . . . ah . . . that's good . . . yes, push against me . . . that's good . . . wait . . . wait . . . I'm going to suck your teats . . ."

"Oh, Albert . . ." I said, "I've been waiting for this . . . those damned positions have made me quite horny . . . your cock feels so good . . . what a splendid cock you have . . . you don't have to hold back . . . I've come twice already . . . yes . . . shoot your gun now . . . shoot . . . ah . . ."

When we had finished we listened to Capuzzi and Melanie who were still busy with each other in the studio.

"No, no . . . don't come yet . . ." Melanie begged. "I need it badly . . . don't come now . . . I need to be fucked much longer . . . give it to me . . . push some more . . ."

"Ha . . . !" we heard Capuzzi grumble. "You'd like to be fucked by Albert, I guess . . ."

"Albert . . . ? He can kiss my ass . . . who needs him . . . ? Just fuck me . . . you're good . . . give me your lips . . . yes . . . and your tongue . . . ah . . ."

The rest was a series of moans and sobs.

Capuzzi asked:

"Can I come now . . . your teats make me too horny . . . I've got to come . . ."

"Yes . . . you can come . . . now . . . ah . . . I don't need Albert any more . . . when you fuck me . . . I don't need anybody else . . . ah . . . you're sweet . . ."

They had finished, but Capuzzi wanted to know:

"Tell me, why does Albert always turn you on . . . ?"

"But, you don't understand . . ." Melanie cooed, "when Albert's prick is in my mouth, or in my cunt . . . or when he puts his lips to my cunt . . . I always think of you only . . . !"

Albert laughed and said:

"Aw, nuts! She's lying . . . you've seen how much she wants me . . . she's even said so . . ."

"Sure," I said, "but why have you never fucked her?"

"It just can't be done . . ."

"But . . . why . . . ?"

"Because that guy is watching her like a hawk . . ."

"But he isn't always at home . . ."

"You never can tell with him . . . he's shrewd and he has a way of turning up at the most unexpected moment . . ."

"So what . . . ?"

"It's not as easy as that . . ." Albert was serious. "You don't know the guy. He's an Italian and like most of them he's as jealous as hell and capable of doing anything. And he's stronger than me . . ."

"He doesn't look it . . ."

"Just wait until you see him naked . . ."

"When would that be . . . ?"

"Oh, sometimes he lets Melanie take pictures of him . . ."

"That's interesting!" I wished he'd let me take Melanie's place in that situation.

"Do you know," Albert asked, "how often he fucks his wife every day . . . ?"

"Well . . . ?"

"Seven or eight times . . . and that's the truth!"

"But how come she's always so horny . . . ?"

"To be fucked by the same guy all the time doesn't satisfy her, I think . . . at least, she told me it's getting monotonous . . ."

Capuzzi called us back to the studio.

"Come on in, we've got to do a new position . . ."

He was in his shorts and undershirt and his face was just as flushed as Melanie's. She seemed to be satisfied and looked more relaxed. Pointing to Albert's limp tool, she said to her husband:

"Look! These two have done it, too . . . !"

She asked me in a low voice:

"Is he good . . . ?"

"He's out of this world . . . !" I said, to make her a little jealous.

Capuzzi looked distressed:

"What are we going to do if Albert has no hard-on?"

Melanie laughed:

"You can take his place . . . I can do the photographing, you know . . ."

Capuzzi undressed and I admired his broad chest full of black hair, and his very muscular arms, but especially that tremendous penis, coming out of his bushy-haired underbelly. He moved toward me, but Melanie protested:

"No ... you can't do that! Do that queer act with Albert, but leave the girl alone ... !"

"We've got a lot of those queer acts ... so why waste a new plate ... ?"

"I don't want you to pose with Pepi ... that's all!"

"You're unfair ..." said Capuzzi. "I let you simulate all kinds of positions with Albert, so why can't I simulate positions with Pepi ... ?"

"Oh, no ... !" Melanie was stubborn. "I know you too well ... you'll get horny at once ... !"

"That's nonsense ... and suppose I do get horny ... then I'll do it with you again!"

Melanie was weakening.

"All right ... but be quite sure you only simulate ... !"

I lay down on the little bench and spread my legs as far as possible.

"Now, this is how we're going to do it," said Capuzzi and put my legs over his shoulders.

"Now, go to the camera ... !" he told Melanie and stuck his prick into me.

"That's too far in ... !" called Melanie. "Be careful ... !"

She needn't have worried, because as soon as Capucci's prick was in me about six inches, half of it was still ouside, but my hole could not hold any more than that.

"One ... two ... three ... finished!" reported Melanie.

Now Capuzzi sat on a chair and planted me on his cock from behind and made me face the camera. He slid his hands under my armpits and got hold of my teats. I began to move a bit, but he whispered:

"Careful . . . not now . . . !"

Melanie also took this picture in a hurry. Capuzzi would have liked to let us pose another group, but since Albert's tool could not be made to stand up any more, we had to postpone it. Capuzzi gave me five guilders and said:

"You know where I live now. Be sure and come the day after tomorrow so we can continue our work."

CHAPTER 24

There was still time to go back to the inner city and look for Zenzi. I met her at St. Stephen's Square and went with her to her room to show her what I'd earned. She was quite pleased, but complained that she hadn't been able to find any customers. She was reclining on the sofa and I saw that my description of all the positions I had to assume at the photographer's place had excited her.

"Damn it," she exclaimed, "now you've made me horny with that story . . . boy, if only somebody would fuck me now!"

I shared her feelings and joined her on the sofa, trying to do the lesbian act she had taught me at home. She seemed to have changed somehow. She wasn't that complaisant, almost passive girl who always yessed Rudolf at home. Her glittering eyes had a new, almost defiant expression. We played with each other's teats, but when I was about to mount her, she pushed me away and said:

"Aw . . . that's not the real thing . . . !"

She got up and opened the door to the kitchen.

"Say, Mrs. Bock . . ." she called to the old woman, "is Karl at home . . . ?"

The old hag came to the door:

"Yes, he's here . . . what d'you want with him . . . ?"

"That's none of your business . . ." Zenzi said in an abrupt manner I had never noticed in her before. "Don't ask questions, but call him!"

To my surprise the old wench didn't say anything and disappeared.

"Who on earth is that Karl . . . ?" I asked her.

"The grandson of that old bitch . . . that's who!"

She took something from the pocket of her dress that was hanging by the door and lay down again.

"And what d'you want from Karl . . . ?"

"A good lay . . ." she said, breathing heavily.

I was about to ask her why she was in such a strange mood today, when the door opened and a handsome boy of sixteen or seventeen entered. He would have been even more attractive if his general appearance and his face had not betrayed a lack of regular meals, and the wise-guy mentality of prematurely corrupted children. He had a half-smoked cigarette sticking from one corner of his full mouth and his grin showed more contempt than friendliness.

"Hi Karl," Zenzi said, "take this guilder . . . and now do it to me!"

He sauntered over to the sofa, grabbed the silver coin and examined it from all sides before pocketing it. Then he began to play with Zenzi's teats as if he were not much interested and kept looking curiously at me.

"Don't take so long . . ." Zenzi said. "What

are you waiting for . . . ?"

He unbuttoned his fly and Zenzi poked her elbow in my ribs:

"Just take a good look at that . . . ! Have you ever seen such a gigantic prick before . . . ?"

Karl grinned complacently and revealed a cock to beat all cocks. It was really unique, almost frightening. It stood up at an angle and reached his navel. The glans alone was as big as another guy's whole tool, and so thick that I couldn't imagine how it would penetrate a cunt without tearing it apart.

"How d'you like it . . . ?" Zenzi asked me. "You got to admit it's worth a guilder . . . !"

Karl threw his cigarette into a broken ashtray and mounted Zenzi without doing anything.

"Hurry up . . . !" she said.

"Put it in yourself . . . !" he replied rudely.

Zenzi obeyed quickly and immediately began to emit a series of weird sounds and endearments:

"Ah . . . Karl . . . my dearest . . . fuck me . . . fuck me . . . not so wild . . . I'm coming . . . you are my darling . . . I love you . . . I want to fuck only with you . . ."

"Who needs you . . . ? You can kiss my ass . . . !" he replied while moving his mighty tool in her.

Zenzi couldn't take that and yammered:

"Why d'you fuck me if you don't like me . . . ?"

"Because you give me a guilder . . . if grandmother gives me a guilder, I fuck her, too . . . ! Who cares . . . ?"

I had judged his facial expression correctly when he entered the room; a blasé cynic of sixteen. The result of growing up in the workmen's slum of Vienna.

Zenzi pushed against him in a wild frenzy, while his thrusts became vehement as if he wanted to punish her. His animal-like crudeness excited me and I wondered whether I shouldn't offer him a silver guilder, too.

He settled my indecision by leaving the room quite abruptly when he had finished with Zenzi. She asked him to stay, but he refused.

"But why don't you want to stay for a while . . . ?" she asked unhappily.

"Because you bore the hell out of me, that's why!" and he banged the door.

Zenzi hurled a drinking glass after him. It broke into a shower of splinters.

"You damned stud, you . . . !" she yelled and then broke into tears. I'd never seen her like that and asked her why she carried on that way.

"He's the only . . . only one . . ." she sobbed, "I really care for . . . that bastard . . . but that's the last time I let him fuck me . . . his rudeness makes me feel so bad after it's over that I'd be better off not to see him at all . . . !"

I was perplexed to hear her confession of unrequited love.

"But what about Rudolf . . . ?" I asked.

Zenzi shrugged: "Well, what about him . . . ?"

"I thought you liked him . . . you always do what he wants . . ."

Zenzi shrugged her shoulders again:

"Rudolf . . . yes, he's a smart guy, but he's old enough to be my father . . . I sort of like him, but I don't love him . . ."

This was the first time that the idea of love occupied my mind again since my experience with that young, well-dressed son of our landlord, Alois. He had inspired in me something more than mere sexual desire. While I'm writing this down, I can see Zenzi and myself sitting on that old leather sofa, in that dark, dreary room, and can hear our conversation all over again. It went like this:

Pepi: "But, Zenzi, you always say Rudolf is the best fucker of them all . . . that he makes you come at once . . ."

Zenzi: "Aw, you say all kinds of things when you feel a big prick in you and your juices start running . . . you talk the same way to your father when he lies on top of you and makes you come . . ."

Pepi: "That's true . . ."

Zenzi: "And after all, what d'you expect . . . Rudolf and I have been together now for eight years . . ."

Pepi: "What? You are no more than fifteen . . . !"

Zenzi: "So what? My mother used to be his mistress . . . eight years ago she died of consumption, and I was left alone. Rudolf took me in . . ."

Pepi: ". . . as mistress?"

Zenzi: "No . . . he just let me sleep on the floor of his tiny furnished room. I preferred it to living in an orphanage . . ."

Pepi: "Why were you afraid of an orphanage . . . ?"

Zenzi: "I don't know . . . perhaps because mother cried a lot when she was taken to the hospital and kept mumbling: 'O God, if I die the poor girl will be taken to an orphanage . . . !' "

Pepi: "And where were you when she was at the hospital . . . ?"

Zenzi: "In Rudolf's place, naturally. Mother

and I lived with him . . ."

Pepi: "And what about your father . . . ?"

Zenzi: "He died when I was only two . . . I can't remember him at all . . ."

Pepi: "What happened next . . . ?"

Zenzi: "Well . . . Rudolf promised my mother he'd let me stay with him and that she needn't worry about it. When she heard that, her last hours were more peaceful . . ."

Pepi: "It was nice of Rudolf to do that . . ."

Zenzi: "Yes, it sure was. The first three or four months I slept on an old blanket on the floor, and Rudolf as usual in his bed he used to share with mother."

Pepi: "And . . . when did it all start . . . ?"

Zenzi: "Well, as I said, after a few months the weather became cold and Rudolf invited me to share his bed."

Pepi: "Did he touch you the first night . . . ?"

Zenzi: "Sure! But he took his time, because he didn't want to frighten me, I guess. He put his finger under my shirt and stroked my slit very gently and then caressed my whole body . . ."

Pepi: "What were you thinking when he acted that way . . . ?"

Zenzi: "I wasn't thinking at all . . . it just made me feel good to be caressed . . ."

Pepi: "But you didn't understand what he was really up to . . . ?"

Zenzi: "I did, too! After all, I often heard at night what was going on when he did it with my mother . . ."

Pepi: "That's interesting . . . it reminds me of my own experience when I watched my parents at night. And what did Rudolf do then . . . ?"

288

Zenzi: "Nothing else . . . at least, not during the first week . . ."

Pepi: "But that way he didn't get any satisfaction . . ."

Zenzi: "Well . . . the second week . . . when his hand stroked my whole body again, he put my hand on his stiff cock . . ."

Pepi: "What did you do . . . ?"

Zenzi: "Nothing . . . I just held it and Rudolf whispered: 'Now *you* are my mistress, my sweetheart . . . just don't tell anybody about us, and you'll have a good life with me . . .'"

Pepi: "And . . . you liked that . . . ?"

Zenzi: "Sure, I liked it. First I was quite proud to have a lover, at my age, and then I was looking forward to having a 'good life,' because I had had a lousy childhood . . . never enough to eat, you know . . ."

Pepi: "That makes sense . . ."

Zenzi: "Then, I was always afraid to lie alone on that blanket on the floor, knowing that my mother was not there any more. As soon as Rudolf let me sleep in the bed with him, I lost all fear and cuddled against his warmth. Besides . . . I'd have done anything he might've asked me to do . . ."

Pepi: "Even if it had been something unpleasant . . . ?"

Zenzi: "Even then! I was afraid he'd throw me out if I didn't obey him . . ."

Pepi: "Did he threaten you with that . . . ?"

Zenzi: "Yes! For instance, he often said that if I'd tattle on him, he'd throw me out at once, and then the police would pick me up and stow me away in some orphanage where the kids were beaten and didn't get much to eat . . ."

Pepi: "Yes, it's much better to be able to

sleep in a warm bed and hold a warm prick in your hand . . ."

Zenzi (laughing) : ". . . or get it into your pussy . . . !"

Pepi: "I don't believe you got it in your pussy, all at once . . ."

Zenzi: "No, not all at once! First, Rudolf put it in my hand and explained to me that a man puts it into a woman's hole, and he touched my pussy very gently to show me the critical spot where a strong male can do so much for us . . ."

Pepi: "You had a good teacher, it seems . . ."

Zenzi: "O yes, Rudolf was a very good teacher. He let me touch his balls and told me that it was there that the human semen was being produced, and that when the man was squirting his fluid into a woman, she becomes pregnant and gives birth to babies . . ."

Pepi: "You had a great advantage over me. I didn't know all these details at first . . . I had to find out gradually . . ."

Zenzi: "Yes, Rudolf was a stickler for details . . . he almost drew blueprints for me . . ."

Pepi: "And . . . that was all you two talked about . . . ? Didn't you do anything . . . ?"

Zenzi: "Sure . . . we did everything . . ."

Pepi: "What d'you mean . . . everything . . . ?"

Zenzi: "Well . . . after he'd explained to me what fucking was all about . . . he straddled me and we did it . . ."

Pepi: "I can't believe that . . . your pussy was much too small . . ."

Zenzi: "Of course he didn't stick it into my pussy . . . he merely rubbed his prick on the outside until he came. He explained to me that my hole was too small and we'd have to wait a few years until he could put it into me . . . but when he fucked me between my thighs I got the idea how good the real thing must be . . ."

Pepi: "Did he never do it from behind . . . ?"

Zenzi: "Sure, he liked it much better . . . as a matter of fact, he didn't always want to shoot off his gun when he stuck it in, in front, only when he could fuck me in the rear!"

Pepi: "You mean in the ass, I know . . . !"

Zenzi: "What d'you mean . . . in the ass . . . ?"

Pepi: "I mean he stuck his prick into your ass, didn't he . . . ?"

Zenzi: "What are you talking about . . . ? That's not possible . . . !"

Pepi: "Oh yeah? Three years ago Mr. Horak fucked me in the ass and squirted his juice in there, because my pussy was too small for his big prick."

Zenzi: "Jeez! I've never heard of that . . . imagine *you* telling me something new about fucking! Is it good . . . ?"

Pepi: "I can talk only of my own experience. I find it quite nice . . . I come at once when I feel a good prick in my fanny . . ."

Zenzi: "But . . . but doesn't it hurt awfully?"

Pepi: "Yes, at first! But when the prick has been lubricated, and especially when it's done the second time and your asshole is still wet with all the semen from the first number . . . it doesn't hurt at all . . ."

Zenzi: "Strange . . . I've got to try that . . ."

Pepi: "But why? Now you can be fucked in your pussy . . . you don't need any substitute . . . !"

Zenzi: "Perhaps not! Well, Rudolf put his prick only between my thighs from the back . . ."

Pepi: "I know that, too. It feels good to have a warm stick rubbing you there . . ."

Zenzi: "And Rudolf liked to come that way!"

Pepi: "Did he do it any other way, too . . . ?"

Zenzi: "Yes, in my mouth . . ."

Pepi: "Did you swallow the stuff . . . ?"

Zenzi: "Sometimes . . . first I used to throw up . . . but then I got used to it . . . after all, it's not poison . . ."

Pepi (laughing): "No, it's not poison . . . and did Rudolf eat your pussy, too . . . ?"

Zenzi: "O sure . . . he spent a lot of time licking my clitoris so that I felt really good and moaned like hell. He said he wanted me to get something out of it, too . . ."

Pepi: "And you always wanted more of it, eh?"

Zenzi: "Sure thing! It drives you plain nuts if somebody has a clever tongue . . ."

Pepi: "Don't I know it! I wish we had somebody here right now who'd do it to us . . ."

I remember that all that talk had us turned on so much that we had to masturbate each other to calm down somewhat. Then I continued to interview Zenzi about her sex education:

Pepi: "How come your teats have become so big . . . ?"

Zenzi: "Rudolf said it's because he fondled them so much and also because of having sex so early . . . when I was nine, my teats had already grown a bit, and I had some hair on my cunt . . ."

Pepi: "And it was only Rudolf who fucked you . . . ?"

Zenzi: "No . . . there were others, but Rudolf had told me always to watch out if somebody tried to fondle me and to be sure that nobody started any rough stuff . . ."

Pepi: "You mean to tell me, he permitted you in those days to have sex with others . . . ?"

Zenzi: "O sure! He said it couldn't do me any harm to get more experience with other guys, as long as I stayed away from young boys. He'd kill me, he said, if he ever caught me with a young boy . . ."

Pepi: "Strange! Wasn't he ever jealous . . . ?"

Zenzi: "No, he said he and I were friends and that was the important thing between us, because we belonged to each other, sort of . . . and it felt good to belong to somebody, especially since my mother died . . ."

Pepi: "Yes, I understand that . . . but, tell me, why was he against your doing it with young boys . . . ?"

Zenzi (laughing): "That's simple . . . they don't pay!"

Pepi: "You mean . . . everybody else gave you money, every time . . . ?"

Zenzi: "I should say so . . . Rudolf explained to me that a woman must get something out of giving in to a man. He said I must get paid even if a guy was only touching my pussy with his hand . . . Nothing is for nothing, he said . . ."

Pepi: "O boy . . . ! If somebody had trained me that way, I'd have a lot of money by now . . . I was really stupid . . . I can see that now . . . !"

Zenzi: "See? And that's why I stay with Rudolf all the time. He's sharp, and you can ask him about anything. That guy knows a lot of answers."

Pepi: "But if he's such a good businessman, why did he let my father fuck you for nothing . . . ?"

Zenzi (laughing): "Don't be silly! What d'you mean for nothing . . . ? When your father started fucking me, we stopped paying rent. Didn't you know . . . ?"

Pepi: "No, I didn't . . . you know, this is really mean . . . !"

Zenzi: "But why?"

Pepi: "Because he fucks me for nothing, your smart Rudolf . . . he never pays me!"

Zenzi: "O yes, he does, though not with money . . . !"

Pepi: "I don't understand . . ."

Zenzi: "The fact that he didn't tell the police when he found out about you and your father is a sort of payment, isn't it . . . ?"

Pepi: "That's a strange sort of bookkeeping . . . ! I don't like that! I won't let Rudolf fuck me any more . . . !"

Zenzi: "Okay, I really don't care one way or the other . . ."

Pepi: "Let's forget it. Tell me how you started earning some money that way . . ."

Zenzi: "Well . . . my first customer was the grocer at the corner store. He always stroked my hair and gave me strange looks, and I told Rudolf about it."

Pepi: "And what did Rudolf tell you . . . ?"

Zenzi: "He told me to do anything the man would ask me to do, but not without asking him for some money . . . !"

Pepi: "And the grocer paid you . . . ?"

Zenzi: "Sure . . . but very little, the first time. Just some small change . . ."

Pepi: "But, God . . . you were so young . . . how did you do it . . . ?"

Zenzi: "It was easy! He often stood in front

of the store when I passed by, and I just smiled at him . . ."

Pepi: "Okay . . . and what then . . . ?"

Zenzi: "And he invited me to come in . . ."

Pepi: "Go on . . . go on . . . !"

Zenzi (laughing): "Well, he showed me the dried prunes that were displayed in baskets . . . also the figs . . . and he said he would give me some prunes or figs . . ."

Pepi: "If you did what . . . ?"

Zenzi: "If I showed him the fig I had between my legs . . ."

Pepi: "That's a new name for cunt . . . what next . . . ?"

Zenzi: "I was silent, at first, and let him repeat his offer . . . I like to eat figs, but I remembered what Rudolf had taugh me and then told the man I didn't want any figs, or prunes . . . He was astonished and asked me what I wanted instead . . . I looked at him with a big smile and said: 'Money!' "

Pepi: "And what did he do . . . ?"

Zenzi: "He looked quite surprised, but then he raised my skirt and played around between my legs . . . then he pulled out his prick and stuck it between my thighs and after a while he came . . ."

Pepi: "And then . . . ?"

Zenzi: "He gave me a handful of small coins and told me not to tell a soul . . ."

Pepi: "And you didn't . . . ?"

Zenzi: "I told Rudolf and gave him the money . . ."

Pepi: "And did you go back to that store . . . ?"

Zenzi: "Sure! I bought everything that Rudolf wanted me to buy. And I didn't have to pay for anything . . ."

Pepi: "Strange . . . ! And who was next . . . ?"

Zenzi: "My schoolteacher . . ."

Pepi: "Your teacher . . . ?"

Zenzi: "Yes, when I was in the fourth grade . . ."

Pepi: "But he couldn't have paid you for it . . . ?"

Zenzi: "That's what you think . . . ! But let me tell you the whole story. There was a girl in our class who was more developed than the rest of us. She already had big teats and every time the teacher showed us some exercises in the gym, he pretended to help that girl when we had to climb up ladders, or were swinging at the rings . . ."

Pepi: "How did he help her . . . ?"

Zenzi: "What d'you think? He grabbed her by the teats, or by her fanny . . ."

Pepi: "And how did you get his attention . . . ?"

Zenzi: "I let him see that I was watching him and he blushed when he saw me smile at him in a certain way . . ."

Pepi: "And did he try to 'help' you, too . . . ?"

Zenzi: "Yes, but he put his hand under my armpits and I told him I was ticklish there. So he switched over to my teats that were still small, but quite distinct. And I kept smiling right in his face, and he blushed each time. One day he'd told that big-bosomed girl she must stay behind because she did something wrong when we exercised at the gym and he would show her how to do it . . . I waited outside the school and when that girl appeared after half an hour, her face was quite red and I knew that something had been going on . . ."

Pepi: "Did she tell you . . . ?"

Zenzi: "Boy, was she stupid! She asked me

not to breathe a word to a soul . . ."

Pepi: "About what . . . ?"

Zenzi: "She said that the teacher had a funny little club between his legs, and he said he would give her good grades if she'd let him stick it between her teats and also between her legs. . . . 'Just imagine,' that silly thing said, 'he rubbed that stick between my thighs and suddenly some water squirted out of it . . .' "

Pepi (laughing): "She sure was silly . . . !"

Zenzi: "I decided to do a good deed and told her the facts of life and from then on she knew what was going on whenever the teacher told her she had to stay awhile after lessons."

Pepi: "And how did *you* get him, at last . . . ?"

Zenzi: "I always smiled at him so impertinently that he got sort of mad, I guess, and one day he told me to stay after gym, because he had to show me what I had been doing wrong when we were climbing ropes . . ."

Pepi: "Aha! I can see what comes next . . ."

Zenzi: "When he helped me climbing the rope his hand got under my skirt and the next moment he was tickling my cunt. We looked at each other and when he saw my steady smile, he took my hand and put it inside his fly. His prick stood at attention and I squeezed it a little and waited for him to say something . . ."

Pepi: "Well . . . did he . . . ?"

Zenzi: "You bet! He said he'd give me good grades if I'd let him put his prick between my thighs . . . I smiled right in his face and said I didn't need any good grades, but he could give me something else. When he asked what it was, I said: 'Money!' He asked why he should give me any money. I told him that was not difficult to guess. I wanted to be paid for being fucked and also for not telling anybody that my teacher had fucked me . . ."

Pepi: "Did he see it your way . . . ?"

Zenzi: "He seemed to hesitate at first, but I lifted my skirt and let him see everything. He grabbed me at once, but he couldn't find a comfortable position for us on that old, broken-down bench in the gym, so I took his prick in my mouth. He was so excited that he came in a few seconds."

Pepi: "And he paid you . . . ?"

Zenzi: "He did, right away. He gave me a half-guilder!"

Pepi: "Boy, he must have been afraid and wanted to be sure you wouldn't talk . . ."

Zenzi: "I guess so, but on the other hand he often kept me there after class, from then on, and he always gave me half a guilder . . ."

Pepi: "And how did you make the transition from Ottakring to the inner city . . . ?"

Zenzi: "Rudolf said that the real money was here in the center of town, and he brought me down here and showed me around so that I came to know the right streets. He also rented the room at old Mrs. Bock's for me . . . she used to walk the streets, too, when she was young, so she doesn't give me any trouble. All she wants is the rent, and one guilder for every man I bring up here."

Pepi: "Rudolf has been quite useful for you . . ."

Zenzi: "Yes, and he says that you, too, could make a lot of money if you only knew the ropes . . . How much did you earn today . . . ?"

Pepi: "Let me see . . . two guilders from the young man on the staircase . . . five guilders from the old guy . . . ten guilders from your

298

whip boy . . . five guilders from the photographer . . . that's twenty-two all together, minus two guilders I've got to pay Mrs. Bock here . . . that leaves me twenty guilders! Boy, father will be surprised when I bring all that money home . . ."

Zenzi: "You're not so silly as to give him all that money . . . ?"

Pepi: "Shouldn't I . . . ?"

Zenzi: "God forbid! Suppose you don't earn anything tomorrow, what then . . . ?"

Pepi: "Then I'll say I didn't earn anything . . ."

Zenzi: "Jeez, are you naive! Look, I'll show you the way I'm doing it. I give Rudolf sometimes five guilders, sometimes only three, the next day maybe six, and another day only two. That way he is content and doesn't bawl me out. I learned the hard way. He used to slap me around when I, sometimes, came home without anything . . . And, what's more, if you give them all the money, they'll buy more wine than usual and drink it all up . . . don't you see . . . ?"

Pepi: "Yes, I guess you're right . . ."

Zenzi: "Besides . . . you are going to need some money for yourself . . . Rudolf or your father won't give you any when you need it most . . . perhaps to buy a dress . . ."

Pepi: "But if I wear a new dress, father will see it and know that I kept something for myself . . ."

Zenzi: "Don't be stupid! You always say that a gentleman gave you a present . . . you always get presents . . . that's a rule . . . And don't forget to be nice to your father. As long as you are nice to him, he'll be quite tame . . ."

Pepi: "Now I know why you flatter Rudolf

so much . . ."

Zenzi: "Sure! Why antagonize him if a little friendliness makes everything simpler!"

We got dressed and took a horse-drawn streetcar home. I gave father five guilders and he seemed a little embarrassed at first, but then he went out and bought some wine. When Rudolf learned of my successful day, he praised me and said I was going to be a first-class money-maker if I continued to be smart and sharp. Afterwards the men got drunk and I spent the night lying under my father.

Next day, and all the following days, I went to the inner city, either with Zenzi, or alone. I caught on very quickly and learned how to treat the various types of my male customers. I made quite a bit of money and gave a certain amount of it to my father every evening. Since he could live on my earnings now, he didn't think of looking for work any more. He accepted my money and invested it promptly in bottles of wine. I didn't like to see him drinking night after night, but since nothing could be done about it, I let him be.

Franz was working in some workshop in the eleventh district, at the other end of town. He was still an apprentice and slept with the master's maidservant. Lorenz, who had found out what was going on in our place, didn't show up any more and all the less so as he couldn't stand Rudolf.

I followed Zenzi's advice and kept quite a bit of the money I earned. It came in quite handy, because my profession forced me to have nice, clean underwear and also good and pretty clothes. Unfortunately, Rudolf never permitted us to put on our most elegant clothes when we were in town "working." He said that, first, we would attract the attention of the cops, and, second, the men would think we were licensed prostitutes, which we weren't. We were so-called clandestines.

In Vienna, licensed prostitution was a legitimate profession. The women had to undergo a weekly examination by the police physician to get a clean bill of health. If one acquired some venereal disease, she was immediately transferred to the police hospital and not discharged until she was pronounced cured.

Therefore, being a clandestine prostitute was the most difficult job in those days. Rudolf introduced me to a doctor who told me what to look for in every customer, to recognize the symptoms of syphilis and gonorrhea as best as I could. It was impossible, of course, to play it safe all of the time. But I was very fortunate never to catch anything. A kind of sixth sense protected me every time when I wasn't quite sure whether a prospective customer was infected or not. In contrast to most of my "colleagues" I made the men talk. I asked them a lot of questions and, once in a while, a man betrayed himself through a verbal slip. Once I asked a very elegant gentleman to have a glass of wine with me but he said his doctor had forbidden him, temporarily, all kinds of alcohol. That "temporarily" put me wise: he had gonorrhea.

Rudolf turned out to be a mine of knowledge and information. He told me never to visit a military barracks unless my customer was an officer. Also never to follow a man to his place if he acted funny in some way. It was always safer, Rudolf said, to ask men to come up to the little room in Dorothea Street. Frau Bock was always at home and at the slightest scream she'd come in, or send Karl who was a strong lad and could take care of any violent visitor.

I don't remember many more details of those first years of my beginnings as a streetwalker, except what I've already written down. I only knew that, thanks to Rudolf, I could get away with remaining a "clandestine" who got the better customers simply because many men are too proud to let themselves be picked up by the "licensed" girls. Men like to believe they went to bed with a "loose girl," who is whoring around privately, which is not supposed to be the same as a licensed prostitute, although, to be honest, the latter is less likely to give him some disease, on account of her undergoing that weekly physical examination.

As I mentioned in the middle part of these memoirs, I would not have followed the career of a prostitute if my father had not found out what my teacher, Father Mayer, had done to me. But being informed of my premature sex experience on the one hand, and suffering from an involuntary continence as a widower, and not having enough money to go to a prostitute, the temptation became too great for him. And it was thus that my fate was sealed. Rudolf's influence was only a natural consequence of that incestuous relationship with my father. It is sad that I can't think of my father with the respect children are supposed to feel for a parent, but I do feel great pity for him. When he was younger, he never had a chance to become more than a saddler jouneyman and he made just about enough money to enable my mother and two brothers, (and myself, of course) to lead the miserable existence of a poor workman's family. Perhaps, if my mother hadn't died so soon, everything would have been different.

Although my later career took me away from the street and into the milieu of better class people, my childhood and adolescence are best preserved in my memory. As far as those early days I spent as a clandestine streetwalker are concerned, they were a tough school and I was glad to exchange it for becoming the mistress of rich men. To earn money by satisfying lots of men, day after day, night after night, amounts to hard work, and it would be monotonous to talk or write about it.

I slept with at least three different men each day, which—multiplied by 365—amounts to 1095 men a year, which, in turn, comes to 32,850 men in three decades. It is difficult to remember to what degree I enjoyed these 32,850 pricks and what their owners looked like, or how they behaved. Apart from that, it is not necessary to mention anything but characteristic episodes that give the reader a general idea of why a very young girl of the Austrian working classes became a whore, and how she went about doing it.

If I should feel the need to write something down again, I may speak of the days when I had already acquired some refinement and what is commonly called culture. In other words, when I had become a high-class whore who looked quite harmless and respectable to the unsuspecting onlooker. For the moment, I feel satisfied to have spoken about the early days of my life which are more easily remem-

303

bered than the later periods.

The uninformed reader will become acquainted with how "the other half" lives, or used to live. Women are called the weaker sex, but when I consider what I had to go through, and how I came out victoriously, I don't believe in ever having been weak. Although I never had any "morals," my moral fiber has been stronger than many a man's.

Women have served men as objects of pleasure since the days of antiquity. Men, poets and heroes, have spoken and written of Love and of beautiful women in the most idealistic terms. And what does it all amount to? When all that talk and declaiming about love and romance ends in a physical embrace, the motions and gestures are always the same. Sometimes the man lies on top, sometimes the woman. Both want to reach as many orgasms as possible. Some call it love, some call it sexual intercourse: that's all the difference there is.